Foolish Puckboy

Also by Eden Finley and Saxon James

Puckboys

Egotistical Puckboy
Irresponsible Puckboy
Shameless Puckboy
Foolish Puckboy
Clueless Puckboy
Bromantic Puckboy
Forbidden Puckboy
Possessive Puckboy
Stubborn Puckboy
Charming Puckboy

FOOLISH PUCKBOY

EDEN FINLEY & SAXON JAMES

canelo

Penguin
Random
House

First published in the United Kingdom in 2023 by Eden Finley and Saxon James

This edition published in the United Kingdom in 2026 by

Canelo, an imprint of
Canelo Digital Publishing Limited,
20 Vauxhall Bridge Road,
London SW1V 2SA
United Kingdom

A Penguin Random House Company
The authorised representative in the EEA is Dorling Kindersley Verlag GmbH.
Arnulfstr. 124, 80636 Munich, Germany

A CIP catalogue record for this book is available from the British Library.

ISBN 9 781 83598 488 8

Printed and bound in Great Britain by Clays Ltd, Elcograf S.p.A.

Look for more great books at
www.canelo.co | www.dk.com

1

CHAPTER ONE

ALEKS

The word "divorce" is supposed to elicit an eruption of all-out screaming and anger. So when Rebecca first mentioned it with a defeated sigh, I was shocked. Not because I didn't expect it but in the way the words were delivered. They might have been whispered, but they held finality, and with one simple sentence, my marriage was over.

I had the opportunity to pack up and leave San José, so I jumped at it, signed with Seattle, and made the move north.

It was the right decision. It's a clean break. New city. New team. New me.

Then why does sitting on the balcony of my new place, drinking scotch, looking out at the water, feel like the same ol' shit?

Coming out as pansexual was supposed to open me up to more possibilities than ever before, but my old PR manager was right. The announcement happening fresh off my divorce has made the public think that I'm actually gay and what Rebecca and I had for all those years was a ruse. Or that I got so over being with a woman I wanted to try dick. It's one stereotype after the other. Lane did warn me, so I only have myself to blame. No, I have society to blame as a whole. I'm only thankful this PR nightmare happened during the off-season, but because of the backlash, I haven't tried to date anyone. Of any gender. Technically, I've gone on PR dates with some models—female, of course—a Canadian actress who films her TV show in Vancouver, and a couple of women my new PR team set me up with, but none of them have been real. They've been photo ops.

When Rebecca and I split up, I was excited to get back out there. Now, I'm too self-conscious to date anyone for real.

I foolishly thought I'd be the next Ezra Palaszczuk or Oskar Voyjik, the two biggest slutbags of the league. Oskar even gave me the imaginary crown when he fell in love with our PR manager.

It's not sitting so pretty on my head right now.

When my doorbell rings, I freeze because the only person who knows my new address is— Fuck. I'm gonna kill him.

I stand and make my way to the side of my balcony and look down to the right near my front door.

I'm doubly gonna kill him.

Oskar Voyjik didn't only show up unannounced, but he brought nearly the whole Queer Collective with him. Almost every queer man in the NHL is at my doorstep, trying to be quiet and snickering to themselves like a bunch of dumbasses.

"No one's home," I call out, and all seven of them look up at me.

"Don't make us drag you out of there," Ezra yells.

Maybe the company will do me good. Real company. Not PR fakeness. I've been whining about things being too much of the same, and if there's anything I can count on these guys for, it's disrupting the normalcy.

I head inside and down the glass stairs of my fancy-ass new house to let them in.

Oskar smiles at me when I open the door. "Hey, fuck-face. Miss me yet?"

"Like a hole in the head." I step aside. "Come on in."

"I dunno," Oskar muses. "The hole in Lane's head comes in very useful."

I pretend to groan at his comment. Not gonna lie, though, I will miss playing alongside Oskar. Even though he only recently found out about my sexuality, being on the same team as another queer player was comforting. As far as I'm aware, I'm the only queer dude with Seattle. Definitely the only out one.

The guys file in, Oskar, Ezra, Ezra's boyfriend and teammate Anton, Tripp and his husband Dex from the Vegas team, and trailing behind them are Ayri Quinn and Asher Dalton from Buffalo—the two other newest recruits to the Collective alongside me. Ayri's been playing for a few seasons already, but Asher's a rookie this upcoming season.

I nod at them. "Asher. Ayri."

Asher wears a stoic scowl, and I can't tell if it's just his face or if he's mad at something.

"Call me Quinn," Ayri says.

Asher adds, "He hates being called Ayri because his name rhymes with fairy."

"And thanks for bringing that up," Quinn says.

"I'm an orphan. You should revel in your childhood trauma like meeeee."

Okay, I really don't know how to take Asher.

"Uh, come on in."

They've been here two seconds, and the other guys have all made themselves at home. Ezra and Anton are on the couch play fighting ... or what might be considered foreplay for them, I'm not sure. Dex and Oskar are on the lower balcony, checking the place out, and Tripp is opening all my kitchen cupboards, looking for something.

"What are you after?" I ask.

"Blender. We bought stuff for margaritas."

"I don't have a blender yet."

"You don't own a blender?"

"When you get a divorce, everything has to be divided."

"She got the *blender*? Dude, how do you expect to make all those shakes the team dieticians always put us on?"

"I was going to buy a new one. Preseason doesn't start for two more weeks."

"Okay, we need to go shopping," Tripp says. "What else don't you have? Plates? Cutlery? Anything?"

"Uhhh ... Yeah, I need all of that too. Rebecca basically got everything. It was easier that way."

Tripp moves to the living room, where the others are. "Everyone back into the rental cars. We have to go shopping."

The room fills with complaints. All except one voice.

Ezra stands. "Yes. This is perfect." He turns to me. "We need to find the nearest thrift store."

"Uh, I can afford new stuff."

"Not for that. After we get the things you need, we're going to pick out attire for the party we're throwing here."

I'm suspicious. "Why does that sound tame and wholesome coming from you?"

Ezra grins. "Because the catch is you'll be blindfolded when you pick your clothes."

"And there it is."

They might be over-the-top, and I'm dreading what we're all going to look like by the end of the night, but hey, this is better than wallowing over my lack of dating life.

–

"I'll go first," Ezra says. "Anton, blindfold me."

"Things Ezra says during sex," Tripp mutters.

Ezra flips him the bird.

I lean in closer to Oskar. "Not that I'm complaining too much, but why the visit?"

"Seeing as you blew us all off for the group vacay at the start of the break to date all those beautiful women, we thought we'd come rescue you from that hell."

I snort. "It really is terrible dating models."

He doesn't need to know it's true. They were all lovely women, but it was all so fake.

"Quinn's single." He nods toward where he and Asher are standing off to the side, murmuring to each other like we are.

"I'll pass. Hockey players are way too much work."

"Truth," Oskar says. "But I'm warning you now, Ez is going to try to push you two together. Quinn brought Asher as a buffer so he wouldn't be forced upon you."

I laugh. "Thanks for the warning."

I glance at Quinn's profile, his messy hair with golden highlights, his flawless skin that makes him look like he's younger than he is, and I have to admit he is an attractive man ... if, you know, it wasn't for the god-awful mustache he's growing for whatever reason. Maybe he hates being pretty.

Either way, I'm not lying to Oskar when I say hockey players aren't my type. We're selfish, we're never home, and our schedules are so messed up we'd never see each other during the season unless our teams were playing against one another.

I'm shutting that down early. Too complicated.

I want something easy but sizzling.

I've done comfortable. I want … *zing*. And the thought of Quinn doesn't give me zing.

Ezra, now blindfolded, gets spun three times and then led to a rack of clothing. Women's clothing. Fucking great. I'm not opposed to bending gender norms or people expressing themselves through the art of fashion. But when it comes to me, I like my jeans and T-shirts. They don't even need to be designer. I hate wearing suits, and the only reason I do it is because the NHL makes me.

Actually, the NHL makes me do a lot of things I'd rather not do, but at least the sacrifices on my diet and my body don't have to be done while wearing a suit. Or a dress.

"We're all going to end up wearing dresses, aren't we?" I ask Oskar.

"Now, it's up to me when I say stop," Ezra says.

Anton guides him up and down the rows of clothing until he eventually says, "Stop."

When he pulls out the garment, it's a one-piece romper with reaaaaally short shorts.

None of us want to do this—okay, Dex, the big puppy dog, does, and he jumps in to go next—but the rest of us are over it before we even pick our outfits. Even so, we're good sports about it because it is only a bit of fun, and it's not like we're going anywhere but back to my house to wear it. That, and by the time we're forced to wear whatever, we'll hopefully be drunk off our tits.

Dex, either cheating and trying to go for a tux in the formal wear section or actually wanting to wear that much tulle, stops on a wedding dress.

How fitting for him.

Ezra cheats when it's Anton's turn because he keeps walking the poor guy around the same clothing rack six times until Anton picks one of the many bikinis in the line.

Asher, led by Quinn because he said he'd rather take a bath in acid than let Ezra touch him—apparently, they have history—manages to score a giant trench coat. Sure, it's a ladies' one, but I would kill to land on something not so embarrassing like that. But then Ez throws in a fedora for free to "match the look," and I realize this isn't a game of chance. It's a game of making fools of ourselves.

Ah, hockey players. We're so evolved.

Quinn lands on an old-school tux, pale blue with ruffled sleeves, and a shirt. Oskar gets a leopard-print skintight dress, and Tripp gets a plain black skirt. Ezra says he'll allow Tripp to keep the shirt he has on with it. Which is a team T-shirt.

That only leaves me. I rub my chin. "Seeing as Quinn was the only one lucky enough to get a suit, what are the chances of me getting something masculine?"

"Just for that," Ezra says, "zero. Kilts are masculine and technically skirts. Clothing is clothing. None of it should be feminine or masculine."

"See, I would totally agree with you. Actually, I do agree with that statement. Wear what the fuck you want. But don't for one second think I believe you're doing this for the nonbinary agenda. You're doing it to make us uncomfortable."

Ezra puts his hand on his heart. "You think so little of me?"

Everyone else answers "Yes" for me.

I step forward. "Okay, let me have it, then. If I can't laugh at myself, I can't exactly laugh at anyone else, can I? Hit me with your best shot."

And they do. After Ezra leads me in what feels like one huge circle, bumping me into nearly everything, I finally get over it when I stub my toe on God knows what. "Ouch, motherfucker, stop."

"Also what Ezra says during sex," Dex calls out. Way too loudly. In the middle of the store.

"Ooh, good news for me," I say. "Surely, they'll kick us out."

"Nope. All good." Ezra removes my blindfold.

Of course I land on ... *that*. It's one of those 1920s dresses with tassels and layers and sparkly beads.

"It's a slapper dress," Dex says excitedly.

We all glance around at each other, trying to silently decide who's gonna tell him.

"It's flapper," Tripp says. "Good try though."

"Nah, slapper sounds right," Asher says. "Because you get to slap the person wearing it."

I turn to Quinn. "Is he always so violent?"

"He's a teddy bear underneath it all," Ezra says. "I saw it. Once. Of course, the next morning, he turned into an actual bear. Grizzly kind, not the sexy kind."

"What is our second rule?" Asher asks Ezra.

"Uh, don't mention that night ever again?"

"So why you doing it?"

8

I glance at Anton on reflex to see if he's as disturbed as the rest of us by this conversation, but he's just smirking at his boyfriend in a dangerous way.

"Because I like to remind you of back in the day when we both made poor choices," Ezra says. "Now we're all mature and smart and—"

"Making half of us wear dresses … or a bikini," I add.

"That's not immature. That's fun," Ezra says.

"Sure. Fun. I can't wait to see what else you think is … fun."

"Patience, oh horny one. Let's go!" As we move to the front of the store to pay, Ezra finds a headpiece with a giant feather on it. "Ooh, perfect!"

Tripp nudges me. "Don't worry. With all your new kitchen tools, I'm going to make lethal margaritas."

"That'll help." But I can see it now. Tonight is going to be messy.

CHAPTER TWO

GABE

The siren cuts the air as we tear through town toward the address we got the 911 call for. A panicked caller and a house on fire. This is why I do this job.

The adrenaline surge isn't what it used to be. It no longer makes me sick or anxious or desperate to get through it. It's level and just enough that I'll be able to jump straight into the task without hesitation.

I lean forward as we eat the distance to the emergency but still don't see a sign of smoke against the black night sky. Since Sanden is driving, my fingers are tapping urgently against my thighs, my knees bouncing, the usual thrumming dance of my body before facing a big job.

I don't think about whether anyone is hurt.

I can't.

We get closer, and I still don't see any smoke, which means the address was completely wrong, or we might be getting out of this easy.

There are no immediate signs of fire when we pull up in the tight, dead-end street, but the address we were given has all the lights on and loud music playing. The driveway is full of big, luxury cars, so Sanden parks the truck on the street before telling the other two guys we're with that we'll go in and check it out. My firemanny senses are telling me this is a no-go, though.

We climb from the truck and follow the footpath to the front door.

The house is fancy. Obviously expensive. Typical of the area and so not typical of anything I'm used to. It'd be a shame for something so interesting and pretty-looking to be burned to the ground. Thankfully, it doesn't look like there's any danger of that happening.

"I'm gonna be pissed if this was a prank call," Sanden says.

"Nah, my money is on drunken shenanigans." These are not my favorite kind of callouts, definitely not the reason I got into this job, but they can sometimes be funny, and we're having a quiet night anyway.

"A place this big?" Sanden's blue eyes track all the way up to the roof and back down again. "Could be some rich person calling over their stovetop burner. Oh, no. It's a degree hotter than it's meant to be," he says, pitching his voice all squeaky.

"Either way, it was this or sitting at the station watching *The Office* reruns with Chief." I lick my lips. "Let's make a bet. If I'm right, you do my kitchen duty tomorrow. If you're right—"

"You'll take my turn to wash the truck." He bounces on his feet. "You're on."

I swear he'll do anything to get out of that.

We knock on the front door, but the music from inside is obviously too loud for them to hear us, and judging by the loud, indistinguishable voices coming from around back, it sounds like they're outside anyway.

I jump off the front porch and take the path along the side of the house and come to a back gate. It's too high to see over, even for me, so I knock loudly and shout, "Fire department!"

"You ordered strippers?" a voice answers.

I throw a wide smile at Sanden, because yep, sounds like I win. I'd be half-worried we're about to walk into a bachelorette party if it wasn't for the masculine voice.

But when the gate swings open, revealing the sight inside, I'm not so sure a bachelorette party would have been the worst thing.

"Holy *fuck*, they don't make strippers like you in Boston," the man who opened the gate slurs. His blood-shot eyes would probably be pretty if they weren't so wrecked, but my attention only lands on him for about a second before it drops to what he's wearing. Some kind of woman's clothing that's all one piece from the neck to the tiny little shorts.

"Ezra Palaszczuk," Sanden gasps from behind me.

The Ezra guy tries to bow but almost goes ass over tit into the bushes.

"Fuck." I jump forward to grab him and stand him back on his feet. "You okay?"

He blinks up at me. "You've got the … the things." He jabs at his cheeks. "Anton, quick, look. The stripper has the face things."

I share a bewildered look with Sanden.

"Ah, dimples?" Sanden asks.

"Dimples!" Ezra throws his hands in the air like he's won the jackpot and staggers into the backyard, leaving the gate open for us to follow.

"Holy shit," I say, trying to get out some of the excess energy before I curl over laughing. "He's so wasted."

Sanden leads us inside the yard, putting on his best fireman voice. "Someone here called 911 and reported a fire."

"It was on the roof," a redheaded guy shouts as Ezra lightly kicks a man lying facedown in a bikini. A thong bikini. And I have to remind myself I'm *working* and not allowed to check out the incredible ass just because it's incredible.

"Okay, the fire was on the roof?" Sanden asks, clearly trying to cling onto some form of professionalism. Lucky one of us is.

"No, it wasn't. It …" A guy wearing a fedora does some complex movements with his hands. "Like, it came from nowhere!"

"It was the fire pit," a blond with a terrible stache says. "It *jumped* out."

"Like a fireball!" a man with no eyebrows in a wedding dress says.

"It was only a fireball because you threw alcohol on it." Surprisingly, the man in the leopard-print dress with a nasty scar down one cheek sounds the most coherent. Until he talks again. "So what's the deal here? You take it off and we pay you, or we pay you and you take it off?"

Someone help me to stay professional.

"Nothing's coming off, gents," I say.

"Not until I get my boyfriend …" Leopard print's phone lights up as someone answers his FaceTime call. An upside-down someone who doesn't look very happy to have been woken at two in the morning.

"Oskar, what—"

"They're about to get naked!"

"It was the roof!" the redhead yells again.

"Who's naked? What's the roof?" the man on the call asks.

You and me both, man.

"Okay," Sanden calls, trying to get back on track. "Can someone"—he points at the redhead—"not you, tell us what happened?"

They all start to talk at once.

"Turned around and—"

"It's like the whole thing went up—"

"Should have thrown this fucking hat on there—"

"A fireball! Bigger than my head—"

"On. The. Roof."

"Do you take hundred-dollar bills?"

I double forward with laughter. Sanden slaps the back of my head, but even that doesn't work. Especially not when Ezra what's-his-name hums some sleazy porn music and starts to dance around him like a pole.

Sanden sends a *help me* look my way. But I can't. This is too much.

Almost as soon as I think that, another guy comes barreling out of the house, enormous bucket of water hugged in his tattooed arms, sloshing it all over the floor and the dress that's flapping around his calves.

"I'm coming!"

He tosses the water in no general direction, but the spray catches bikini guy, who launches to his feet.

"Where's the fire?" he shrieks.

Leopard-print guy—Oskar—is assuring his boyfriend he'll keep him on the phone for the show, even as the poor man is begging to go back to sleep. Wedding dress man is patting his singed eyebrows, the redhead is staring vacantly into space, and the man with the water, who's easily the hottest one here, fixes his eyes on me. His feather from the

14

thing on his head droops pathetically over one eye, and he staggers toward me.

"You." He points, and I'll give him props, his finger is almost aimed in my direction. "You're *so* hot. Why don't the supermodels I look date like you?"

Eh, his attempt at talk was still kinda understandable? "If you're dating supermodels, somehow I think you're doing okay."

His eyes cross the closer to me he gets. "I wanna suck on your apple's Adams."

Now Sanden is trying not to laugh, completely ignoring Ezra and his porn soundtrack.

"No, babe, don't go," Oskar shouts. "Aleks is about to fuck the stripper!"

The call disconnects as the one wearing a fedora shouts, "Lane, take me with you!"

I quickly set a hand on Aleks's shoulder to keep him an arm's length away, but instead of deterring him, he turns his head and licks my hand instead.

"Okay, buddy," Sanden says, steering Aleks away from me and over to the outdoor furniture. "If there's no fire, we're going to go. I suggest you all stop drinking and sober up. I can't imagine any of your teams would be impressed to see you like this."

"Teams?" I ask.

Hockey players, he mouths.

That explains the house and the fancy cars outside.

Doesn't explain the fire, but I get the feeling we'll never know what happened there.

Bikini dude staggers over, his top askew with one nipple hanging out, and he shoves his finger in my face. "Smile."

15

I hesitate for a second but do it because it's not like this whole thing isn't hilarious anyway.

He grunts, then turns, grabs Ezra, and drags him toward the house. Ezra spanks that incredible ass the whole way inside, which is obviously the only reason why I'm watching it.

There's so much skin and muscle and drunken stupidity on display here that I'm getting hot under the collar.

Which is a feat for someone who runs into actual fire.

Aleks, now planted in his chair, turns and looks up at me with big eyes. "I'd have your babies." And I'm assuming that was meant to be quiet, but he fucking shouts it.

Sanden looks up from where he's turning off the gas fire in the middle of the back deck. "Now that's an offer you can't refuse."

"Can and will."

Sanden approaches me, nodding toward the back gate we came through, and I hesitate instead of taking the lead.

"You really think we can leave these guys here without one of them dying?"

"Hey, if it's any of them but Aleksander Emerson, that can only work in our favor for the Stanley Cup this year."

I throw my head back. "I forgot you do sports."

"I'm surprised you don't."

"Too many rules, too much going on." Concentrating for that long isn't something I'm good with either. Maybe if I actually *liked* a sport or had a reason to watch it— drinking games are *always* a good reason—then it'd be fine. But a bunch of guys on the field/ice/court all fighting over a tiny object? Yeah, not for me.

"Leave the hockey to these insanely rich idiots, and let's get back to *The Office*," Sanden says.

Still, I can't make myself go. "Maybe we should get them inside first? They might be safer?"

"Sure, near the kitchen and the knives. I could have sworn one of them said something about putting his hand in a blender."

"Yeah, but if they die that way instead of by fire, I won't have it on my conscience."

He purses his lips for a second. "Yeah, good point."

"It's going to be like herding cattle, isn't it?"

"Drunk, horny cattle."

"Drunk and horny is nothing we haven't dealt with before."

"Except this time, the attention is coming from people on the same team as us."

"What?" I look at the group with fresh eyes. "They're all queer?"

"Apparently."

"I didn't know sports people did that. You know, make that kinda thing public or whatever."

"You've been missing out." He shoves me toward Aleks. "You take your future husband."

I tell him to shut up but do it anyway. I've been hit on a lot in my line of work; drunk people equal accidents—*who knew*? But this might be the first night I've been hit on by someone smoking hot. If we were two men in a club, I'd be taking him home.

But we're not in a club. And Aleks is in no state for anyone to be taking him to bed, unless we're talking literally, because I'm damn near having to carry him inside.

He's another rich guy who gets paid way too much to do way too little and is slurring his words so badly I can't make out what he's saying.

As soon as I get him to the couch, he flops face forward onto it. I turn to go help Sanden with the others when Aleks grabs my thick work pants. His bicep pops beneath his tattooed skin, and I swallow and drag my eyes away from it and up to his. In the soft light inside, his eyes look … blue? Green? A nice color.

He doesn't look away. Just stares. And this shivery sort of awareness runs through me.

"Zing," he whispers before passing out.

CHAPTER THREE

ALEKS

I startle awake at who the fuck knows what time, my skin itching from all the beads in my dress.

Why am I still wearing this stupid thing? And why is there a feather tickling my damn nose?

I blow on it to get the stupid thing away, but it falls back in my face.

Last night's events are blurry, but fuck, I needed a night like that. I can't remember the last time I did stupid shit for no reason.

I sit up, realizing I'm on the couch and not in bed. Quinn is on the other side of the long U-shaped couch, but I have no clue where the others are. The house is lit up, but it's still dark outside.

Standing is more difficult than I thought it would be, and I almost fall headfirst into my glass coffee table. I'm surprised none of us actually did that last night; we were so messed up.

I strip off on the way to my bedroom so I can get a few more hours' sleep, walk past a guest room with the sound of sex coming from it, and then pray that the other loved-up couple in this group isn't doing the same thing in my bed.

Thankfully, my bedroom is empty, and when I climb into my high-thread-count sheets and my head hits the pillow, I land in that weird space of time where I'm still lucid enough to know I'm dreaming but go with it anyway.

In my dream, I'm being carried by a hunky fireman. He's faceless, but my skin tingles, and the warmth spreading through me takes away all the seediness of being hungover.

I let the dream take me, and it takes me to some dirty, dirty places. That's when lights blind me, and he puts me in a chair center stage. I realize he's not a real fireman but a stripper, and I'm definitely not complaining.

He's so sexy as he grinds up on me. His muscles are insane, his pecs dancing under the suspenders of his fireman uniform.

I want to lick them and touch his abs. Hell, I want to have his babies—

I startle awake and get an overwhelming sense of déjà vu. Not the stripping part—the fireman part.

The sun is up, and I don't know how long I was sleeping for, how long I was dreaming of that hunk of man who wasn't a figment of my imagination but someone I completely made a fool of myself in front of last night.

By screaming at him that I want his babies. Which is absurd, considering I don't want kids.

I can't exactly remember what the hot man I shame-lessly hit on last night looked like. I can't remember his features; I just remember … him. But if there were actual firemen here, that means …

I jump out of bed and run downstairs, not caring that I'm only in my boxer briefs. Quinn's still passed out on the couch, but now Tripp and Dex are up. They're on the couch too, drinking coffee and having an intimate conversation.

Dex looks up at me, his eyebrows completely gone.

"Was there a fire here last night?" I ask.

Tripp points to his husband. "What gave it away?"

"You singed off your eyebrows?"

"I was trying to help," Dex yells, startling Quinn awake. He groans. "Why are you all so loud?"

"Where was the fire, and was there any damage? I don't own this place, and I just moved in. Don't really want to piss off the landlord yet."

"Out back," Tripp says.

I head outside and don't see any damage until I get closer to the fire pit. There's a huge burn mark in the grass near it, and one of the white Adirondack chairs that came with the house has a black fire stain up one leg.

Not horrible in the big scheme of things. How hard could it be to replace a patch of grass and a chair?

There are footsteps on the back deck, and I assume it's the guys coming out to look with me, but when I turn, I'm either still drunk dreaming, or this is actually happening.

I'm standing in my yard, practically naked, and the man of my literal dreams is walking down the back steps toward me with another man who's vaguely familiar, so I guess he was here too last night.

They're both in jeans and T-shirts, out of uniform, and smiling at me as they approach. That's when my gaze catches on dream guy's face. His eyes are a striking blue. People say my pale green eyes are mesmerizing, but they've got nothing on the deep, rich color of his. His short hair is messy on top, kind of fluffy, like he's the type of guy to run his hands through it often. He has the squarest jaw I've ever seen and even has one of those cute chin dimples that goes with the dimples in his cheeks when he smiles.

But his body ... Damn. All muscles and bulk, and I think I'm drooling.

"Do you remember us?" the other guy says.

I chuckle and force a nonchalant attitude. "I do. Uh, moments of it anyway. Did the guys actually think you were strippers? Or did I think you were real firemen and you're actually strippers? That bit is hazy."

Their smiles widen.

"I'm Sanden. This is Gabe."

Gabe. My dream man has a name.

"We're actual firemen who responded to a call here last night. We wanted to check in and make sure everyone is alive after what we walked into."

"I've only seen three of the seven other guys that were here, so I don't actually know."

When I allow myself to glance back at Gabe again, his attention is on me too. My bare abs, more specifically.

I'm almost too self-conscious and want to cover up, but at the same time, I like the way my skin heats at how obviously he's checking me out. I might like it too much.

I'm basically still half-hard from the weird stripper dream I had of him, and this is making my situation worse. I have to stop watching him watch me.

Clearing my throat, I say, "Let's go check on the others." I step past them when Sanden's voice stops me.

"Ah, so there was a fire here last night."

When I turn back, he's pointing at the burned grass.

"A little one. I don't even know how it started."

Both of them laugh.

"Yeah, none of you were very forthcoming last night," Gabe says, and his voice is deep and smooth. Not what I was expecting with his clean-shaven baby face.

"Unless it was about having my man's babies." Sanden puts his arm around Gabe's shoulders.

My face falls, but I try not to show it. Of course a man like Gabe would be taken by a man like Sanden.

Seriously, when they do firemen calendars, do they use real firemen? Both of them could be in one.

"He means partner," Gabe says.

"Yeah, I got that—"

"No, *work* partner." Gabe pulls out of Sanden's hold.

Oh. Work partner. "My man" as in … friend?

A moment passes between Gabe and me. Or maybe I'm still drunk and imagining it. Then reminders of what I said last night to him flood my brain, and I about want to cry.

"I want to say I'm so sorry for everything you witnessed last night. It wasn't appropriate behavior, and you guys don't need to be objectified while you're trying to work. All of us here know what that's like, so we should've behaved better."

"Aww, no Aleksander Emerson and Gabe Crosby babies? I'm disappointed," Sanden says, but I get stuck on the last name.

"Crosby? Your last name is Crosby? Are you any relation to Sidney?"

"Who?" Gabe asks.

Sanden shakes his head. "It hurts how someone so pretty can be so … Gabe."

"You're telling me," I mutter.

"Is it a sports ball person? Because no. Not related."

"And now I'm so heartbroken I really will have to revoke the babies offer."

"Damn," Gabe deadpans. "Because I was so close to taking you up on that offer."

"Really?" Okay, there's way too much hope in my tone.

"No. Let's just say …" He glances back at the house. "I really wouldn't fit in your world."

Before I can ask him what he means, Ezra and Anton emerge from the house, and Ezra yells, "Did we forget to pay the strippers?"

I sigh. "Again. Sorry. You can't take him anywhere."

"Says the man wearing only underwear," Gabe says.

When his blue eyes lock with mine again, another memory flashes. One where we shared another moment like this last night.

I whisper, "Zing," just like I did then too. It's reflex. He does something to my insides that I haven't felt for a really long time.

He frowns.

Ezra and Anton are upon us now, and Ezra takes out his wallet. "How much?"

I face-palm. "Ez, they really are firemen."

"Oh." Ez turns to Anton. "Maybe we should set more fires."

"So it was you?" I ask. "I can't even remember how it all happened."

Ezra looks guilty as he says, "I might have been joking about burning off Quinnie's horrible lip sweater he's trying to grow? And then, well—"

Anton cuts in. "My boyfriend is a dumbass and dropped the lighter. The grass caught fire, and then the

24

chair, and then Dex thought he'd put it out … with his margarita. He's damn lucky he didn't burn his face off."

"Explains the missing eyebrows though," I say.

"Little D was the one to put it out," Anton says, referring to Asher. "He's had a lot of practice with his evil twin brothers. I've never met them, but Ez says they're a handful."

"Where is Asher?" I ask.

"He got an Uber to a hotel after everyone went to bed," Anton says. "Ezra patted his head, which apparently broke rule number one."

Ezra nods. "No touching the Little D."

Sanden snorts. Both he and Gabe have been watching our exchange, ping-ponging back and forth between us like a tennis match.

"So we're all accounted for, then?" I ask. "What about Oskar?"

"Haven't seen him," Ez says, "but I'm sure he's fine. Now that he has Lane, he doesn't do public hookups anymore, so we don't need to worry about this being bad PR or anything."

A strangled noise comes from somewhere nearby, and we all look toward the house, trying to pinpoint the sound. We move as a group and find Oskar facedown in the grass, his leopard-print dress up around his waist and showing off his bare ass.

"Dude, have some dignity." I shove his dress down.

"Where's the fun in that?" He rolls over. "Who slept with the strippers?"

"Oh my fucking God." I turn to Gabe and Sanden. "As you can see, all of us are accounted for and not dead, so thank you for coming to check on us."

Sanden grins. "Trust me, it was worth it. I had no idea hockey players were so …"

"Normal?" Oskar says.

"Crazy?" Anton adds.

"Awesome?" Ezra suggests.

Sanden shrugs. "I was going to go with moronic and immature, but sure, any of yours work too." He turns to Gabe. "I can't wait to tell the guys back at the station."

It's like Sanden took a class on how to make a bunch of hockey players shit themselves at once. Because this can't get out. We all have sponsorships, endorsement deals, and contracts riding on our upstanding reputations … okay, upstanding for hockey players, anyway.

"Hey, uh, do you mind maybe not mentioning this?" I ask.

"Yeah, please don't make me call my boyfriend and tell him I fucked up and he needs to fix it," Oskar says. "He's done enough fixing of my image to last a lifetime."

"Can we tell them the story but not that you're famous?" Sanden asks.

I'm in crisis mode, not wanting to get on the wrong foot with my new team before I even start playing for them, so I blurt, "What about season tickets? Will that keep you quiet about this whole thing?"

Sanden says, "Fuck yes," while Gabe says, "No, thanks. Don't like hockey."

And now Gabe has taken the same fuck-with-hockey-players lesson Sanden has.

"Don't … hockey?" Ezra asks.

"I don't understand," Oskar echoes.

"He also has the surname Crosby and doesn't know who Sid is," I tell them.

"Just when I thought we could be friends." Ezra storms off.

"Ignore him. He's dramatic when he's hungover." Anton follows.

"He's dramatic always." Oskar leaves too, and only Gabe, Sanden, and I remain.

"Sanden can take the tickets," Gabe says. "I won't say anything."

For some reason, I believe him.

I take Sanden's details so I can get him the tickets, but before they leave, I make sure I look at Gabe when I say, "I hope to see you at one of my games."

I almost have hope when he stares at me with heat in his blue eyes, but then he says, "Not likely," and all that hope sinks, weighing me down like lead.

CHAPTER FOUR

GABE

It only takes two weeks of Sanden asking before I give in. I tried, I really did. Even though deep down I knew I'd say yes eventually, I really thought I could hold out longer than this.

Turns out the memory of an almost naked Aleksander Emerson is hard to argue with.

I have no idea what I'm hoping to get out of going to this game, considering the arena is huge and loud and Aleks will be focused on his job, but even if he doesn't know we're there, who cares? I'll get some fun eye candy, shut Sanden up about the season tickets, and then we'll head out for drinks.

"I bought you a present," Sanden announces loudly as he walks into my kitchen.

"What if I was naked in here?" I ask.

"Why do you think I yelled out before I walked in? Here, this had your name all over it."

Material hits my face, and when I peel off whatever it is he threw at me, I stare at it a moment before throwing him a look. "*Really*?"

"Thought your boyfriend might like it."

The name *Emerson* stares back from the jersey.

I know he's expecting me to fight him on it, but these things are fucking expensive, and I know how to take a joke. "Fuck the boyfriend. I'm always down for gifts. Even stupid ones."

I strip out of my shirt and pull the jersey on instead. And then I look at it. "Did you get the wrong size on purpose?"

"No clue what you mean," he says, hands forming a halo above his head.

That fucker.

And hey, the shirt might be tight, but at least I'm not going to be mistaken for a stripper tonight.

"Whatever. Ready to go?" I ask.

"Someone's eager."

"Someone wants to get this over and done with."

"Uh-huh. So *someone* isn't all excited to check out a certain sexy hockey player?"

I grab my keys. "*Someone* will be doing that anyway. It's literally the entire reason for going."

I follow Sanden out to his truck. It hasn't been long since I moved out of the share house I was living in and into my one-bedroom bungalow, but my new neighborhood already feels like home. It's good to be on my own for once, but I know if I ever need them, my five ex-roommates will be there for me. It just got to the point where I wanted to stand on my own two feet and be an adult.

Work is around the corner, and in the other direction are the gym, shops, and bar. Everything is within walking distance, so I didn't bother to buy a car when I moved in, and while sometimes that's a pain in the ass—rainy days aren't my favorite—mostly I like that I have to walk everywhere.

There is no fucking way I would walk to Climate Pledge Arena though. When we get there, the parking situation is ridiculous, and my hands drum out a constant rhythm on my thighs while I wait for Sanden to find a spot.

For the first game of the regular season, Seattle's fans have turned out in droves. People funnel from the sidewalk into the venue, and even though sports might not be my thing, the atmosphere absolutely is.

It reminds me of going to a concert, only more boring.

It's bright inside the foyer, loud, and constantly moving. Sanden leads me into the arena to our seats, right down in the front row, and a teeny tiny—never to be admitted—surge of hope hits me that Aleks might actually see us here. Until I look at the people directly across the ice from us and realize that all we'll be to the players is a blur of faces.

Maybe I should have turned up in my work uniform instead of this jersey since apparently that's the key to attracting queer hockey players. And it would give me a fuckload more protection against the cold.

There have been a few times in the last few weeks where I've been tempted to google the guy and find out what his deal is—the whole notion of out professional jocks just blows my mind—but I've held off. I wish I could say it was because of self-control and *not* because of my incredibly short attention span, but I'd be lying.

"Okay, give me the most basic of rules to follow this thing," I tell Sanden.

He launches into an explanation of forwards, defensemen, and illegal moves, most of which goes completely over my head. I follow enough to know that the teams are aiming for the net and they constantly rotate through lines, and that's enough for me.

The whole arena is buzzing, even though it's more than half-empty. The seats nearest us are filling up, people getting loud. My focus ping-pongs around from the people to the ice to the screens high above and the lights ringing the upper levels. The guy wearing the baseball hat to the hockey game. The bright orange jersey in the sea of blue. The chaos is kind of amazing.

"Yasss!" Sanden shouts, grabbing my arm and shaking me. "Look out for your man."

Players have started filling the ice, pucks everywhere; something is announced, but it's drowned out by the music pumping through the speakers.

My gaze immediately latches onto the blue team, watching player after player speed by, trying to catch a glimpse of Aleks. I feel like a teenage girl at a Harley Valentine concert, desperately hoping for attention that isn't going to come, and while I'm being a complete dork about this whole thing, I'm okay with it.

"When you were describing hockey," I yell to Sanden over the loud music, "I was expecting something more structured than this." I point to where a player is smacking puck after puck into the net. "He scored, like, twenty times. What is happening?" If this is hockey, I can get behind it.

"This is the pregame warm-up." He loses his shit laughing at me. "This isn't the *game*."

"Oh." I flop back into my chair. "To think I was enjoying myself."

"Does that mean you'll come again?"

"Not a chance."

His face falls a little.

"You know who'd love these seats? Eman."

Sanden waves a hand. "Eh. That guy. He's always busy with his *fiancé* these days."

He says fiancé with so much disdain I'm tempted to ask why he hates Remy.

But before I can, he shoots forward in his seat. "There he is."

My head snaps in the direction he's pointing, and if I thought an almost naked Aleksander Emerson was a sight for the spank bank, it's nothing on him skating, lightning speed, in full padding.

My tongue swipes my suddenly dry lips as I'm glued to every powerful movement.

"Damn, he's fast," I say.

"Hard to believe that's the same guy who could barely walk straight."

I glance around to make sure we're not being over-heard. "I'm torn on what suits him better. The dress, the briefs, or all this." I gesture toward where he is on the other side of the ice.

"The man looked good in all three, so he's possibly one of the sexiest men alive."

Sanden has a point.

"I'm willing to bet he'd look even better in none of those things. I'd pay to see that sleeve tattoo again. His dark hair all messy with sweat …" And I'm getting way too into that image. I shift in my seat.

Sanden eyes me. "Oh, you are *so* sleeping with the guy."

"Except you forgot one thing." I point out at the team. "Famous hockey player." Then I point at my face. "Poor, little ol' me."

"We both saw his face when we showed up that morning. I don't think I've ever seen a hockey player blush before. Also, you're not little, you stupid huge tank of a human being."

"I'm not *that* big. And he wasn't blushing." He's way too tan for that.

"Ah. My bad. That was you."

I shove him, hating that he's right, and he almost face-plants off his chair. For as confident as I'd been the night we got the callout, the next morning, I could barely put two words together. Not only because I was surrounded by half-naked men, and Aleks was acting weird, and one of them was literally passed out in the yard, but … they were intimidating. Even after I'd seen them at their worst. They all live a life way beyond anything I could ever dream of, and no matter what I do, what I accomplish, I could never measure up to all that.

I'm used to having nothing. Guys like Aleks have everything and a bottomless bank account to get more. Once upon a time, I had dreams, until I realized that living off ramen and having five roommates to make ends meet wasn't worth it. I trained to be a firefighter, and I've never looked back. I love it, but it's not exactly glamorous work.

So while it was awesome that Aleks could flirt with me when he was drunk, and a total ego boost to know he thinks I'm hot, when it comes down to it, he's him and I'm … *me*.

And I like me, but even I know I'm a complete nobody.

Guys like Aleks might fuck nobodies when they're drunk, but that's about all we're good for.

Hey, I'm up for it if he is, but I just have to remind myself that's all it could ever be.

I watch Aleks for a few more minutes, but he's completely consumed by what he's doing, so I drop back in my chair and open Google. Then I type in, *who is Sidney Crosby?*

When the results come up, it's easy to see why those hockey players went wild over my name.

Turns out the guy is kinda a big deal.

A loud *thump* breaks me out of my search, and when I glance up, my nerves shoot into my throat. There, on the other side of the glass, is Aleks, shit-eating grin in place.

"What? We're not interesting enough for you?" he taunts.

I lean forward, slapping my phone, screen out, to the glass. He reads what I was looking at and throws his head back with a laugh.

"You're only looking that up now?"

"It's possible I forgot about it until this second."

Aleks gasps, gloved hand flying to his chest as he skates back a step. "It's like you want to break my heart." His gaze reluctantly slides to Sanden. "You got him here."

"He didn't put up much of a fight, if I'm honest."

The need to shove him again is strong.

I'm too busy glaring at Sanden that I don't see Aleks move until it's too late.

He swings his hockey stick around, scoops something up, and then *flings*. What feels like a snowball hits my head as shards of ice slip down the back of my shirt.

My neck practically turtles into the jersey, and when I glance back up at Aleks, jaw hanging open, I'm a mixture of amused and in shock.

He holds his arms out to the side. "Do I have your attention now?"

I shake the loose ice from my hair and stand up, getting as close to the glass as I can and totally failing at keeping my smile in check. "Just for that, every time you're on the ice, I'm gonna be too busy to watch. You have a lot of teammates I can google."

"Uh-huh." His gorgeous eyes run from my head to my waist and back up again before quickly pinging away. "Nice jersey."

"Thanks." And then, fuck it. I turn around so he can see his name and glance back at him over my shoulder. "I'm told he's an okay player, but I haven't had a chance to look him up yet."

"*Damn*." Aleks slaps his helmet, bright eyes fixed on me, and only snaps out of it when his team starts to leave the ice. "I gotta go. You better watch me."

"Why the fuck do you think I'm here?"

CHAPTER FIVE

ALEKS

Even though I hit the ice with determination to show off and I'm killing it, I'm yet to put one in the net. I've had countless shots on goal, but Anaheim's new goalie, Caddel, is on a streak and shuts down every attempt I make.

Something Oskar likes to point out every time he skates by me. It's the first time playing him this season— our preseason games were against Vancouver, Calgary, and Edmonton. He was once my teammate; now we're playing on opposite sides, and it's weird but also comforting.

It's a shame we don't have Oskar on our team because that man can defend a zone like no other. Though he's either going easy on me, or my resolve to impress a certain firefighter in the stands is outmaneuvering Oskar's talent.

After another failed attempt on goal where play is stopped, Oskar skates up to me.

"Did I see the firemen guys in the stands?" he asks.

"Yep."

"Ah. Is that why you're playing so shit? Because your future husband is watching?"

"Excuse me, it's future father of my babies. I'm never getting married again. Get it right."

Oskar laughs. "Sorry for getting the details wrong. You going out with them after this?"

"I dunno. I hope so, but he's already made it clear he doesn't want to be here. Every time I'm on the ice, he's got his head in his phone."

Oskar punches my shoulder with his gloved hand. "Then let's get his attention. Get the puck." He skates off before I can ask what he's going to do, but it becomes clear when the next time I'm in possession, he charges at me like a Spanish bull and slams me into the boards.

The loud bang as I hit the plexiglass echoes around the arena and is followed by gasps from the crowd.

He has the skill to make it look like a legal body check, but I lose the puck, and it's picked up by one of Oskar's teammates. Who then scores.

I'm called off the ice, but Oskar blows me a kiss.

Worst wingman ever.

By the start of the third period, I'm tired of constantly being shut down by Caddel, but my line mate, Dennan Katz, is having more luck, so I focus all my energy on getting him the puck.

To go from a 1-1 tie going into the last period to a 4-1 win, thanks to Katz's two goals with my assists, I'm not even going to rub the upset in Oskar's face. Much.

I'm obviously a bigger person than he is.

And when we run into each other in the corridor while I'm heading for the press conference and he's leaving it, I don't even mention the loss. I smile—a totally innocent and non-gloaty smile.

But then he says, "It was so noble of you to give up scoring so one of your teammates could do it for you."

"I need to show Gabe that I'm a giver."

Oskar shakes his head. "You're so getting married. I'll meet you out front because I need to witness this train wreck in person."

I wave him off. "By the time we get out of here, I'm sure he'll be gone."

That makes Oskar run for the locker room, and now I'm worried he's going to try to wingman for me again, and after his attempt on the ice, I think I'll be better off without his help.

I breeze through the press conference, spout how welcoming my new team has been and how Katz and I have immediately connected on the ice, and kiss my new coach's ass by saying he's a genius for pairing us up. I'm talking up Seattle because, if I'm honest, it's not that I'm *not* getting along with everyone, but I'm still an outsider.

Everyone is great and professional. They're all cordial. And maybe it's because I'm used to having friends like Oskar and Ezra, where insults are how they show affection, but this whole respectful encouragement I'm getting from everyone is freaking me out.

There are drugs in the water in Seattle, aren't there? Only explanation it could be. Actually, it's probably because they're so close to the Canadian border. All that politeness filters through.

By the time I do my press conference duties, shower, and get dressed, Oskar's waiting outside the Seattle locker room for me.

I step close to him and lower my voice while other teammates file out behind me. "On the extreme off chance he's still out there, do not embarrass me in front of Gabe. I am begging you."

"If your future husband can't love you for who you are, do you really want to marry him in the first place?"

38

I shove him. "Don't mention marriage. Joke all you want about us ending up together, having babies, whatever, but I'm trying to get laid here, okay? Hell, not even full-on sex. I could really go for a blowjob."

"Sorry, I'm a taken man now." Oskar starts walking toward the player's exit, and I follow.

"From Gabe, you hoser."

"No need for name-calling. And don't worry, I'll get you that blowjob, even if I have to pay him."

"That's prostitution."

"Nothing wrong with sex work."

"Except you've already accused Gabe of being a stripper multiple times when he's not. Can you please try not to be so shameless tonight?"

"Ugh. You're starting to sound exactly like Lane." His voice goes high-pitched. "'Have pride in who you are and what you've accomplished, Oskar. You deserve respect.' You're both gross. If I wanna be cheap and nasty, let me be cheap and nasty."

"Okay, but you're getting regular sex. I'm not. I haven't even …." Nope. Not going there.

"Haven't even what?" Oskar grabs my arm to stop me as we reach the exit.

"You know … since Rebecca."

His eyes widen. His mouth drops.

I have the very real fear that I have broken one of the best defensemen in the league.

"You are an abomination to the manwhore crown I gave you! I bestowed greatness upon you, and you … you … For *shame*." He's ridiculous, but it's also why I like him. Because even though this is a sensitive topic for me, he can make light of it. It's what I need to remind myself that sex isn't a big deal.

I was looking forward to the freedom of being able to bang anyone I wanted, but the theory is much less scary than the reality. I've only ever been with one person, and we were comfortable with each other. Being with someone new, what if it's awkward? What if I come in, like, two seconds? What if I'm bad at giving blowjobs? Hell, I think part of the reason I didn't hook up with any of my PR dates, other than not feeling the whole set-up part of it, is what if I'm actually bad at everything and Rebecca was too nice to tell me?

It's not something I'm going to talk to her about either because while we ended on good terms, we ended things for a reason, and I think we're lucky we didn't have kids because this gives us a clean break.

A clean break where I have no idea what I'm doing and I'm truly on my own for the first time in my whole life.

Cool.

Totally fun.

Not at all daunting.

"We need to fix your dry spell, stat," Oskar says and pulls me through the exit. "Did you drive here?"

"Yeah, my car's in the team parking lot."

"Lead the way."

"Wait ... what about—"

"You think I didn't run out there and track down your future h—hookup and his friend? They're meeting us at Salty."

"Worst name for a gay bar ever," I say.

"I dunno. It works on so many levels. You're either going to meet bitchy queens or give someone a blowjob. Either way, everything is salty."

"Shouldn't you be bonding with your new team instead of going out with me?" I ask.

"Eh, they all already love me."

"Is that your delusion talking, or did you bribe them with new cars or some shit?"

"Come on. You know me."

"Delusion. Got it." I drive us to Salty, and the only reason I know where it is is because I looked up gay bars when I first got here. Have I had the guts to go inside one yet? No. And I'm so glad I didn't say that out loud because I can already hear Oskar's retort: That goes for people as well as gay bars.

Maybe I should get this first hookup over with. Gabe is hot, totally my type—if I had a type, which I don't, so I guess that doesn't really mean much. He's seen me at my worst, so really, anything I do in bed can't be too much of a disappointment.

Right?

"I'm overthinking this," I blurt before we get out of the car.

Oskar grunts. "Okay, here's the deal. Supportive Oskar is going to come out, but I'm warning you, it's for a limited time only. Here goes." He turns and locks eyes with me. "You don't have to do anything you don't want to do."

"I want to. It's just … I'm in my head about it all. It's been so. Fucking. Long. I don't really even know how to flirt anymore. I'm sure *I want to have your babies* is not something you're supposed to yell at hot people."

"To be fair, you're not supposed to yell that at ugly people either."

41

"Ah. Supportive Oskar is already gone. Good to know. Can you at least drag me in there if you're going to force this upon me?"

"Is that you giving me permission?"

"Yes. Please make me do this because I really want to, but it turns out I don't like change. I like comfort and familiarity, and the only adrenaline I like is when I'm on the ice."

But as I walk into that club, my gaze ping-ponging all over to find my guy, my eyes finally land on a booth where he's sitting there watching me.

His muscles, his cocky smile, the nest of mess that is his hair …

Suddenly, this type of adrenaline rush is all worth it.

CHAPTER SIX

GABE

Showing up at his game, basically racing him to this club … I might as well have the words *Fuck Me* stamped on my forehead because the whole time Aleks approaches, I can't look away.

"You are not subtle," Sanden points out.

"I can't help it. The man is hot."

"Must be why you're coming across so thirsty."

"Shut up. It's your fault. You forced me to go to his game."

Sanden's laugh is loud enough that the people at the table next to us turn and stare, but I don't care.

"No, no, you're right," Sanden says. "All my fault."

"Glad we agree."

"I can't wait to see where this goes."

"Probably nowhere, but hey, if he asks me into the back room of the bar, I'm not gonna say no." We knock our beers together, and I take a long drink as the two hockey players reach us. Nerves buzz through my limbs, and I have to shake them out before I start bouncing in my seat.

"My favorite strippers," Oskar says, opening his arms.

"As much as I know you're fucking with us, I wouldn't be at all surprised if you really had favorites," I retort, then drag my gaze back to Aleks. "Hey."

43

"Yeah, hey." He immediately breaks eye contact and slides into the other side of the booth. Opposite Sanden. Basically as far from me as he can get.

Well, damn.

Maybe that's the answer to where this could go: nowhere.

My excitement crashes as I suddenly worry that I've read into something that isn't actually there. Though how many ways can you misread someone offering to have your babies? But I've been wrong in the past, and the thought of me being here could be making him uncomfortable doesn't sit right with me.

I take a long drink of my beer, and when I set it down, Oskar is across from me, very obviously looking between me and Aleks. Before I can say a thing, Oskar dives off his seat and onto the floor beside us.

"*Jesus.*" I jump up to help him to his feet.

"Aleks," Oskar snaps. "If you wanted to sit next to Gabe, you could have said—you didn't need to manhandle me. Only Lane gets to do that."

Then before I have a chance to catch up, Oskar shoves me into his vacated chair and drops into mine, looking entirely too proud of himself.

I glance over at Sanden. "And you said I'm not subtle."

"No idea what you mean." Oskar picks up my beer and finishes it off.

"Another round?" I offer flatly.

"We'll get it!" Sanden jumps out of his seat, and Oskar follows so fast it's like he's on a pull string.

Apparently, subtlety is out the window today.

I slip into the booth next to Aleks. He's not as big as Oskar is, and neither of them is near as wide as me, but Aleks has that type of body that's lean and toned. He has muscles and is obviously fit, but without his skates or pads, he's kinda small.

Aleks sighs beside me. "Why am I getting flashbacks to sitting on the back of the bus in middle school with all my friends crowded around me and Susie Shepner, waiting for us to kiss?"

"Yeah, I don't think *that's* what those two are waiting for." I turn and pump my eyebrows at him, and Aleks bursts out laughing. He drags a hand over his face and turns to face me.

"Gah. This is … I'm sorry this is awkward."

"Does pointing out the awkwardness make it less awkward or more awkward?"

"Maybe we need to say 'awkward' one more time."

"Don't think that helped." I'm joking, though, because with only a few words, the tension seems to have left him. "You didn't look worried when you were dumping ice over my head. What happened?"

He shrugs. "I was on the ice. It's my domain. Nothing can touch me out there."

"Except your buddy who was slamming you into the boards."

Aleks rolls out his shoulder. "That was for your benefit, by the way."

"It was?"

"Yeah." The playful shove he gives me lights up my excitement again. "*Someone* wasn't watching again."

My smile is fucking ridiculous. "Ah … but someone else was, huh?"

"It was distracting."

"Is that what you're going with? You were too distracted to score any goals? I thought the point of hockey was to put the ball thing in the net thing?"

"Ball thing," he mutters. "I got two assists. That's considered a good night."

"Mm. I've heard of that. It's like when my friend had gallbladder surgery, he gave all the praise to the nurses instead of the doctor. Makes total sense."

"You'll have to keep coming to my games until you see me put one in the net."

I lean in. "Is that your way of asking to see me again?"

Aleks goes to reply, then changes his mind, glancing in the direction Oskar and Sanden disappeared. That weird twisting feeling grips me again. There's something going on here that I'm missing because I'm *sure* he's flirting with me, but …

A rotten question hits me, and I ask it before I can change my mind. "Seeing as subtlety doesn't exist tonight, I'm going to be straightforward. Are you seeing someone, or …? You seem interested but also not. If you've got a boyfriend or something, I'm not into that."

It's not at all reassuring when he immediately grips his left ring finger. *If this bastard is married—*

"No, I'm …" He pulls a face. "I'm divorced. Recently. And it's just occurred to me you're the first person I've actually had to tell that to, and it's something I'm going to have to say again and again …"

Wow. That's heavy. And explains a lot.

I drag my hand roughly through my hair. It doesn't change anything here because as long as the guy is available, I'm down to hook up, but being unattached and actually being *available* to hook up are two totally different things.

"You don't have to tell anyone you don't want to. Maybe if you really were my future husband and father of all these apparent babies"—I nudge him so he knows that is a total fucking joke—"then you'd probably need to give me the heads-up, but if you're just looking for a fun night, that's not something you have to talk about. I think. I should clarify that I'm *not* divorced, so I'm not an expert, but when it comes to me, you don't need to say." Fuck, that was a lot of words. "And now I'm going to stop talking."

"You, uh … you'd want to hook up?"

I finally turn back to him to find those piercing green eyes on me. "Sorry, was coming to your game and showing up here not me broadcasting my interest?"

Aleks rubs the scruff on his jaw for a moment. Then he gives me an absolutely heart-stopping smile.

Damn, little hockey player.

"It's been that long since I've had anyone flirt with me, I might need things spelled out some more."

Sanden and Oskar loudly announce their arrival, and I'm almost disappointed to see them again. With Aleks jumping between flirty and nervous, I need more time to bring him out of his shell, so when Sanden hands me my beer, I pick it up and pretend to look at the label.

"You know what, I feel like something stronger. Aleks, help me with it?" Then I close my hand over his and slide out of the booth, relieved as fuck when he follows. Instead of heading toward the bar, I lead him over to a shadowy corner and fall back against the wall, pulling him in after me. He stands between my legs, not touching anywhere, but so fucking close. My heart is beating madly as my gaze drops to his lips, and I'm so desperate to taste them, reveling in this moment of pre-make-out expectation, that it takes me a moment to notice his mouth is forming words.

"So … do you come here often?"

Is he for real?

Aleks is feigning interest in the totally black wall behind me, and I fight my instincts not to tease him.

"Ah, yeah. A bit."

"Cool." He clears his throat. "I've never … you know, in a gay bar, that is."

"Really?"

"Married, remember? I can't imagine my wife would have been thrilled with me turning around and saying, *hey, babe, going to grind up against a bunch of men tonight, back later.*"

I smirk. "And yet, I can't help but notice the lack of grinding so far."

He throws a thumb over his shoulder toward the dance floor. "What do you call that?"

"A good time. That we're not a part of."

Uncertainty crosses his face. "You wanna go out there?"

"If I did, I'd be out there." I swallow, taking a risk, and lightly set my hands on his hips.

Aleks tracks the movement, and when he looks up, his eyes seem darker than before. "Tell me what it's like."

"Dancing?"

"With other men. Grinding and stuff."

Grinding and stuff. I never thought I'd find a professional jock *cute*. "It's hot. Literally, because of all the sweat and the dancing, but being surrounded by that many bodies? By men who want to fuck you? I defy any queer dude to not be turned on."

He glances back that way, and while I definitely, one hundred percent want to be the one who gets off with him tonight, I recognize that look. A man who's wanted something for a really long time and never been able to

48

have it. I felt the same way when I walked into a gay club for the first time. And sure, not every bi or pan or whatever-he-is guy needs to be with another man, but Aleks clearly *wants* to.

"Hey." I wait until he looks at me. "If you want to dance, I'm okay with that. If you want to know what it's like to have a bunch of men with their hands all over you, we can do that too. My future husband should have whatever he wants."

That finally seems to relax him. "No more future husband jokes, fuck. I just got out of one marriage, and I'm not interested in another anytime soon. Maybe ever." He shifts closer. "But I appreciate the offer. You're …" He wrinkles his nose. "Kinda cool. Which I don't think you're supposed to tell your hookups, but there it is."

"Technically, we haven't hooked up yet."

He hangs his head back. "See? I'm fucking it up already."

But he's smiling. And I'm smiling. And when he looks back at me again, his green eyes hook my attention and send a surge of lust through me.

I make my move. Slowly, because I'm not a dick, and I want him to know this is all up to him, I lean in. One breath … two … then my lips graze his. Want shivers through me, a powerful desire that threatens to knock me off my feet.

He's so fucking hot. *Cute.* Jumping from confident to uncertain and back again in a way that's got my interest. A flash of him on his knees, piercing eyes looking up at me, stubble scraping my balls, fills my mind, and my cock jumps to life at the thought.

His warm breath is minty, lips soft, and this time, Aleks drags them over mine. I almost whimper at the not-quite contact, because no way is this anywhere near enough. My brain is screaming at me to dive in, take it deeper, but I'm really putting my patience to work as I try to read where he's at. My hand settles on his face, the other gripping tighter to his hip, and Aleks takes my subtle pressure for the invitation it is. He shifts forward, chest meeting mine as his mouth opens and I swallow his shuddery breath. Something lurches below my belly, and when his tongue grazes mine, my groan fills both of us.

I keep things slow, deep, tasting and savoring and hoping that this is doing everything for Aleks that it's doing for me. I'm fucking floating at the direction the night has taken, at the way he feels pressed against me, at every stuttered breath making his chest move against mine.

There's nothing like a first kiss. Nothing like that band of possibility stretching tighter and tighter until you're both so turned on you're ready to rip each other's clothes off.

Aleks's hands form fists on my jersey, his kiss turning aggressive and needy, short-circuiting my brain. His stubble, the sudden confidence ... My cock is a fucking steel rod in my pants, and in an effort to desperately seek friction, I pull his hips toward me.

His hard cock meets mine, but before I can sink into the bliss of it, he's torn away from me.

My eyes snap open to find Aleks stumbling backward. "Ah, give me a minute?" he asks before almost bolting for the bathrooms.

My forehead knots as I watch him hurry away. Then I stand there like a fool and give him a few minutes—okay, *ten* minutes—before I accept that he isn't coming back.

And when I get to the table, it's only Sanden and Oskar there.

"You guys seen Aleks?"

Oskar's head snaps my way. "Wasn't he with you?"

"He was, and then ..." I kissed him when he probably didn't want me to, scared him off, and now I feel like shit. "He wasn't."

"Fuck." Oskar jumps up and throws some cash on the table. I catch sight of a hundred-dollar bill in there.

"Why do you have cash on you?" I ask him.

"Call it my contingency for tonight."

I get the feeling I don't want to know what he means by that.

"Did Aleks say where he was going?" Oskar asks.

"He headed for the bathroom, but that was a while ago."

I don't need to say more. The three of us know I've been rejected. Fun times.

Oskar goes to turn away when he pauses and glances back. "In this case, I can promise that it's not you. It's definitely him."

"Not making me feel any better either way."

"Does it help to know that before I met my sex jailer, I would have done you?" He glances at Sanden. "Probably both of you, if I'm honest. At the same time."

Sanden laughs. "Yeah, but it's *you*. I don't think that counts if the things I've read are any indication."

And while I have no fucking clue what they're talking about, I can safely say it doesn't help. Aleks ... fuck. One kiss from him was enough to rearrange gravity, and it kinda sucks to know I couldn't do that for him.

CHAPTER SEVEN

ALEKS

When there's a knock on my door around twenty minutes after arriving home, I'm tempted to hide and pretend I'm not here.

Because it's either Oskar or Gabe, and I hope it's Oskar. He's the better choice of the two. If Gabe followed me home, I'm going to have to admit that I freaked out. His mouth was warm and perfect, his kiss unlike anything else I'd ever experienced before.

It started soft and sweet, but the minute his tongue met mine, I was drowning. Drowning in doubt and in pleasure. It confused the fuck out of me, and instead of explaining myself like an adult, I ran out of the fire exit to the club to try to get some air.

Then, by the time I got myself under control, I realized I was going to have to go back inside and explain myself. I didn't have the words, so I chickened out completely and left.

Because I'm that guy now. Apparently.

I've never been flaky before, but ever since I moved here, I don't know what's up, what's down, or what I'm doing half the time.

The only definite thing in my life at the moment is hockey.

The doorbell goes off again, but this time it's followed up with Oskar saying, "I know you're in there."

I go to the door and check the monitor on the wall to make sure he's alone. Oskar ribbing me about disappearing is only slightly less embarrassing than Gabe doing it.

I let him in but don't let him talk. "I don't need to hear it."

"Hear what?"

I have to give him credit; his innocent tone is impressive. "That I'm a loser for running out on a supersmoking-hot guy who, with one kiss, sent me into a spiral of insecurity. I already hate myself enough."

"I … that …" Oskar blinks at me.

Oh look, I broke him again.

"I need to call Lane." He takes his phone out and hits his boyfriend's number. "I need help" is the first thing he says down the line.

I can hear Lane's response from feet away. "What did you do, Oskar You-Better-Not-Have-Had-Public-Sex-And-Cheated-On-Me Voyjik?"

I laugh.

Oskar does not. He turns away and whispers into the phone. "Baby, why is that your first reaction to me needing help?" There's a beat where I can't hear what Lane says. "That old habit has to die a horrible death. Because I love you. Only you."

I fold my arms impatiently.

"I need help because Aleks is being emotional about *insecurities* and *feelings*, and—"

Okay, the laugh coming through the phone is even louder than the yelling.

"So glad my torment is hilarious," I call out so he can hear.

Oskar puts the phone on speaker.

"Sorry, Aleks," Lane says. "I'm not laughing at you. I'm laughing because Oskar doesn't know what to do. If you need an adult to give you advice, I'm here."

Oskar hands me the phone and then follows me as I move to my living room and slump on the couch.

"I don't need advice. I need …"

"He needs to rip off the Band-Aid and get laid," Oskar says, and I mean, he's not wrong. "Hey, that rhymes!"

"Ah," Lane says. "So, you never … with any of those PR dates you went on?"

"Nope. Didn't even kiss them other than a peck on the cheek. Tonight, I kissed a guy and then ran away because I'm scared shitless."

"Can you pinpoint why you ran away? What scared you off?"

It's easy to say it's because I've never been with a man. I'm worried about not knowing how to give good head and that it will be an awkward experience, but if I look deeper, I think those are only surface-level issues.

"I'm scared I won't be enough."

"Sexually?" Oskar asks. "Need some pointers? I've got lots of advice."

"I think he means overall. Am I right?" Lane asks.

"This guy is, like, perfect. I even told him my situation, and we agreed we wanted to just hook up, but when it came down to it, I froze. I couldn't push past that."

"Honesty is a good start," Lane says. "Tell him that you're nervous. Tell him that you might freak out, even if it's irrational. If he's not okay with you needing to take a break or to stop, even if you're halfway through a blowjob, then he's not the guy you should take this step with."

"Well, there's no way Gabe will ever want to see me again, so I'll keep that advice for the next guy."

Before I know it, Oskar charges into my kitchen and brings back a lighter. "I know how you can see Gabe again." He lights it.

Lane can't even see Oskar, but we say at the same time, "No."

"Whether it's with Gabe or someone else, I hate to say it, but Oskar's right. You need to rip off the Band-Aid, but you also need to do it in a safe environment and be up-front with whoever you go there with."

I run a hand through my hair. "It's like I'm back in high school."

"Just don't use the words 'no-no areas,'" Oskar says. "It's really not a sexy way to word it. I once had this guy where he—"

"And I don't need to hear any more," Lane cuts in. "Oskar, be a good boy, and I'll see you when you get back from your road trip."

Oskar somehow preens under being called a good boy. "No-no areas" bad. "Good boy" is hot. Apparently. I'm not going to think about that too hard.

What I am going to think about is how I went from hoping Gabe turns up to my next home game to hoping I never see him again at all. Even if I want to.

–

Our following game is also at home, and even though I tell myself not to look, I can't help but check if Gabe came. He didn't. Neither did Sanden. Those seats stay empty the whole game.

After that, it's an eight-day road trip for the team, and I have to say, throwing myself into hockey works as a good distraction. On the ice, I'm in the zone. It's after the games, at restaurants and bars with the team, going home alone, that I start to think of Gabe and how I fucked everything up before anything could even happen.

Oskar's advice constantly flits through my mind, telling me I should go out and hook up with someone. Anyone. Like he said, rip off the Band-Aid. But there's something holding me back. Nerves. The idea I might regret it. Everyone else not being Gabe.

He's the first guy who's ever gotten under my skin after one meeting. The only man to send a shiver of want down my spine.

Yeah, I could go out and hook up with countless people, and I've been looking forward to doing that, but now that I have the real opportunity to carry it out, I'm realizing one huge personality trait I didn't know I had until now: I'm not the hookup type.

I want to be, but I don't think I have it in me.

At the next home game, I've all but accepted that those season tickets will go to waste now, but as we hit the ice for the warm-up skate, I notice two figures in the stands. My heart leaps into my chest when I see Sanden, but it sinks again when the guy next to him isn't Gabe.

It's a guy wearing a Colorado jersey … to a Seattle versus Carolina game. Makes sense.

I nod to Sanden, who gives me a wave, and the guy who I will refer to as Colorado forever and ever bops up and down in his seat like a kid full of sugar.

Even though I'm disappointed Gabe's not here, at least that means I can focus on hockey. At first, I think that's a good thing until I have the game of my life, score a fucking hat trick, get an assist, and realize that Gabe missed it all.

I shouldn't care, but I do.

Which is why, immediately after the final buzzer goes, I skate up to the area Sanden's in and wave him down.

Some kids from the stands run toward me, so I get the team equipment manager to throw me some pucks to hand through the slits in the plexiglass to them, but to Sanden, I say, "I need Gabe's number."

Sanden folds his arms. "Yeah, Gabe's not into whatever game you're playing. And I don't mean hockey."

"Though he hates that too," I add.

He laughs. "True."

"He's going to be at my engagement party tomorrow night," Colorado says behind Sanden.

Sanden nudges him. "Dude."

"What? I'm not giving up a chance to have an honest-to-God sports legend at my party. Gabe can tell him to fuck off if he really wants to."

I wince because there are still children being handed pucks, and even though hockey players are known to swear like sailors, we try not to in front of the kids. "I'll be there," I say just to get Colorado to leave. "Where is it?"

"Fox Brewhouse. We're starting at ten."

"See you then." If I can get the courage to face Gabe, that is.

CHAPTER EIGHT

GABE

I'm late getting to the engagement party. The Brewhouse's private area isn't as loud as the main part of the bar, but it's full of people, and it takes me a moment to spot Sanden.

And the look he's wearing immediately puts me on guard.

I'm not even sure why I was invited to this thing. I know Remy professionally, and I know Eman through Sanden, but we're not exactly close. Sanden looking like this so early in the night makes me think the engagement party isn't going smoothly.

Which doesn't surprise me at all with Eman involved.

Eman is … a lot. He used to go to school with Sanden and comes along to all the events our station puts on, which is how he met his fiancé, Remy, who's a paramedic for Station 21, the closest station geographically to ours. There's a friendly rivalry between the stations, but Remy seems sweet. Maybe too sweet compared to Eman's abrasiveness. Eman's the kind of guy who thinks he's best buddies with everyone, but there's always been something about him that's a little off. And it's nothing I can put my finger on, so half the time, I wonder if the issue is with me and not him.

So when I see Sanden's face, my first thought is that Eman is being his a-lot-ish self, but then I place the expression: guilt.

"What's going on?" I ask cautiously as I approach where he's drinking alone at a cocktail table.

"Yeah, nothing, all good, buddy."

Buddy is what we call people when we're trying to either calm them down or get them to follow directions.

"Let me guess, you signed me up for extra chores next week?"

"Nope, geez, what kind of guy do you think I am? Signing you up for chores. Like I'd do anything *that* horrible, and in fact, the thing that I knew and didn't tell you is almost angelic in comparison."

Uh-oh. I'm really not going to like this. "Yeah, you're gonna have to tell me before my brain starts spinning out."

"Eman came with me to Seattle's game last night, and when Aleks came over, Eman got excited and invited him to come. Here."

My face floods with heat because oh, holy shit. "He said no, right?"

"Sure. Of course he did. And that's definitely not him over there being drooled on by Eman."

I snap around so fast I'm surprised I don't trip over the stool beside me. It only takes a second of searching before my gaze catches on Aleks, where he's sitting in a lounge area with Eman and some other guys.

I swear I can't breathe for a minute. This consuming mix of lust and want folds over me before it all crashes down again at the reminder of the last time I saw him.

I turn back to Sanden. "Nice of him to make Eman's night like this."

Sanden hums. "Nice. Yeah."

Fuck. There goes my fun night of having a few drinks and forgetting myself for a minute. Because if Aleks is here, there's no way I'm going to be able to relax when he's literally taken over my brainage. The door is closed when it comes to him. I get it, and I respect his decision. There are more than enough queer guys here for him to move on from his divorce with.

It doesn't stop me from wanting him though. That one kiss is seared into my memory bank as the hottest kiss that was cut off way too quickly. But I have to let it go.

Maybe he's only recently coming to terms with being queer. Or he's still questioning himself. Either way, I'm going to be the bigger person.

Instead of making things weird between us, I'm better off keeping my distance and letting him enjoy his night.

"A heads-up would have been nice."

"I know." Sanden at least has the decency to look sheepish. "I kept going back and forth on telling you, but he asked for your number, and even though I told him no, it was clear he wanted to talk to you. And *I* knew that if *you* knew that he would be here, you would have found an excuse not to come. Even though you really want to see him again."

I give Sanden a tight smile. "It doesn't matter what I want though."

"Unless you both want the same thing."

"If we both wanted the same thing, we would have hooked up already. Just leave it."

"I'm telling you, he—"

I hold out my arms. "I'm here. I'm going to enjoy myself." Yeah, *right*. "If he wants to talk to me, I'm not exactly hard to miss."

Sanden chuckles. "Okay, we'll leave it all up to the pro hockey player who can get body slammed on the ice but is scared of a little kiss."

It was *not* a little kiss.

I shush him instead of pointing that out. "I only told you that because you were there and got to see the epic display of my rejection. You're not allowed to spread it around. Aleks is … he's in a weird place, okay? Drop it."

"It's dropped." Sanden holds out his hands like he's proving they're empty. Then his gaze cuts to something over my shoulder, and he scowls. I follow his stare to where Eman is *still* hanging off Aleks. Aleks is talking to him but subtly leaning away.

"You would think Eman would be spending tonight with Remy, though. I mean, it *is* their engagement party. They *are* the ones getting married."

I eye Sanden. "You want Aleks for yourself or something?" It would make sense. Sanden is a hockey fan, and Aleks is hot, so it wouldn't be totally out-there to consider.

Sanden shoves me. "Your sloppy seconds? Not a chance."

"Okay, but …" It hurts to even say this. "If you both … you know … and then …" I take a breath and remind myself I'm not in high school anymore. "You don't need to worry about me. If anything happened between you two, it's your business."

Sanden eyes me. "He asked for your number, not mine."

Maybe he asked for it to apologize for leaving me hanging, but I'm not the one for him. I don't need to hear that.

"I'm going to get a drink."

"Wanna get me one too?" He mutters, "I'm gonna need it."

Whatever the fuck that means.

I head for the bar, where Eman and Remy blessedly have a tab set up, and grab two beers. While I'm waiting, my eyes stray back to Aleks, and this time, he's already watching me.

His expression of sheer terror at the sight of me totally fills me with reassurance about him wanting to talk.

"Here's your beers."

I jump at the voice and quickly grab the bottles the bartender is holding out. Drinking is suddenly the last thing I want to do, but I take one quick, deep gulp anyway.

All I need to do is get through tonight. Maybe if I find a guy of my own, I won't care about what Aleks is up to.

Eman's loud laughter pulls my attention back to them, to where his hand is resting on Aleks's shoulder as Eman leans right into his space. It's ... uncomfortably close. If he was my fiancé, I'd have words about how he's ignoring everyone else in favor of a famous face. One glance back at Sanden, and his expression mirrors my own.

Another loud burst of laughter, and this time, Eman sloshes half of his drink over Aleks's knee. Aleks tries to move away, but there's a guy on the other side of him, and when he glances up and his eyes catch mine again, there's only one word in them.

Help.

I try to whine to myself that the hockey guy isn't my problem, but the fire roaring alive in my gut calls out the lie. Before I can stop myself, my feet head in his direction.

"Eman, hey," I call as I reach them. "Remy needs you."

Eman waves a hand toward me. "He knows where I am."

"Yeah, he said something about the card left on the bar. You've hit your limit ... or they've spent over your limit ..."

Eman's eyes fly wide. "Fuck." Then he scrambles drunkenly from his seat, and the second he's swallowed by the crowd, I grab Aleks's hand, yank him away from the other guy, and pull him after me. I don't stop until we reach a small seating area half hidden from the rest of the room by a large potted fern.

I release his hand and drop into a couch without a word, setting down both beers I'd been clutching in my other hand, and wait to see if Aleks stays. At first, I think he won't, but then he flops down next to me, and my entire focus funnels to where his thigh is pressed against mine.

"Is he always like that?" Aleks doesn't have to be specific for me to know he's talking about Eman.

"Don't really know him."

"Then why were you invited?"

I rub my jaw. "Most of my station was, but I'm not sure if that's because of Remy or Eman. Remy works at another station, and Eman's sort of made himself an honorary—but not really—member of ours."

"I get the feeling you don't like him much."

And maybe that's true, but I'm not about to sit here and talk trash about a guy when I'm at his party, drinking his beer. Besides, it's obvious what Aleks is doing. "You really want to talk about Eman?"

He lets out a self-conscious *heh* and runs a hand down his face. "No, I ... fuck. I want to apologize."

"What for?"

63

"Running out on you the last time."

My jaw tightens for a second, remembering that heavy weight of rejection. "You don't need to do that. I know you've been out of the game for a while, but it's okay to say no. In fact, I encourage it if you're not feeling it. I'm a big boy. I can handle it."

And I can, even if I'm disappointed.

Aleks watches me out of the corner of his eye, and I wish I knew what thoughts are going through his head.

Everything from the scruff on his face to his sleeve tattoo and the way he carries himself screams confidence and sex appeal, but it's the insecurity behind his bright green eyes that gets to me. The man is fucking sexy. But so are a lot of guys here tonight.

Yet, he's the only one I want to pay attention to.

While he was sitting with Eman, it looked like he was managing conversation fine, even though he was uncomfortable under all that attention. Here, his hands keep flexing, moving, his shoulders are pulled tight, and then he lets it all go in one long exhale. It's like seeing a totally different guy in front of me.

He reaches forward to snag the second beer, turns in his chair to face me so his still-damp knee replaces his thigh against mine, and when his eyes meet mine, they're steady.

"How about we try for a do-over?" he asks.

"A do-over?"

"Yeah. Like, last time was practice. This is the big game."

I eye him, trying to figure out if I want to play. The guy obviously has baggage, and this is a lot of work to go through to get him naked.

Even though I know I should walk away, I also know I won't.

Not when he looks at me like that.

Not when I can feel his anxiety rolling off him in waves.

And not when—*son of a bitch*—the nerves trickle into me too. I'm not a nervous guy. In my line of work, you learn to control it, or you get hurt. Around Aleks, I'm completely out of fucking control.

I hate it because when he fucks with me again, it's gonna hurt.

But watch me walk right into the fire anyway.

CHAPTER NINE

ALEKS

"I feel like I owe you an explanation first," I blurt and then rub my sweaty hands over my jeans. "A proper one."

"I don't want to hear if I fucked up somehow—"

"You didn't. Fuck, you so didn't." My skin feels hot under my collar, and adjusting it does shit all. "This is … well, not embarrassing but kind of hard to get out. I … Okay, I met my wife in high school. Like, early high school. And we were married for ten years. And since splitting, I've been with exactly zero people."

Do the math for me, please, because I don't want to say it out loud.

Realization dawns. "Oh. So you've only been with—"

"One person. My entire life. I kissed Oskar last year before he was with his now partner, but it was only because I thought it would help me move on and be comfortable. Didn't help because we're only friends, and that's all we'll ever be. I'm not only inexperienced with sex, but even kissing anyone other than my wife." I wince. "Ex-wife. And with me coming out so close after my divorce, it's been a bit of a PR debacle, so I've been going out on dates set up by PR people, but it was all for show, so somehow, the pressure of doing it for real has become overwhelming, and I'm … I'm freaking out. So it really, honestly has nothing to do with you. You're great. Our kiss was … great. Everything about you is, uh, great. But I realized I had no idea what I was doing, and as much as I wanted to hook up with you, I was feeling inadequate."

Gabe smiles, but he has to be humoring me or is amused by my total awesomeness and how smooth I am at this.

"I can be that guy for you, you know," he says.

"What guy?"

"Your first time with a man. I get you're coming out of a long relationship, you're probably not looking for anything serious, and you're hot enough that I'm okay with taking things slow and at your pace. I mean, oh no, I have to get all those first experiences out of the way with you! How horrible for me."

I let out a loud, relieved breath. "You have no idea how much I needed to hear that." *I* had no idea until now.

"We'll start slow."

"How slow? Because I really want to kiss you again."

"Dancing." He glances toward the small dance floor in the sectioned-off area for this party, where the two grooms are slow dancing.

"Slow dancing?"

"We have to work our way up to grinding." Gabe stands and holds out his hand.

"I don't want to interrupt their moment." They're the only two out there, and isn't that like a wedding no-no, upstaging the ones getting married?

Gabe doubles over and winces as if he's in pain. "Ouch, fuck."

I jump off the couch. "What's wrong? Where hurts?"

"My pride," he croaks. "I'm feeling rejected again. The only cure is dancing. Help me, Aleks. Help meeeee."

I shove him, but he's so big and brawny he doesn't budge. "I thought you were legit in pain, you dick."

He laughs. Hard. "Okay, in all seriousness, you don't have to dance with me, but you're not getting a chance to kiss me again until you do. Your call."

When Sanden hits the floor with a woman who was introduced to me as Remy's sister earlier, I'm comfortable enough to go out there.

I take Gabe's hand. "I'll do whatever it takes to earn your lips again."

Gabe leans in and says in my ear, "If you play your cards right, you might get my lips somewhere else … eventually."

My cock perks up, and damn it, it won't let me forget how long it's been since I've had sex. But as much as I'd love to fuck around with just anyone, going slow is what I need. I'm appreciative Gabe is willing to go there with me, knowing I'm a mess.

When we reach the dance floor, he takes the lead. He pulls me against him, his thick arms wrapping around my back while my hands rest on his wide chest. It's not only the muscles and rough hands that are new to me but the size difference as well. I'm not a small guy, but compared to Gabe, who's taller and wider, he eclipses me.

If I had my skates on, we'd be the same height, but I think I like this. He lowers his head, touching his forehead to mine, and yeah, I really like that he's bigger than me.

There are a lot of eyes on us, but I don't care because being this close to someone, having their hands on me, their body pressed against mine, we're the only two people in the room.

"How are you doing?" Gabe asks. "No freak-out yet?"

"No freak-out. I want more."

"Hmm, I can feel that against my thigh, but patience is a virtue. Or so I've been told."

I groan, which earns a soft chuckle.

He moves his lips to my ear and murmurs, "I can't wait until you're ready for me to give you everything. For me to move inside you. To have you on your knees."

Wow. Okay. That's new. My dick thickens so fast that all my insecurities disappear. That might change if I ask for him to follow through though.

Slow and steady.

Slow. And. Steady.

"I'm going to turn you inside out, wreck you, and still have you begging for more."

I throw my head back. "Fuck, please kiss me again."

"I guess I did promise if you danced with me ..." Gabe pulls back, his blue eyes piercing through me. His lips quirk, and then he surges forward, his mouth meeting mine.

His lips are warm, his tongue slipping between them and teasing me to open for him. I let him inside, and my knees almost buckle.

The slow, romantic song fades into the background to where I can't even hear it. The loud noises of the people surrounding us disappear too. It's just Gabe and me, tasting, exploring, getting lost in one another.

This time, I'm not worried about what this will lead to. I'm not stressing over hooking up and not living up to expectations because there are no expectations. I'm able to enjoy the moment and get what I want. What I need.

One loud crash breaks through the din and pulls us apart.

We turn to the noise to see a very drunken Colorado— uh, Eman—abusing one of the waitstaff with broken shards of glass all over the floor beneath them. Both Remy and Sanden rush to Eman's side to calm him down, but it's too late. The damage is done when Eman takes a swing and totally misses, almost falling over in the process.

A manager comes over to them, screaming that this party is over.

"Are your friends' events always this dramatic?" I ask.

Gabe laughs. "Says the guy who throws parties in drag and calls the fire department for a fire that doesn't exist."

"Hey, there was a fire, but uh, fair point. I'll give you that."

"Though if you think this is chaotic, I don't want you to meet my ex-roommates. They're basically the only family I have, but hot messes doesn't even begin to describe them."

We're all ushered out of the private area, grabbing our jackets and belongings on the way, and escorted outside. Sanden claps Gabe's back while Remy tries to wrestle Eman into a cab.

"I guess the night really is over, then," Gabe says.

The cold Seattle air whips at my face, but I don't want to say good night.

I turn to him. "I mean, we could … my place is—"

Gabe steps closer and cups my cheek. "Small steps, hockey player."

I grunt, knowing he's right but still wanting to be selfish anyway.

"When can I see you again?" he asks.

"I have another home game tomorrow night—"

"I start my rotation tomorrow."

"What does that mean?"

"I'm on for twenty-four hours, then off for twenty-four for three shifts in a row."

"Damn. After that, I go on a road trip, but it's a short one. Only four days."

"You should get home on my days off then."

I nod. "I want to go on a date with you."

"A real proper date?" He pretends to fan himself.

"Fair warning, the last time I dated, I had braces. You'll be lucky to get a movie and ice cream out of me. It was my go-to move back in the day."

"Back row?" Gabe's hand slips inside my jacket and presses against my chest. "Get any hand action?"

"If I lie and say yes, will you give me a handjob on our date?"

He mocks offense. "Excuse me, I'm nothing but a gentleman."

"Mm, the things you were whispering to me on the dance floor sounded anything but gentlemanly."

"You'll have to wait and see. Give me your phone."

I do, and he puts in his details and then calls himself so he has my number too.

"Don't go selling that to any fans," I joke. Sort of.

He frowns. "Who would do that?"

"It's happened before."

His lips press together. "How much money could I get for it?"

"Not as much as I'd give you not to give it out."

Gabe's smile lights up his whole face. "I don't need your money."

"What do you need?"

"Patience. I don't know if I was born with enough to be able to handle you."

"You seem pretty restrained and in control to me."

He shakes his head and steps back. "You have no idea how close my control is to snapping. See you next week,

71

hot stuff." He turns and walks away, and I'm left standing on the side of the road, freezing my ass off.

These next three games need to fly by.

CHAPTER TEN

GABE

I've never been more grateful for twenty-four-hour shifts than I am right now. Only when they're followed by a whole day off, I have too much room to think. Sure, I meet up with friends during the day, but at night, my TV accidentally lands on Aleks's game against Dallas and Buffalo, and then the one night I'm off and he doesn't play, I can't help texting him. A lot. Really, really filthy things.

> You're a fucking sadist. I spent all night at the bar with a permanent hard-on around my new team.

> Did you leave the bar alone?

> Would you care if I didn't?

Yes and no. You can hook up with whoever you like, but my texts are to get you eager for me. Not some other guy.

I'm alone. I meant it when I said it's too hard to take that step. At least with you, I know there's no pressure.

Except the pressure in your pants.

You gonna take care of that for me when I'm back?

Patience, little hockey player. By the time you're back, you're going to want me so badly, you'll forget all about how scared you are.

With Aleks on the road, I told him I'd organize our date, and I've got the perfect idea. Considering my financial situation is what I'd call *barely keeping my head above water*, I don't have a lot of money to dish out, so I'm really hoping he's not the kinda guy who wants expensive dinners or, I dunno, gallery openings or whatever.

It's just good old-fashioned spending time together.

He gets back to Seattle midmorning, and I spend the day manscaping, picking up the things we'll need, and texting him all the creative things I'd love to do with his body. I'm careful to make sure he knows I'm not pushing, but I figure if I get him used to the idea, *in theory*, it'll make it easier for him to get over that hurdle his brain has built up. I still have no idea whether I'll take things further tonight, even if he wants to, because the last thing I want is for him to freak out or panic. It's lucky for me this guy is so easy to read.

And as if that thought is a trigger for him to prove me right, my phone lights up with a text. An image. *Fuck*. Aleks is wearing gym shorts, hand gripping the base of a very impressive imprint. Want floods my body at the sight, but it's the following text that does it.

> Thought you'd be interested to know I haven't even let myself jerk off today. Someone is NOT happy.

> (This is how you do the dick pic thing, yeah?)

I crack up laughing and hurry to assure him he's got the "dick pic thing" very, very right.

My ex-roommate Madden arrives to lend me his truck, and I drop him back at Big Bertha, the nickname of our old share house. Like I told Aleks, the guys who live there are the only family I have, and I strangely miss living with them, even if they have no sense of boundaries. It was the right move though.

It was time to be a grown-up and be independent, to give up my long-lost dreams I once had of being an artist and focus on the career path I happened to fall into but have loved every minute of.

After checking in on the guys, I hit the road on my way to pick up Aleks. I'm a few minutes late, and he's waiting out the front under a streetlight, looking mouthwateringly good. He's wearing fitted jeans and a long-sleeved Henley that strangles those lean biceps. A T-shirt I want to help him out of later.

He jumps in the cab almost the second I've pulled to a stop.

"Nervous?" I ask.

"Would you believe me if I said no?"

"Maybe if your hands weren't clenched like that."

"Shit." He flexes his fingers, and when he looks at me, it's with a lot more confidence than I'm used to from him. "You're a cruel bastard."

"Why? Didn't you like my messages?"

"Too much. And you fucking know it."

He's trying to look mad, but even in the dim light, it's clear he's playing.

"Hey," I say, pinching his rough chin before I lean in and kiss him. It's a quick one, more of a promise for later than anything else, but he presses into it eagerly. His mouth is greedy, tongue so demanding it takes me a second to remember to pull away.

"Sorry," he says, stare pinned on my mouth and not looking sorry at all.

"Geez, at least let me get our date started before you jump my bones. I'm not *that* cheap."

"Bullshit."

He's got me there. "Okay, so *you're* not. I really don't have standards."

I pull away from the curb, mainly to stop myself from kissing him again, and start on our drive out of the city. I'm taking him to a property half an hour away that's owned by a friend of a friend who uses it on weekends and holidays. No one is up there tonight, making it the perfect place for a fire and stargazing from the truck. But driving half an hour together makes me slightly anxious that we'll have nothing to talk about. My brain has been running at a thousand all day trying to come up with a store of conversation topics that I forgot the second I glimpsed him.

"You really don't have standards?" Aleks asks after a few minutes.

"Not really, why?"

"Because you're fucking gorgeous. I'll bet you have your pick of any guy—or *person*?"

"Guy. And yeah, I don't have an issue picking up, which sounds kinda braggy, but it is what it is. Plus, I've told you all about the things I can do with my tongue." I send him a cheeky grin. "Gets me a reputation."

"So how many guys have you used that tongue on this week?"

I think he meant that to come out casually, but it just … didn't. It's a real effort not to show him how cute I think this jealous streak is. "Hmm …" I tap my chin, pretending to think, but when his face scrunches up, I can't even play with him. "None, you idiot. Fuck. I've been too busy working and watching stupid hockey games."

"Watching *my* games?"

"Well, considering I think the sport is stupid, what other reason would I have to watch?"

He scowls. "I'm torn between wanting to thump you for saying the sport I love is stupid and being all cocky that you watched me play."

"Stick with cocky."

"I'm trying, but how can you *hate* hockey? It's the greatest sport of all time."

"What makes it the greatest?"

77

"Dude. Huge men. Hard hits. Tiny puck. And we play on fucking blades on ice."

Half to stir him up and half because it's true, I lift one shoulder and say, "Eh."

"*Eh?*"

"You play a game a couple of times a week."

"And practice basically every day. Coach puts us through hell."

"You think hockey playing is hard? You should try running some of our drills."

He snorts. "With my eyes closed. Have you ever skated before?"

"A couple of times."

"I bet you can't even stand up in skates."

"I bet you can't even lift a fireman's hose with those scrawny muscles."

"Hey, maybe tonight we'll find out."

Damn. I didn't mean the innuendo, but I'm on board with it.

"And I'll have you know," he continues, "I'm not scrawny. You're built like a tank."

"Everywhere," I helpfully inform him. I mean, my cock isn't some huge monster, but it's in proportion with the rest of me. Whereas from the glimpse I had earlier, Aleks's looks bigger than average.

Aleks laughs. "We'll see."

"*If* you play your cards right."

And for all my worrying that the drive would be silent and awkward, Aleks and I find conversation easily. He's fun to tease, and when he's not stressing over sex or what comes next, he's easy to get to know. He grew up in a town outside of Detroit, has been playing hockey all his life, and gets along well with both of his parents. His life has been *pretty simple*, as he puts it, without knowing how much I would have killed for that kind of simple life. What he's talking about—supportive, present parents—it's the kind of life every kid deserves. One I want to be able to provide one day.

Before I know it, I'm pulling into the long drive that leads to the field behind the main house. It's dark out here; trees mark the property boundary, and the large house is shadowed and eerie, but once we pass through the gate and pull up in the long grass under the stars, everything else melts away.

"Where are we?" Aleks asks.

"On our date. I figured since you're so high school, you never knew the thrill of sneaking out to a bonfire with a six-pack of cold ones. And while I would have loved to organize a huge-ass party so you could get the full experience, I sorta wanted you to myself tonight."

Aleks's smile gets super big at that. It sets off these fun little butterflies in my gut that I do my best to ignore as I climb out of the truck and round it to the back. I've got a cooler with food and beer, as well as a fuckload of blankets and some firewood.

"I thought a firefighter would be against an outdoor fire?" he says, joining me.

"I'm against *unsafe* outdoor fires. And, say, drunken hockey players setting each other on fire." I grab the firewood out of the back. "But this I can handle."

"Want help?"

I point to the blankets. "Get that all cozy for me."

I find the fire pit we've used in the past and clear all the area around it. It's ringed by rocks and dirt and far enough away from the grass I'm not worried about an accident.

There's no breeze, and we've had enough rain here that everything is green and thriving.

By the time I've got the wood burning, Aleks is already lying back on the blankets, sipping his beer, watching me steadily.

"Like what you see?" I ask.

"Probably too much."

That's promising. I spring up into the truck and maneuver myself so I have a hand resting on either side of his torso. "Can I kiss you?"

"You didn't ask before."

"You didn't look so worried before."

The lines in his brow immediately smooth out. "I'm not worried. Surprisingly."

"Good." I lean down so my lips brush his. "All I want is a kiss. And so you know, if that's all I go home with, I'll be more than happy."

His inhale brushes my lips, and then his hands lock behind my head, and he crushes me to him. Aleks's mouth immediately opens, tongue surging forward and tangling with mine. He kisses like it's the last time he'll ever get to do it, and the desperation goes to my head. Ah, both of them. I'm light-headed and horny, and I wasn't lying when I said a kiss was enough because the way Aleks kisses … yeah, I could probably come like this. I groan into his mouth, his fingers tangling in my hair and sending prickles of pain across my scalp. He's all warmth and need, a hint of beer on his tongue, and for all the shit I give him about being little, my arms are straining under the pressure of holding myself above him.

He's arched up to meet me, but I can feel him trying to pull me down with him. On top of him. It feels like I'm fighting us both as I hold firm because I don't know how far to take this. I know *I* want more, and he's giving me good signs, but it all feels too fast.

The plan was to snack and talk and drink and maybe make out.

Take it slow.

Then Aleks's teeth sink into my lip, sending a zap of pleasure from my mouth to my cock, and the moan I release makes it very clear to us both where I'm at with it all. Still, I manage to keep the barest thread of sanity when I pull back from him and ask, "Is this okay?"

CHAPTER ELEVEN

ALEKS

Is this okay?

"Hell no, it's not okay," I say, but Gabe totally gets the wrong idea and pulls back. I grip his shirt and hold him against me. "It's not okay because, fuck, I need more. I need ..." I roll my hips.

"Want me to take care of that for you?"

I nod because making words is impossible. I wait for that overwhelming sense to hit me—the reminder that I have no clue what I'm doing—but it stays silent, and the relief is strong. And I know why. Gabe. I completely trust that he'll be okay with whatever happens, and it makes it easier to let myself sink into it and enjoy what comes next.

"We'll go slow?" Gabe asks.

"Fuck, go as fast as you want."

He chuckles. "I mean in terms of what you want to do. Want me to use my hand? My mouth?"

I nod again.

"Both wasn't an option."

"Why not?"

"High school rules. It was only ever one or the other."

I really want his mouth, but flashing back to those awkward high school years where I first explored what I like, it was always a tit-for-tat situation, and as much as

I'd love a fucking blowjob, I'm not ready to reciprocate when I've never even touched another man's dick before.

"Hands," I say. "Let's do hands."

Gabe smiles. "You going to touch me too? You don't have to. Whatever we do, I know where you're at, and you don't have to do anything you're not comfortable with."

"I'm not a virgin—I've done the sex thing, but I'm at rookie level with you. I want to touch you. Suck you. I want to do everything with you. Just …"

"Not tonight." He hovers over me, and I try to work out if he's disappointed by that, but his face is giving away nothing.

"Is that … Like, I know you say you're cool with this—"

"I'm more than happy with this arrangement. You know why?"

"Why?"

Gabe leans in, touching his soft lips to mine. "Because if we knock off all the bases in one night, I'll have to come up with a different excuse to see you again."

Best answer ever.

"There are lots of excuses you could use."

He lowers his head, kissing along my rough jaw and neck. "Like what?" His hand moves between us and pops the button on my jeans.

"Uh, none that I can think of with your hand so close to my dick."

He has my fly undone now. "The hockey player can't do two things at once?"

I'd refute him, but I literally can't. "Not when it comes to being filled with this much lust."

He strokes my cock slowly. His callused hand rubs me in all the right fucking ways, mostly pleasure with only a

83

bit of pain from being dry. As if sensing that, he releases me and lifts his hand to his mouth and spits.

I'm so mesmerized by the move all I can do is grip onto his shoulders and watch as he takes me in his fist once again.

Our breathing syncs, Gabe panting as much as I am. His hard length is against my thigh, still confined within his pants, and as much as I want to reach for him, all my concentration is selfishly on me. On Gabe's hand and the wicked things he's doing to my cock.

He flicks his wrist on the upstroke, smears precum down my shaft, and switches between fast strokes and sensual ones.

Handjobs, jerking off, all I've ever experienced has been fast and hard because when there's other, more advanced stuff to have fun with, this was always a means to get off as quickly as possible.

Gabe makes it a fucking art.

When he comes back to kiss me, his lips on mine, I explore his mouth, loving the slight sting from his freshly shaven upper lip and chin. Even kissing a man is so much different than I imagined.

And I've imagined it. What it would feel like. If it would be different. Mostly, it's not, but that scrape of rough skin against mine, the heavy weight of him on top of me …

I squeeze my eyes shut and break my lips from his. "I'm not going to last much longer. This is … there are no words. It's …"

"Stop thinking and just feel," Gabe whispers. "I want to see you come. I want you to look at me while you do it."

"Nrgh." That's not even a word, but I don't care. "Gabe ..." I suck in a sharp breath and unleash.

It's been so long—so fucking long—since anyone else has made me come that it seems to last for an eternity. Waves of pleasure hit me, along with dead tiredness and aching muscles.

I'm like Jell-O when I finally come down and he releases me.

He sits up, straddling my legs. "I assume you guys in the NHL get regularly tested like we do in the fire department?"

"Tested?" I'm so drunk on my orgasm it takes a second to register what he means. "Oh, for like, STDs and stuff? Yeah, we do. But also, considering my very long body count, you wouldn't need to worry."

"Good." He raises his hand and licks my cum off his fingers, and fuck, I swear that makes me come some more. "Have you ever tasted yourself before?"

I shake my head.

When his fingers run along my lips, I open for him and suck one into my mouth. The faint salty taste is different but not all that surprising. It tastes how I imagined it would. And I have no fucking idea why I never thought to try my own cum before.

Gabe pulls his finger free, and when I open my eyes and look up at him, the heat in his intense gaze warms me all over.

I reach for him and run my hand down his chest, settling on the bulge in his pants. "Can I taste you next?"

He cocks his eyebrow. "Depends on what you mean by taste because I remember you asking to only use our hands."

I swallow hard because in this moment, I do want to use my mouth. After that, he could ask for anything and I'd give it to him, but we made a deal. "I'm happy to still use my hand to get my taste."

Gabe moves my hand away and undoes his pants. Inch by small inch. So fucking slowly. Considering I just came my brains out, I'm still impatient as fuck. I already know this handjob is going to be the kind I'm used to. Rushed. Because I want my prize, and I want it now.

What can I say? Hockey players aren't known for their patience.

He barely has his cock free before I'm wrapping my fingers around it. Like he did, I pause to quickly gather some spit to use as lube.

It's ... wow. I've jerked myself off countless times before and didn't think another cock would be all that different.

I was very, very wrong.

We stay in the position we're in, me on my back with him straddling my waist. My gaze flicks between my hand working him over and his gaze as he stares down at me.

His lips are parted, and in the dim light, it's still possible to see his flushed cheeks. He's so fucking sexy.

As if using muscle memory, my hand does its own thing, and I jerk him like I would if I were doing it to myself.

His breathing increases.

When I break my gaze from his face and look down at the swollen tip of his cock sliding in and out of my fist, I instinctively lick my lips. He must like that because precum dribbles from his slit, and the urge to sit up and take him in my mouth is overwhelming.

I was worried I'd be bad at this or it would make me uncomfortable. I've always been attracted to men in a hypothetical way, but this … this is real. This is bone-deep attraction.

"Are you ready for it?" he asks breathlessly. "Unless you want to switch positions so I ruin my own clothes, you're going to need to do laundry when you get home."

My underwear is still damp from my own release. "I'm doing laundry no matter what, but I want to feel you on my skin."

With my free hand, I lift my shirt, revealing my abs.

"Oh, fuck," he cries and then tenses.

Cum shoots out of him, landing on my abs, some up my chest that gets my shirt anyway, and the rest covering my hand.

Gabe slumps forward, pressing his chest against mine, and buries his head in my shoulder.

I clear my throat. "Your shirt is kinda soaking up what I was after."

He lifts up his middle section but keeps his head buried. I bring my hand up to my lips and taste him. It's headier than mine. Sexier. The taste of him makes my cock twitch and contemplate another round.

The idea of being the one to make him come, of him doing it for me, is a power trip.

"So," he says. "First shared orgasm with a dude. What do you rate it?"

I pretend to think. "Out of ten? I'd say a nine point seven five."

He sits up again. "Excuse me?"

"It was amazing. Top-notch. But …" I bite my lip.

"But what?"

87

"I wish I'd had the guts to suck you instead. I want to experience it all."

Gabe smiles down at me. "You're so impatient."

"It's my number one trait."

He leans in and kisses me, long and deep. "Don't worry, hockey player. You'll get to experience me again. And, if I'm lucky, again and again and again and again. We're nowhere near done making you comfortable with another dick yet."

I'm not so sure about that. Because we've only had this one time, and I'm already ready for more of him. The nerves have dissipated somewhat too. It's difficult wanting everything while also trying to pace myself, but I'm going to do it.

Somehow, I think Gabe's going to make all my first experiences worth the wait.

CHAPTER TWELVE

GABE

My stomach strains against my waistband, and I have to face the fact I've eaten too much. Between arguing with Aleks about how to make the perfect s'mores to arguing over who could put away the most food, we've cleared out everything I brought with me.

I sit back against the cab, legs stretching along the bed of the truck.

"I'm done. No more," I say.

"Are you saying I win?"

"Fuck no."

Aleks rests his hand on my abs and presses down. "You sure about that?"

"Fine. *Mercy*. Damn, you don't play fair."

The spark in his gaze is promising, but I'm way too full to be able to get it up again. That handjob he gave me was hot enough to keep me going for a while. It started hesitant but turned confident fast. And seeing Aleks let go like that, it removed any lingering doubts about whether he's as into this as I am because I could feel the need coming from him.

He drops down beside me, and I immediately move closer. I'd wrap my arm around him, but I feel like I might burst, so instead, I grab his arm and pull it around my shoulders. We've both taken off our cum-covered shirts, so he's a warm, large mass beside me, and I take a moment watching the fire dance and just … being. Under the stars, with a hot man who's actually better company than I would have expected from a professional jock.

"You make yourself comfortable anywhere, don't you?"

I tilt my head back to see him, but all I get is a glimpse of the side of his face. "What do you mean?"

"Roaring fires, drunken house parties, hockey games, middle of nowhere in a truck with a stranger …"

"From memory, you were comfortable at all those places too."

"I pretended to be."

I'm skeptical. "You're going to tell me you're not comfortable on the ice?"

"Okay, I'll give you that."

"And … here?"

Aleks's tattooed arm squeezes me tighter, and fuck, it feels nice. I'm almost glad we only got one of the sexlist items checked off because I don't have to worry about when this will happen again. The answer? As soon as we can possibly arrange it.

Which, considering his work schedule and mine, might not be for a while.

I shift against him, nudging him for an answer, which prompts a sexy chuckle.

"Yes."

"Yes?"

"Yeah, this is pretty great."

"Pretty great?" I gasp. "Let's see what you come up with for our next date."

"There's going to be a next one?"

"Isn't there?" Considering everything we talked about before, both of us seem to be on board with more. Unless … "Don't tell me now you've got the hang of a dick you're done with me."

"Well, it didn't take you long to come, so I'm going to go ahead and assume I'm basically a pro now."

I smirk. "If that's what you want to tell yourself."

"Ooh, you've done it now. I'm in professional sports. I have an ego and a reputation to live up to."

"Did I bruise your poor ego?"

"Nope. Just made me more determined than ever to fucking nail that blowjob."

"Oh no, your threats. They hurrrt!"

Aleks pinches my side, and we shove against each other a few times, but we're both too sluggish and full for it to escalate to more. Instead, we end up lying side by side, shoulders touching, on the floor of the truck bed.

"Question," he says.

"Mmm?"

"Is this what all your dates are like?"

I turn my head to the side to face him. "What, out here?"

"No … *fun*."

Fun? A jolt of happiness passes through me. "I actually don't date much."

"Really?"

"Is that surprising to you?"

Aleks's eyes are dark as they trail down my face to my chest and back up again. "Hmm, you do make s'mores all wrong, so not really."

"Oh-ho. You better be planning an epic fucking date, just warning you."

"What'll you give me if I win?"

Now, *that's* a question. There are a million thoughts flying through my mind, but given the look Aleks is giving me, I know what he's waiting for.

I lean in, lips at his ear, and say, "I'll suck your cock like a goddamn lollipop, and between my tongue on your balls and my finger up your ass, you won't know which way is up."

His head falls back against the blankets, choked laugh trying to escape as he runs a hand over his face.

"Too much?" I ask.

"The opposite. It's my newest addiction. Outside of porn, I've never heard anyone talk like that."

I almost ask him what his wife was like, but I leave it. That isn't information I need to know, and honestly, I don't want to think about anyone else with Aleks. I'm having fun bringing him out of his shell, and even if he sees me as a temporary thing, I'm going to make sure this brief fling we have is memorable.

I get a thrill out of the thought of ruining every other man for him. "I'll talk like that any time you want because I'm already thinking all that and more. You have no idea of the things I want to do to your body."

"Like?"

"Patience, little hockey player."

"Fuck off with that little hockey player shit already. I'm not that much smaller than you."

"Whatever you need to tell yourself."

We drift into an easy silence. Most of the time, I'm not interested in coaching a baby gay, but Aleks makes it easy. He's not looking for me to promise the world; he's not trying to get me to settle down and commit. He's here for a good time, and that's something that I can provide.

"So why don't you date?" he asks.

"Time," I say. "My work schedule doesn't give me much time to build a foundation with someone, and most people are too impatient to give a relationship the time to grow. And before I moved out, I was in a share house with five other guys. They're my brothers—we've always had each other's backs, but there are no boundaries at all between us, and a lot of guys don't know how to take it. Most of the guys I've tried to date didn't believe me when I said that none of us had ever looked at each other that way. That's not us."

"But you've moved out now? What made you take that leap?"

"For lots of reasons, but mostly, I was ready." I look back over at him, and he's already looking my way. "What happened with your wife?" This, at least, is a question I'm comfortable with.

"She wanted to settle down and start the next stage of our lives, but … I'm hockey. I wouldn't know myself without it, and even though I didn't know it then, she wanted me to walk away from hockey for her. She never would have asked me to though, and I never even thought to offer."

"So you grew apart?"

"Yep." He takes a breath. "It took a while, but I'm okay with it."

"Do you still love her?"

His whole face screws up. "That's a heavy question for a first date."

"Yeah, but we're not really dealing with actual dates here, are we? Hanging out, getting off … we're going to have a lot of time to talk unless you're planning on running out on me each time."

"Ah, so that's why you kidnapped me and brought me out here. So I couldn't escape."

"You know it." Even though both of us are well aware he didn't answer the question, I let it go. He's right. It's heavy, and it's not my business. He's giving me his body, and fuck if that isn't enough for me. That doesn't entitle me to every other part of him. "Think you'll want to date much once you're done with me, or are you looking to get back out there? Have some fun after years of commitment."

"I … don't know. Most guys in my position would default to fucking anything that moves, wouldn't they? It's what I want to say. It's what all my friends are expecting, and it's what I was hoping would happen for me. I'm just not sure I have it in me. We'll see, I guess."

"Lucky for you, I still have a lot to teach you. You'll have plenty of time to decide."

"True. Do we need to set up a schedule or something? Your nights of freedom around you playing teacher with me."

"What do you mean?"

"I have more away games coming up. You'll probably have days off … go out …"

It takes me a second to get what he's saying. He's asking if I'm planning to hook up with people while we do this. And, sure, there's no actual reason why I couldn't, but why does it feel wrong?

"I'll make you a deal," I find myself saying. "I'll keep all my cum stored up for you, if you do the same for me. After all, I wouldn't want you learning bad habits from other sloppy teachers."

"What are you, the grand master of orgasms?"

"I don't remember you complaining. I *do* remember you shooting so hard I was having flashbacks to the hose at work."

"You really think a lot of yourself, don't you?"

"Do you disagree?" I send him a teasing look. "You'll want to be very careful with your answer."

"I already complimented you. Stop fishing."

"For what it's worth, you were a nine point seven five too."

"Oh, *really*?" His voice lowers. "What would have scored me a ten?"

"Seeing you impaled on my cock."

All the air rushes from his body, and his eyes get that sharp look of lust about them. "Okay."

I shake my head. "You're jumping ahead a few paces. Let it happen when it happens."

"If I'm not dead by then," he grumbles.

"You need more practice. Don't worry, we'll turn you into a grand master yet." I roll over onto my side so I'm hovering over him again, letting my hands trail over his body. His muscles are sleek and lean, and I love the look of every one of them.

"Yes," he says suddenly.

I raise an eyebrow in question.

"Yeah, you've got a deal. No sloppy other guys. Just … just you. Until …" My fingers find the end of his briefs, and his abs bunch up tight. "Just until."

I lean down to kiss him. "Just until."

Then I remind him of how good my handjobs are.

CHAPTER THIRTEEN

ALEKS

We hit the locker rooms, sweaty and tired from practice. After dumping my helmet in my cubby, I immediately go for my phone. Nothing.

Katz, already pulling off his practice jersey, chuckles. "I know that look."

"What look?"

"The look of desperation. Who is she? Or he. They?"

I love that everyone on the team is cool with me being openly pan and that Katz didn't assume it could only be a woman I'm waiting to hear from. "He. And he's no one. Just a guy."

"Mmhmm. That's why you're looking at your phone, wondering if it's broken because there's no message."

Touché.

Cody Bilson, on my other side, says, "No message, no love. That's my rule."

"Explains why he's been married so many times," Katz says. "Anytime a woman messages him, he proposes."

I snort.

"Excuse me," Bilson says. "I'll have you know it takes at least three dates for me to propose, fuck you very much."

Katz smiles over at me. "So much better. We have the night off. Why don't you message him?"

"He's a firefighter, and I was hoping we'd be done before six when he starts his next rotation, but by the time I shower and dress and get out of here, he'll be at work. This whole dating around a schedule thing sucks."

"You think dating is hard, try being married," Bilson says and then realizes … "Ah. Sorry. I forgot you were."

Katz nudges me. "Divorce doesn't mean anything to a serial divorcer."

"I prefer serial monogamist. My perfect person is out there somewhere."

"You know, you don't *have* to marry them before working out if they're the one for you," I say. "I've just started dating, but it's fun."

"Fun is how it all starts. Then you have too much fun, and then you're suddenly drunk in Vegas and marrying a person you hardly know." Bilson finishes stripping down and walks toward the showers.

"I guarantee that will never happen," I say to Katz. "I'm never getting married again."

Katz slaps my still-padded shoulder. "Yeah, I've heard him say that too." He disappears next, leaving me to stare at my empty notifications.

I send Gabe a text.

> I was really hoping to get out of here before your shift started so I could come say hi, but it wasn't meant to be. The team leaves tomorrow for another road trip. See you when I get back?

He responds immediately.

> This whole work thing is getting in the way of sex, and I don't like it. You should quit your job. I promise my mouth would be worth it.

> I should quit? How do you propose I make ten million over the next three years if I'm not playing hockey?

> Your bank account doesn't impress me, baby. I save lives for a living. Therefore, my job is more important.

> I'll give you the saving lives thing, but hockey is my life.

> Damn. My skills weren't enough to make you want to give up hockey for dick? Guess I'll need to try harder next time.

I smile, but it fades quickly. It's a joke, I know it is, but it brings up a very real issue I've had to deal with the last couple of years. When will my career no longer be my number one priority? Will it ever happen? Will I ever be ready to actually settle down, realize I want kids, and prioritize my personal life?

Before I know it, Katz is back.

"You said your guy was a firefighter?"

"Yeah, why?"

"My brother is one back in Des Moines. You do know that all they do on shift is sit around and wait for a call, don't you?"

"That doesn't sound right."

"Well, basically."

I frown. "What's your point?"

"Mom and Dad still show up with enough food to feed the entire station every time it's my brother's turn to be in the kitchen. I think pizza brought to them by famous hockey players will get you in the door."

"Players? Plural?"

"I want to meet this guy. He needs team approval."

I narrow my gaze. "Does everyone on the team have to run their dates by you?"

"Nah. Only the people I like."

With five words, Katz makes me feel the most welcome I have since signing with Seattle.

Bilson is back now too, and Katz can't help himself.

"Besides, if I had to approve of every partner, I'd never get to play hockey. It would be a revolving door of meeting Bilson's future wives."

Bilson gives him the finger.

Katz ignores him. "Hurry up and shower so we can go feed a bunch of heroes."

"Feed? Heroes? You taking me out for dinner, Katz?" Bilson asks.

"Nope. But you're more than welcome to join us. We're meeting Emerson's boyfriend."

"Not my boyfriend," I clarify. "A guy I'm kinda, sorta, trying to date, but hockey and firefighting keep getting in the way."

"I'm in," Bilson says. "A firehouse full of guys means there's no chance of meeting the next Mrs. Bilson."

99

I don't even have time to panic about Gabe thinking I'm some kind of pushy stalker by turning up at his work. I'm too excited to see him again.

–

When we walk into the firehouse, Sanden glances at us from where he's wiping down one of the trucks. His face lights up.

"Is that him?" Katz asks.

"You're Brennen Katz," Sanden says and then turns to my other teammate. "And you're Cody Bilson."

"Not him," I say. "My guy wouldn't even know who you two are."

"Then I definitely disapprove." Katz approaches Sanden and throws his arm around his shoulders. "You should date this guy instead. He's a fan."

Sanden laughs. "Sorry, Aleks is so not my type."

"Ah. Straight?"

"Nope. Just not into the big and brawny thing."

Bilson looks confused. "Wait … are we … are hockey players not attractive in queer circles? Why does this feel like an abomination on society as a whole?"

"Are you sure you want to go with queer people are an abomination?" I ask.

"Anyone who doesn't find me attractive, then yes." Bilson pouts.

"Only Bilson could be offended for not being attractive to someone he's not even interested in," Katz says. "You watch, now he'll have to run out and find his next wife so he can have that validation."

I turn to Bilson. "You have issues, man."

"Don't we all?" Bilson spots a woman in uniform heading up the stairs to the upper level. "What can I say?

I have a weakness." He automatically follows the blonde, and when I watch him go, my eyes catch on someone coming down the same stairs. He looks so fucking sexy in his navy uniform, but I do wish he was wearing his fireman pants with the hot-as-fuck suspenders.

I smile and hold up the billion pies we ordered.

"You wanted to see me that badly you felt you needed to bribe me and my coworkers with food? How cheap do you think we are?"

"Did it work?"

He points to the balcony above us that overlooks the truck bays. "What does that tell you?"

There are six guys watching us.

"Are they looking at me or the pizza?"

"Definitely the pizza," Gabe says and takes half of the boxes from me. "Come meet the team."

Sanden puts down his towel. "Break time."

"Truck doesn't look clean," Gabe sings without even looking at it.

"How does he know?" Sanden complains and gets back to work.

"You don't let the poor man eat?" I ask.

"He needs to get his chores done first."

"You'd make the meanest parent ever."

"I plan on it."

I ignore the trickling guilt about kids because unlike in my marriage, Gabe doesn't mean with me. Anytime Rebecca brought up the topic of kids, I'd find an excuse to change the subject. I don't need to do that here because Gabe and I won't ever get to that serious point.

I know that. He knows that.

We're dating. That's it.

Gabe introduces me to everyone, but I forget their names as quickly as he says them. It's daunting, almost like a meet-the-family thing, but all of his team are hockey fans, and they're easy to converse with. When in doubt, mention hockey.

Katz and I are talking to Gabe's chief when Bilson comes over to us. "I'm in love."

"Oh boy, here we go," Katz says.

I add, "So much for a firehouse being safe from Bilson's love life."

Gabe's hand lands on my bicep. "Can I steal you for a moment?"

Anytime.

His hand trails down my arm, and I interlace my fingers with his as I follow him outside and around the corner into an alley.

"What are we doing out here?"

Gabe slams me into the wall, backing me against it, but then laughs. "Oops. I thought you hockey players knew how to brace for hard hits."

"When we're expecting them, but that was nothing. Actually, it was kind of hot."

"Only kind of?"

I lick my lips. "Mm, I can think of a way it could be hotter."

Gabe presses against me, lowering his voice. "Yeah? How?"

Instead of answering him, I fuse my lips to his and push my tongue inside his mouth.

He moans, and my cock strains against my pants. His hands roam my chest while mine settle on his ass and pull him flush against me.

When he's had his fill, he pulls away breathless. "As much as I'd fucking love to get your cock out right here and now, I'm on duty."

"I know."

"Considering we live in the same damn city, you'd think we'd be able to see each other more than our one date."

"It doesn't help that I'm never here, and when I am, you're working."

"We have to figure out a system."

I nod. "We really do. I'm starting to worry you're all talk. How do I know how awesome your dick really is if I can never get near it?"

"When are you back from your road trip?"

"Eight days."

Gabe grunts. "Another reason for me to hate hockey."

"You know, every time you mention that, the hockey gods smite the closest hockey player. You wouldn't want to smite me, would you? I have a Stanley Cup to win."

"A Stanley who?"

"Now you've done it. Don't jinx me. I need to impress my new team."

Gabe sighs. "Fine. Go sports. Rah, rah." He pretends he's holding pom-poms.

"That's better. Even if it's sarcastic."

Gabe smiles, but his face falls when a ringing alarm echoes from the building. "Damn. Gotta go." He kisses my cheek and runs back inside, calling out as he does, "I'll text you later."

And as I watch his crew suit up and jump into the truck, I'm filled with a new kind of worry. Because all of a sudden, his job of fighting fires and saving lives is all too real.

The chances of it being a drunken stupidity fire like our callout are high, but I can't help but think, what if it's serious?

What if he gets hurt?

I'm even less a fan of his job now than I was when it was merely keeping us apart.

CHAPTER FOURTEEN

GABE

One of the things I love most about this job is how no two days are the same. We can go from slow downtime, tasting pizza on an incredible guy's tongue, to tearing down the street, alarm wailing, as Sanden briefs us on what the fuck we're walking into.

No two fires are the same. No two emergencies are the same. Thinking that we know what we're up against is a dangerous mindset, and in this job, the only thing we can expect is the unexpected.

We're all highly trained. I've worked with these guys for years and trust them to have my back. Our only rule is that we all make it back in one piece.

In my career, I can count on one hand how many times we've been called out to something massive, but large fires aren't common, and emergency situations with casualties are the one thing I hope to avoid every time I climb into the truck.

"Fire at Lawton Park animal shelter," Sanden says. "They're evacuating the animals. Office is roasted."

"Shit." *Not the animals.*

Unlike the fire we were called to at Aleks's, it's easy to see the smoke as we approach. It takes us three and a half minutes to pull up outside the location, and there are people everywhere. This is the part I hate. All those nosy people who come by for a glimpse of tragedy and do nothing more than get in the way.

The second Sanden parks, we jump out and get to work. Despar and Loren split off for the hose, and I approach the building for recon. Sanden's asking questions somewhere behind me, and as I'm watching, a woman comes running out behind five terrified dogs. They bolt off in every direction as I grab her.

"Is anyone else inside?"

She shakes her head before devolving into a coughing, hacking mess. Thank fuck.

I help her toward Sanden, and the sound of incoming sirens announces backup and hopefully EMTs from Station 21.

The office looks to have taken the brunt of it, fire licking out of the windows and blackening the frame. Smoke has covered the parking lot, and I turn to signal to Despar and Loren before clearing out the people in our way.

It's stifling in my suit, the heat a comfort I'm used to, a reminder of what I'm doing, of the importance of my job.

"Over here," I tell the two men who look like they're about a second from running back inside.

"I don't see Rascal," one of them says.

I extend my arms to either side of me and keep instructing them to back up. My attention doesn't leave them because I know that look, that panic. "Keep moving." I'm not above restraining him if he makes a move that could get him killed.

"Rascal's not out. He's still in there."

"The woman said the building is clear. Move *back*."

"I can't leave him in there!"

Through the smoke and the loud blast of the hose and the mass of people and animals running everywhere, there's no way to say *who* or *what* made it out, but I know for a fact there's no going back inside now.

A second truck pulls to a heavy stop, the team immediately jumping out for a second hose as Remy pulls up in his ambulance behind it. Sanden leads the woman who was coughing over to Remy, and I wave my hand to get Sanden's attention because if this guy really wants to get in there, he'll find a way to do it. I need backup.

"Fuck this." The man makes a move, and in my split second of turning away, he's almost too fast for me.

Stupid fucking idiot.

I take off after him, and unlucky for him, I do this for a living. I gain on him in seconds and tackle him to the ground. He struggles, stray elbow thumping my shoulder, but I throw my weight down and pin him against the hard concrete.

"You don't understand," he begs.

And, fuck, my heart goes out to him. I get it. I understand the hopelessness and feeling completely out of control. The sickening knowledge that this is happening and there's no way to determine if everyone is okay.

"What I understand is if you go in there, you die."

"It's not burning around back yet. I'll be fast."

"It's not the fire you need to worry about, buddy. You'll pass out from the smoke before you burn alive. Now, you need to let us do our jobs and get this thing under control before anyone gets hurt."

He goes limp. He's crying. It threatens the same emotions from me, but I lock that shit up tight, and when Sanden reaches us, we both haul the man to his feet and drag him back. Not that he's putting up much of a fight now.

We get to the back of the crowd, where people are disastrously trying to herd animals into cages, and life jumps back into him.

"Rascal!"

He breaks from our hold and runs toward a fucking *iguana*.

Jesus. "I thought Rascal was a dog," I say weakly.

Remy jogs over to us. He's almost a head shorter than me, lean and slim, with messy, tawny-brown hair. "She's on oxygen in the ambulance. Anyone else who needs me?"

I point him toward the guy and his iguana. "Might want to check him out for shock."

"Those guys were all in the building when it started," Sanden says, pointing toward the people struggling with animals. "But good luck getting any of them to stop what they're doing."

Remy cringes at someone trying to pin a panicked German shepherd. "Should we help?"

I glance back at the fire, which the team has almost got under control. "They're good there. I have a feeling this is what we'll be doing with the rest of our night."

Sanden laughs. "Aren't you allergic to cats?"

I groan. "Fucking hellions."

"I'll take them. You take the dogs," he offers.

"I'll help, too, when I can," Remy says, then claps Sanden on the shoulder and heads toward iguana guy.

Sanden rubs his shoulder like it hurt, which is overly dramatic considering Remy's much smaller than us.

I shove him toward the animals instead of asking him about it. "You can ice that later. We have work to do."

Sanden is a great guy. We joke we're work husbands. And while we're friends outside of work, we don't really have the type of friendship that is deep or important. Out here, we have each other's backs, but I'd feel out of place asking Sanden to open up to me about whatever's changed between him and Remy's fiancé, Eman.

We begin to chase down all the loose animals, and I'm tossing up which is worse: putting out a fire or trying to track down close to fifty animals. By the time the fire is out and we're cleared to go inside the building to collect cages, a lot of the animals have disappeared all over the neighborhood.

Rabbits are found in people's front yards, dogs tearing across roads, and cats stuck up goddamn trees like this is a fucking Disney movie. People are hard to deal with when it comes to fires, but animals are one thousand times worse. No amount of "there, there" and "it's okay, buddy" will calm them down, and we resort to having to catch the fuckers by force. Most of the people who were standing around gawking at the fire have left, but a few stayed to help out, and on a wild thought, I pull out my phone and call Aleks.

"You busy?" I ask.

"No, why?"

"We're on an animal hunt, and there's no rule against volunteers helping out …"

"I have no idea what you're talking about."

I fill him in on the callout as I make my way down a street, looking for any signs of our strays.

He's quiet for a moment. "I thought you were trying to convince me your job was hard."

"Why don't you get that hot ass of yours down here and find out?"

"On my way."

And he mustn't have been lying about that because he shows up fifteen minutes later. It's only when he's walking toward me, asking where to help out, that I take a moment to stop and think through what my invite actually means.

I'm working. There's absolutely no chance of orgasms here. Hell, we won't even get to make out like we did at the station, but I called him anyway. Because he's leaving for eight days, and this is my last desperate chance to see him before he goes.

Sanden throws me a *you're fucked* look the second he spots Aleks, but I ignore it and lift my hand to Aleks instead.

"I think I have a fireman kink," he says as he approaches.

I throw my head back and laugh. "You and the rest of the world."

"Yeah, but the rest of the world doesn't get to see you *out* of that uniform." He pauses. "At least for right now."

Yeah. At least.

I don't give that thought a chance to take hold. "Come on." I start walking south. "We're looking down this way." I hand Aleks two of the leads I'm carrying but keep the cage. And normally it's so easy to talk to him, but now I've had that moment of realization, that acknowledgment that all I wanted to do was spend actual time with him, I'm a bit lost for what to say.

Orgasms I can do. Conversation that doesn't lead us to that point? Apparently, I've found my weakness.

"Maybe I shouldn't have called you," I say.

"What? Why?"

"Well, I'm just putting together that this is weird."

"I can handle weird." He points at his face. "Hockey player, remember?"

"Is that what you do? You haven't mentioned it five times today already. I was in danger of forgetting."

"Dick."

"You love my dick."

"Crazy but true."

"Once you've become even more acquainted with it, the world will be a buffet of cocks and pussies for a star player like you."

He gives a noncommittal hum. "We'll see."

I have no idea how Aleks can doubt it. You don't look the way he does and earn *ten-million-dollar* contracts without gaining the attention of everyone around. Look at my teammates' reactions when he walked into the station.

And sure, what Aleks does is hard, but it's *sports*. His paycheck is in the fucking millions, and I barely make enough to scrape by, even on days when I put my life on the goddamn line. It's hard not to think about things like that.

"Is that one of them?" He points at a puff of white fur, barely visible under a shrub.

"Looks like it." I pass off the rest of the leads and silently approach. I'm slow, cautious, and before whatever it is can bolt, I lurch forward and wrap my hands around the squirming thing.

A loud, angry *meow* fills the air.

Cat.

It takes everything not to drop the squirming animal, and Aleks hurries to open the cage before I stuff it inside and he slams the door behind it.

"Damn it."

"You okay?" Aleks asks, but it's not the struggle that's worrying me.

My eyes are already starting to water, nose itching and prickling. "Fine. But now I'm regretting inviting you here."

"Why?"

"Because I'm allergic."

He almost laughs. "To cats?"

"Yep. And in a couple of minutes, my eyes are going to be swollen and red, and my whole face will turn splotchy. Prepare to fall in love."

Aleks picks up the cat. "You are almost too good-looking. Now I can walk beside you without feeling inadequate."

"Your concern for me is heartwarming. Truly."

"I guess this means once we're married with all those hypothetical babies, we won't be getting them a cat."

"My house will be a dog zone only."

"Damn. But I'm a cat man."

"Oh no," I wail. "I can't believe you hid that from me. The betrayal. The shock. It's like I don't know who you are anymore."

"Our relationship is already doomed."

All of my self-control is going toward not rubbing my eyes, that the words come out before I can stop them. "For you, I could make an exception."

And I don't even think I'm joking.

CHAPTER FIFTEEN

ALEKS

Flying out the day after a long, long, tiring night chasing animals down and then hunting for an all-night pharmacy so we could get Gabe some Benadryl is depressing. Because even though it was a rough night, hanging out with Gabe was amazing.

We're headed to the East Coast for the beginning of this long-ass road trip, so about three hours into the flight, I get out of my seat and make my way to the back of the plane, where management and PR sit.

"You look like you're about to keel over," Coach Dane says. "Are you sick?"

"No, sir. Just tired. I was out until all hours doing my civilian duty."

Coach holds up his hand. "I don't want to know what that means. Make sure you nap during your downtime today."

"I was thinking of napping after I talk to Frank." I point to the team's PR manager.

"You do that."

"You need something?" Frank asks as I slip into the seat next to him.

"I had an idea for a team charity event."

"We're always looking for new projects."

"Last night, there was a fire at the Lawton Park animal shelter, and now there's a bunch of animals without anywhere to go or stay. I think the plan was for them to go home with some of the workers and to find volunteers, but I'm thinking we either do an adoption day or a fundraiser to help rebuild or to supply temporary housing for the animals. The only thing is, it would need to be done quickly because it's an emergent situation."

Frank opens his laptop and takes some notes. "I'll get on it."

That was easy. I head back to my seat next to Bilson.

I do what I said and nap, and then the second we land, I turn off airplane mode and open my messaging app.

Before I can type out a message to Gabe, a photo pops up on my screen. I wince.

"Ooh, is it nudes?" Bilson asks and tries to look over my shoulder.

I shove him. "I wish, but no. Gabe had an allergic reaction last night." I turn my phone toward him, and he winces like I did.

"How did that beautiful man's face get so messed up?"

"Cats. Also, you think he's beautiful?"

"I have eyes. Even as a straight man, I can appreciate a hunk."

Give me *things baby bisexuals say* for five hundred!

"Or ... what used to be a hunk. He's tainted goods now. You should ditch him and find someone new."

I can see his point. Gabe's eyes are puffy, and he has a rash down one side of his face, but still. "And you wonder how your marriages never work out."

"It's because no one can match my level of awesome. It's not a mystery."

It isn't, but not for the reasons he's thinking.

Hope you feel better soon, I text.

He replies:

> I'll be back on my feet in no time, and if you still want to see me again after witnessing the horror that is my cat allergy, it'll all be cleared up by the time you're home.

It's alarming how quickly I'm becoming addicted to Gabe. Not to him, but to seeing him. Last night was as fun as the date we had in the back of his friend's truck, and it didn't even include orgasms. Hell, it didn't even involve much affection at all other than that scorching hot kiss up against the firehouse.

While I've always disliked away games because of the travel and not having the advantage of a home crowd, this is the first time I've ever legitimately wished I was home.

In retrospect, I should have seen problems in my marriage a hell of a lot earlier than I acknowledged them.

And as illogical as it might be, I use that want to hype me up on the ice because the sooner I can win these games, the sooner I'll get home. I don't care if that doesn't make sense—it works. The team pulls off three out of four wins, which means we're going home on a high.

Frank grabs me on the way onto the plane before heading back for Seattle. "Everything's set for when we get back. We couldn't organize anything big on short notice, but I've been in contact with the animal shelter, and they're going to bring some of the animals down to the practice rink to get footage of you guys with them, and then we'll run an online campaign for donations. We'll also give out information on where they can adopt."

"Awesome."

"And now you get to handle the fun part."

That makes me nervous. "Fun part?"

He nods behind him. "Asking two or three of the other players to surrender their night off to do the campaign."

Well, shit.

Even though I'm close with Katz now and Bilson is growing on me, I wouldn't say I'm comfortable asking either of them for a favor.

We're the last ones on the plane, so instead of taking a seat, I stand in front of everyone. "Hey, I know I'm the newbie and not in a position to be asking for favors, but …" I bite my lip and decide to go a different route. "Who loves dogs?"

The team looks around at each other with confused expressions on their faces.

"The Lawton Park animal shelter near where I live burned down last week, so we want to get some shots and video of us on the ice with their animals to get donations. If any of you can spare your time, I'd appreciate it."

"Who the fuck cares if you're new, Emerson?" Bilson says. "After firing that many bullets into the net, you can have anything you want."

And that's how my entire team volunteers for the job.

I'm touched.

Seattle is starting to feel like home.

-

I text Gabe to come to the practice arena, and then I leave his name with security so they'll let him in. We get our team jerseys, put them on over our civilian clothes, and get out on the ice with our skates and sticks.

There are dogs of all sizes, all ages, and all breeds with handlers in the stands. Cameras, crew, and photography lights point toward the ice.

"Emerson, you can go first," Frank says and turns to the dogs. "Ah, we'll have … this red guy up first."

A person wearing an LPAS polo steps onto the carpet they laid out on the ice, bringing a large labradoodle-looking dog with bright red hair with her.

I skate up to it, but the dog's a bit skittish.

"He was found chained to a vacant house," the handler says. "Seemed well looked after, but it's like the owners moved and left him behind."

Fuck, I hate people.

I lower myself onto my knee. "Hey, buddy."

I let the dog come to me and sniff the air. He moves closer, and then closer again, until he's close enough to lick my face.

I gently pat him. "You remind me of my friend Tripp with your red hair. Though there's only one man he licks." Next thing I know, he's pinned me on the damn ice and is trying to kill me. Death by face-licking.

I'm too busy pissing myself laughing that I don't notice the cameras on me until the handler finally gets the dog back under control.

"See if he'll chase the puck," Frank says and sends one sliding my way.

I hold it up to Dog Tripp's face, and he immediately tries to bite it. When I stand and throw the puck at his feet, he wags his tail and bows like he's getting ready to attack.

I tap the puck and send it sailing, expecting the dog to chase after it, but instead, he goes for my stick, gets the blade in his mouth, and runs off with it.

The entire arena breaks into soft chuckles while Frank throws me a thumbs-up.

But when I notice Gabe's brawny figure standing in the corner of the arena, the dog is all but forgotten. I skate over to the barrier toward Gabe.

"You made it. How long have you been here?"

"Long enough to see you get mauled by that cutie over there." He points to the labradoodle, still running around with the big hockey stick in his mouth. "What is all this?"

"Fundraising campaign for the animal shelter that was on fire."

Gabe glances around again. "You did this?"

"The team is always looking for ways to give back to the community. What do you think?"

Gabe lifts his finger and beckons me in closer. When his mouth is practically next to my ear, he says, "I think I've never been jealous of a dog before." He licks my earlobe. "How long until you can get out of here so I can lick you in other places?"

"Frank?" I call out. "You got enough footage from me?"

"We just need you to film the plea. We've got cue cards."

"Think you can wait that long?" I ask Gabe.

"I can try."

Now, let's see if I can get through this taping as fast as possible with no mistakes.

CHAPTER SIXTEEN

GABE

The second Aleks steps off the ice, I don't give a fuck he's in skates. My hand closes over his, and I all but drag him out of the arena. Until we get outside and I realize I have no idea where to go.

"Let's grab my bag from the locker room, and then you can take me wherever you like," he says.

But we don't make it that far.

We pass an empty office with its door wide open and lights off, and it gives me a fantastic idea. I pull Aleks back and drag him inside, then slam the door and back him up against it.

"What's all this?" he asks, smile twitching the corner of his lips.

The click of the lock echoes behind him. "You organized that."

"Yep."

"For those animals."

"I was worried they'd force you to house them, and then I'd have to deal with your face constantly swollen and red." He pokes my cheek. "I like these dimples way too much."

"Joke all you like. I see you, Aleksander Emerson."

He draws a breath. "And what are you going to do now you've gotten me here?"

"I'm going to show you what a blowjob is meant to feel like." I press a quick, bruising kiss to his lips before falling to my knees. In his skates, his cock is perfectly positioned for my mouth.

"What if someone comes down here?"

"They're all too busy with the photoshoot, and …" I suck my finger into my mouth and wink. "I've got a secret weapon to get you there faster."

"Fuck."

"Patience. We'll get there too."

Aleks's hand holds the door handle beside him to keep him steady as he drags his fingers through my hair. "I'm ready."

And since green means go, I make fast work of the buttons on his jeans and yank them and his briefs down far enough that they sit under his ass. God, his cock is pretty. I'd been right about him being big, but he's not too thick, perfectly straight, and his balls are goddamn magnificent, which isn't something I've ever thought about a guy's nuts before. He's already hard, balls tight, and I'm taking that as a good sign that we won't be here long.

"I'm going to deep-throat you and play with your prostate until you're cross-eyed. Fair warning."

His grip in my hair tightens, all nervousness gone as his dark stare locks on mine. "Do it."

Yeah, baby.

We don't have time to waste, so I swallow him right down, relaxing my throat and loving the way his smooth head pushes deeper. My tongue goes to work on the underside of his cock as my finger sneaks around behind him.

As soon as my finger slips into his crease, Aleks tenses up, and I pull off, replacing my mouth with my hand.

"You need to relax, or it's gonna hurt."

"I'm trying," he pants. "Kind of hard to do that when I'm already on the edge."

I wink up at him. "Told you I was good with my tongue."

"You've got no fucking clue."

I stop stroking him. "Relax. No tension. Also, try not to kick me with those skates. I get the feeling it would hurt."

Aleks steadies himself and tries to do what I tell him, but as soon as I rub his hole, his muscles lock up again. I keep eye contact, his grip in my hair tightening, and I work small circles on the area.

"Whenever you're ready," I tell him.

He takes a deep breath, and the second he relaxes and bares down, I slip my finger inside.

"Ah, fuck, that's weird," he rasps.

"Want me to stop?"

"I don't know yet."

I press in further, searching around until …

He cries out, my scalp burning under his grip. "Holy fuck."

I dive on his cock again.

Because we need to make this fast, I don't give him time to adjust or catch his breath, just continue my all-out assault on his dick. I finger him gently, alternating between pressing in and out and tapping that bundle of nerves that rewards me with a burst of precum each time.

I pull off him again, jerking him fast, and run my tongue over his balls. Round and round both of them,

I alternate between licking and sucking them into my mouth until Aleks's muscular thighs tremble.

"God, you taste fucking incredible," I tell him. "Absolute sex. My dick is rock hard, you have no idea. The things I picture doing to your body—I wish I could strap you to my bed and play with you until you stop driving me so fucking crazy."

He grunts. "What would you do?"

"Edge you. Get this cock nice and thick and swollen and angry until you're begging for release. Then I'd stretch my hole out and impale myself on your dick."

"Oh, fuck, quick. I'm close."

I close my mouth back over him, tongue working madly as I peg his prostate over and over and then—

"*Nrg, Gabe.*"

His cum hits my tongue in a salty stream that I greedily suck down. He tastes so fucking good, making my head spin, addicted, and so fucking glad we made our agreement to keep this between us until … well, I'm not going to think about that.

Once he's done, I pull off him and shove back to my feet.

"Applause is welcome."

He slumps against the door. "Can't. Boneless. Fuck. The only reason I'm still standing is because I was worried about my skates."

"Tell me that wasn't a ten?"

"Hard eleven."

He reaches for my fly, but I step back. "No time."

"But … you did me. Don't I have to—"

I cut him off with a kiss. "There's no have tos. I did this because I wanted to, knowing that you wouldn't have time to reciprocate and knowing that you might not even want to."

"I want to."

That makes me smile, but hell, the promise of a blowjob from *him* would make anyone smile. "Good. But before we do that, we're grabbing some dinner. Burgers? Then your place?"

"Perfect."

"Go grab your bag."

I Ubered here, so we take Aleks's car to a burger place and huddle into a booth. It's an out-of-body experience when a dad and his kids come over and ask Aleks for his autograph, and I stare the entire time, wondering what my role is here.

When they leave, I lean over the table and drop my voice. "Did that actually just happen?"

Aleks shrugs. "You're dating a celebrity now."

Sort of dating. Temporarily. I don't let those words out. "You did score a whole bunch of home runs in your games."

Aleks pretends to faint like I knew he would. "You're determined to break my heart, Crosby."

"You played really well, hockey player."

He eyes me. "Wait … you watched my games again."

"Might have done."

"You're turning into a hockey fan."

"Never."

He points at me. "You're converting."

"Sure, make it sound *less* like a cult." I give him a dry look that only makes him laugh.

"You'll be a true Crosby yet." He props his head on his hand. "Did you watch *all* of my games?"

I busy myself with the menu. "Might have done."

123

"What about the one I played while you were working?"

I clear my throat, pretending to be really interested in the burgers they have on offer. "It's possible the whole station watched."

"Yes." Aleks fist pumps. "Were they super impressed with me?"

"You put a disk in a net. Calm down."

"So that's a ten-level impressed?"

"You were barely even on the ice that much."

He gasps. "That's an eleven. Fuck, you want to marry me now, don't you?"

I can't even pretend to feign disinterest because he's being an idiot, and I really like this side of him.

"You might be an eleven on the ice, but I'm the eleven in the bedroom."

"How about we agree that we're both awesome?"

"Sure." I grin. "But I'm awesomer."

"At least you think so." Aleks pushes aside his menu and crosses his arms. "I think I'm going to adopt Tripp."

I stare at him for a moment. "Umm … isn't that your friend?"

"No. Well—technically, yes—but I mean Dog Tripp."

"There's a Dog Tripp?"

"The one I was making out with earlier."

I point at him. "I approve of this adoption, but if you come home with dog breath, I'm going to get jealous. Wait, how will that work if you're never home?"

"I'm going to convince management to get him as a team dog. Other teams have them, and they're awesome for morale. Plus, it means while we're all on the road, there'll always be someone to look after him." Aleks turns serious. "The poor guy deserves it."

Okay, Aleks needs to stop being so perfect now, or I might actually have issues here. "That sounds amazing. Do you think they'll go for it?"

"It came as news to me, but apparently, my new team will do anything for me. I'm *kind of* a big deal."

"In fantasyland."

"Because of that, you get to pay for dinner," he says, passing his menu to me.

"Okay, ten-million-dollar man."

"Hey, I'm an equal opportunist."

I get up to go and place our orders, catching him checking out my ass while I'm at the counter.

When I get back to the table, instead of taking my seat, I slide in beside him instead.

Leaning over to his ear, I say, "Like what you see?"

"Yeah, I don't think it's the burgers I'm hungry for."

My hand closes over his thigh. "Hey, Aleks?"

"Yeah?"

"Eat fast."

CHAPTER SEVENTEEN

ALEKS

As soon as we make it through my front door, we're all over each other. Mouths, hands, kissing, groping.

I push him up against the wall in my foyer, but he flips us and pins me. Considering how many hits I take on the ice and never once got turned on by it, it's amazing how much I'm enjoying Gabe manhandling me.

His strong body up against mine, his thick thigh between my legs. The way he looks *down* at me.

"You're killing me," I say against his lips.

"Mm, wait until you're inside me. Then you really will feel like you're dying."

"You're so sure of yourself."

Gabe grabs my wrist and lifts my hand to his chest. Slowly, he drags my hand down his body, stopping above the bulge in his pants. "You have no idea what it will feel like to have my ass bearing down on your cock. For your dick to fill me up while I fuck into your fist. If you don't move fast enough for me, I'll take over, pushing back onto you over and over again. You'll be inside me, all around me, and you'll want to give in to the pleasure, but I'm not going to let you. You're going to wait until I've had my fill before you fill my ass full of your cum."

Holy fuck. Those words. His mouth is filthy, and I love it.

Now that he's got me well and truly worked up, he drops my hand, undoes his pants, and shoves them down his thighs.

"Touch me," he begs, and he doesn't have to tell me twice.

My fingers wrap around his long cock, and I stroke lazily. I love watching as the head of his dick passes through my hand, his slit red and angry while leaking like crazy for me.

"Can I taste you?" I ask.

He pauses. No, more like stiffens. Gabe pulls back, looking me in the eyes. "Do you want to use your mouth on me?"

"So fucking badly. I might be bad at it, and I might not be able to make you come, but fuck, I want your cock in my mouth more than I've ever wanted anything. Except maybe a Stanley Cup."

"At least my dick is one of your priorities. Get down on your knees."

A shiver of want runs down my spine.

"You want to follow my lead or use your instincts?" Gabe asks.

"Just tell me if I do anything wrong." I sink to the tiled floor and lick my lips. There's a brief moment of panic that I have to push away before I make my move.

"You have no idea how hot you look down there, staring at my cock like it's your last fucking meal." Precum leaks from his tip.

I lean in, running my tongue over his slit and lapping up the salty drop.

Gabe shudders, and when I glance up at him, he gives an encouraging nod. "Keep going." His words are breathless, his chest heaving.

I suck his tip into my mouth, but before I can take more of him, I'm hauled to my feet.

"Nope, nope, new plan. I need you inside me right now." Gabe pulls his pants back up enough for him to be able to walk without tripping over. "Bedroom."

I drag him up the glass stairs to my room. I try to push him down on my bed, but he turns us so I'm the one flat on my back.

"Get naked." The neediness in his tone goes straight to my balls, and I scramble out of my clothes.

Gabe does the same and then stands before me, gloriously naked. "Condom?"

I'm too busy admiring his muscles and long torso, which leads to his amazing cock to really take in the word. "Huh?"

He laughs. "Condom. Do we need one?"

"Uhh ..." I know I have a box somewhere. I stocked up when I planned on taking the slut world by storm, but clearly, I have no memory of where I put them.

Gabe grabs his pants from the floor. "I have one. And travel lube. But I'm tested regularly, and I'm on PrEP." He holds it up. "Yes? No? Your call."

Condoms were always a given when I became single, but as I think about why, the number one thing that pops into my mind is to prevent pregnancy. Which obviously won't happen here. All those sex-ed lessons I had as a teen only focused on that side of things because same-sex relationships were never talked about or encouraged. And of course I know STDs are a thing, and condoms should always be used when you don't know someone, but as I stare at Gabe, the trust I have in him overrides everything else.

The only thing at the front of my mind is that I want to feel all of him. "We don't need one."

"You sure?"

I have no doubt. "Definitely."

He takes the travel lube and rips open the packet. "Move up the bed."

I shuffle my way up until my head hits the pillow and watch as Gabe's knees hit the mattress. He bends over, planting one hand next to my hip while the other reaches behind him.

"Are you …"

"Am I prepping myself? Yes, but only because I'm so fucking desperate for you. I'll give you a chance to do it next time."

Hey, I'm okay with that. Especially because it means there will be a next time.

My cock points upward, straining, begging for attention, and when Gabe's eyes flutter closed and his mouth drops open in pleasure, I have to take matters into my own hands.

I grip my cock and stroke lightly. Not enough to bring pleasure but something to take away from the desperate need tingling in my balls.

"I want to see," I beg. "I want to see you work yourself open."

The look Gabe sends me is downright sinful, and in one quick move, he turns, maneuvering so he's facing away from me but straddling my thighs.

He bends even more, giving me a direct line of sight of his two fingers moving in and out of his ass.

My mouth dries, and I freeze. I want to take over for him; I want to lube up and thrust inside this very second. I'm impatient and nervous at the same time, but when Gabe lets out a long whine, something inside me snaps.

"I fucking need you now."

Gabe pulls his fingers free, shuffles backward up my body until he's in position. And without turning back around, he opens another packet of lube, reaches behind him to stroke my cock with a slippery hand, and guides it toward his hole.

I watch as he sinks down on my dick, my shaft disappearing inside him. I have to hold my breath because it feels so fucking amazing, and I'm worried I'm going to blow my load way too fast.

Gabe takes his time, riding me slowly to begin with, and I can't get over how fucking hot he looks.

The muscles in his back are insane, leading to a narrow waist and delectable ass. It's round and firm and muscular, just like the rest of him.

He picks up the pace, and we find a rhythm. I lift my hips as he bears down, our bodies meeting over and over again. My fingers bite into his hips, and if I could, I'd keep watching as my cock slips inside him, but I can't.

It feels too good. I'm too close. I close my eyes and arch my back, trying to get myself under control, but it's no use.

"Gabe," I let out in a harsh whisper.

"I need your hand," he says. "Jerk me off."

"Wait, wait, wait." I grip his hips even harder to stop him. "I want to see your face when you come." I slap his ass lightly to get him to get off me, but as soon as he does, I sit up and tackle him to the mattress so I'm on top.

His legs wrap around my waist, and his hole is right there. I push back inside him.

The moan he lets out sends a zing right to my balls, and all I can do is chant in my head to make it last. Make it last.

"I still don't have your hand," Gabe complains.

The rhythm in my head changes from trying to drag our orgasms out to challenging myself to make Gabe come as quickly as possible.

I reach between us and pull on his cock with hard, fast pumps of my hand.

My hips snap forward, and I take his ass over and over again. He's so tight. So warm.

He's fucking amazing.

"I'm close," he promises. "Keep going."

I'm riding the edge with him, so close to falling off it.

I thrust inside him one more time, sure my legs are going to give out at any second. His ass tightens around me. It pulses and contracts. And when I glance down between our bodies to see his cock emptying onto his own stomach, I unleash inside him.

I can't breathe, I'm sweaty, and my hamstring is cramping, but the rippling pleasure pulsing through my veins and out of my dick is all worth it.

Grunts fill the room. Heavy breaths.

I'm not sure if it's a man thing or a Gabe-specific thing, but that was so fucking hot. Hands down the best sex I've ever had. And I want to do it again.

–

I wake with Gabe next to me, passed out on his stomach but still on his side enough to have one of his arms thrown over me.

131

I'm on my back, staring at the ceiling while I still have time to do it. I have a weights session today at the team gym, a run on the treadmill, and then a game tomorrow night, but this morning, I'm a free man to do whatever I want.

And I want Gabe. Just like this. The heavy weight over me, the bigger body next to mine ... I still don't know if I have a type because I find all shapes, sizes, and genders attractive, but Gabe might be my ultimate type.

He definitely doesn't make me want to get out of bed anytime soon.

I'm sharing more than sex with him. I'm giving him my first experiences, and in return, he's giving me amazing memories that I will cherish for years to come.

He stirs beside me, rolling over to face me, but his eyes remain closed.

I lean in and kiss the tip of his nose. "Good morning."

"Glemorglin," he rumbles, and I laugh.

"Not a morning person?" I ask.

Finally, he opens his eyes, those bright blue irises making my breath catch. He's so gorgeous it's criminal. His light brown hair is messier, even more so than usual.

"Not when I don't have to be," he says. "What's your excuse?"

I roll to my side and pull him close. "How perfect you are."

Gabe snuggles in and closes his eyes again. "I am great, aren't I?"

He's being sarcastic, but he has no idea how easy he has made this whole thing. I'd been dragging my feet with moving on, with finally taking that next step. Because of nerves, because I wasn't ready, but most of all, because I hadn't found anyone that made me want to try.

"You've made this first-time thing so easy on me," I murmur.

"Not the first time I've been called easy," he deadpans.

I squeeze his ass. "I mean it."

He looks me in the eyes as he says, "It's not like it's been a struggle for me. I ..." He subtly shakes his head. "I didn't expect you."

I smile. "I've never been so thankful my friends are idiots who tried to set fire to my backyard."

"Technically, they did set fire to it."

"True. Maybe their wingman skills aren't as terrible as I thought they were. I'll have to remember to thank them at some point." I get an idea. "Actually, I could do it now." I reach onto my bedside table, where my phone is charging, which I hold up, opening the camera app.

Gabe buries his head in my shoulder. "What are you doing?"

I take the pic, loving the way we look together, even though Gabe's not even looking. I look so goddamn happy.

"Can I send it?" I show him.

"Are you allowed to? What if it gets out?"

"The guys wouldn't do that."

"Don't phones get hacked?"

Doubt creeps under my skin, making me uncomfortable. "If you don't want me to, I won't."

Gabe holds me closer. "I'm cool with it, but I don't want you to get in trouble."

I kiss the top of his head. "It's sweet you're worried, but even if I did get hacked and the photo got out, not much will happen. I'm openly out to the world now, and while it wouldn't be ideal, it won't be a huge scandal."

"Then send it."

I open the Collective chat and post the pic.

Thanks for the assist.

Then I turn off notifications, put my phone facedown on the bedside table, and give all my attention to Gabe. Or, more specifically, his cock.

I start by kissing his neck, his collarbone, his chest, moving my way down his insanely cut body.

I want to finish what I started last night. I want a real taste, to drink him all down.

Gabe's hand runs through my hair and grips tight when I reach his deep V and run my tongue along it.

He forces me to look up at him. "You don't have to do anything you're not ready for."

Thanks to him, I'm more than ready.

For anything.

And as I take my time, slowly sucking him into my mouth, teasing his head with my tongue and testing how deep I can get him, it's unlike any other experience I've had. Foreplay has always been the lead-up to me getting off—something needed so I can get some action in return.

I don't even need to come. I fucking want to, but this right here is about exploring, learning what drives Gabe crazy, and I will never get enough of it.

He lets me do what I want, doesn't complain or get impatient, but when my jaw starts to hurt, I glance up at him and realize how hard he's holding on to a single thread of control.

"You finally ready for it?" he asks.

I bob my head and hum an affirmative because I don't want to pull off him, even for a second.

"Thank fuck. It's not going to take much to send me over the edge." He tests out a small thrust, lifting his hips off the bed.

His cock hits the back of my throat, but not too deep. "That okay?"

Even though my eyes are watering, I give a small nod.

He does it again, and then again. Not rough. Not fast. Just testing me. Each time he hits the back of my throat, my eyes water more. I try to swallow, but that's awkward, and I think Gabe can tell.

"Grip the base," he says. "That way, you can control how deep I go."

I do as he says, and that's the game changer. Now when he thrusts into my mouth, he does it with ease, and I can take it.

The heel of my hand that's gripping him presses against his balls, and he lets out a curse.

"If you're having doubts or don't want my load, you better move away. Fast."

Like I'm going to do that when I'm so close to what I want.

Give it to me.

Give it all to me.

As if hearing my silent plea, Gabe throws his head back and unleashes in my mouth.

His cum slides down my throat, and I love the salty taste. It's strong and heady. I want more.

More of him.

More of us.

I just want … more.

CHAPTER EIGHTEEN

GABE

I'm an idiot. Such a fucking idiot. I went and got greedy, and now … I puff a breath into my hands, then jump off my bunk and grab my phone. I'm on shift, crawling out of my skin, knowing Aleks is home and I'm here and there's nothing I can do about seeing him.

And I have no idea if he even wants to see me again.

Our agreement was to ease him into moving on. To get him comfortable, and given our last time together, he's well and truly comfortable. My plan of introducing a new sex act each time went out the window when I jumped on his cock, and so now I'm scrambling to figure out what happens next.

Does he want to try bottoming? Can I convince him that rimming is something he has to try? With me and only me. How many of these things can I come up with? And once we've crossed off our hypothetical sexlist … does it … end?

I don't think I'm ready for that.

It's getting hard to ignore the connection between us. I want to kick myself over it because this is what people talk about. This is what people mean when they say to steer clear of guys who are experimenting, who are new to this. Aleks is going to want to branch out—and rightly so. I've had years to sleep around and build my experiences. I've been with multiple guys at once. I've hooked up in seedy bathrooms, and dated all the wrong people, and spent time working out who I am and what I'd want in a partner.

And fucking Aleks is ticking all those boxes.

Except the big one.

Whoever I end up with, I need to be end goals. I'll treat my forever like a goddamn king because if I'm going to spend my life with someone, it's going to be someone I genuinely like. Someone I can have fun with, and talk with, and build goals and a life together. I love sex, and hopefully we'll have a healthy sex life as well, but if I'm honest, it's further down my list than even I would have picked.

Aleks and I are fire in the bedroom, but we're also compatible in every other way out of it.

Our work schedules get in the way, but that's something I'd be willing to work around.

If only he was in a different stage of his life than the one he's currently in. Maybe if we'd met after he'd become more confident in who he is as a single man, but he's gone from being married to divorced to being set up on fake dates with women he doesn't know to whatever the hell we're doing.

So the question remains: do I like him so much that I'd stand by and wait for him, hoping he'll come back to me?

I stare at my phone, wanting to message him but obsessing over *what*.

Want to meet up tomorrow?

I delete it.

> Think you'd want to ride me next time?

Not a question to send over text.

> What are you doing?

Nope, too needy.

I need to talk to someone unbiased, but my best friend is touring with a play he's in and would probably be onstage, and the rest of the guys I used to live with probably wouldn't understand it. Half of them think bothering to settle down is a stupid idea, and the other half will take the *you know better* route.

Out of the four of them, Madden is probably the best option. He's a holistic nudist jock with a big heart and the one whose truck I desecrated on my date with Aleks. I'm not sure he'll have advice for me, but he's surprised me in the past.

I head out into the main living quarters and hit Call.

Madden answers almost right away. "Yo."

"Yo to you too."

"What's up? Aren't you working today?"

"Yeah, I'm at the station, but it's been a slow day."

"Gotta love those."

As much as I enjoy the adrenaline and the rush I get from racing out on a job, I have to agree with him most of the time. It's the emergency part I don't like. Being active and single-mindedly focused on the job, not having a second to think of anything else, that part I love. "I do, but it's also giving me too much time to think. I'm going out of my goddamn mind."

His lazy tone immediately turns concerned. "What's wrong?"

"You know that hockey player I took out?"

"The one you won't name in case I turn all fanboy? Yup. What about him?"

"We have an ... arrangement." I can't exactly give Madden all the specifics because a newly divorced player in Seattle? It doesn't leave a whole lot of options. "He's never been with a man before, so we agreed he'd get comfortable with me, and that would make it easier."

"Uh-oh."

My throat gets oddly tight. "I knew what I was doing when I made the offer."

"And let me guess, now you regret it?"

I press my palm into my eye socket. "I wish I did. Maybe then I'd be okay with walking away. But ... I don't want to. He's fun, Mads. We have a really great time together, and the sex is good too, but now I'm finding myself trying to think of other sex acts I can come up with to keep him around."

He hums. "Depending on how kinky you want to go, you could keep him around for a while."

"I know, but it feels manipulative, almost."

Madden cracks up laughing. "Out of anyone I know, you're the last dude who needs to worry about being manipulative. Look, make the offers, and let him answer. If it's a no, I know you'll respect that. If it's a yes, it's his choice. Just take it as it comes."

"Which is great advice, but our agreement was that we'd do this until he's comfortable. And he got there way too quickly."

"You know the great thing about agreements? They can change. Communication, man. It's important."

"Yes, but if I talk to him about this, I'll have to tell him that I kind of like him, and those aren't words I throw around easily."

"You tell us you love us all the time."

"Yeah, because you're my brothers, and I know there's no way any of you would hurt me. He ... he really could." And that's the terrifying part. The thought of Aleks hearing that I've overstepped the role I'm supposed to play and getting uncomfortable. Wanting to end things. I know him well enough to know he'd never hurt me intentionally, but if he's not feeling this, I also know he won't have any issues with walking away to save us both that ongoing stress.

"Look, I want you to protect yourself. You're my boy, and this hockey player is just another person to me. If you're not comfortable having that talk, then don't. Keep doing what you're doing and see where things go. If you have the talk and it ends badly, you know where we are. Come back to the house, for as long as you need to, and we'll smother you in attention and baby you until you feel better. We've had more than enough experience with Christian."

Yes we have. My best friend is incredible, but he's not the most emotionally secure person.

"You're the best," I tell him. "And I have a feeling I'll be taking you up on the blanket burrito sympathy sometime soon."

"I'll stock up on the rum."

"Love you, Mads."

"You too, brother."

We hang up, and while I didn't get the advice I wanted, I do feel better. Knowing the guys are there for me, that I'll always have their support, does a world of difference. I don't know how people without a support network get through.

I'm not sure what Aleks's family life is like other than he gets along with his parents, or what his relationship with his ex-wife is like, and it makes me realize that while I know a lot about him, there are still a lot of missing pieces there. He has his hockey player friends, who all seem to love him. I'm glad he has that.

It makes me remember him taking that photo of us cuddled up together, and a flood of warmth passes through me. Before I can overthink it, I open our messages again and type one out.

> Think you can send me that photo of us?

His response comes through so quickly it makes me wonder if he's been wanting to text me too.

> Why?

> To jerk off over, obviously.

> Well in that case …

The photo pops up on my screen, and I quickly tap on it to enlarge. *Fuck.* I didn't get a good look yesterday, but I'm drinking it all in now.

My first thought is how hot we look together, but that thought devolves into something softer. Something that focuses on the way his eyes are crinkled in the corners, the way his head is rested against mine, the way his smile isn't too bright, too wide, just … relaxed. Easy.

"What are you getting all heart-eyed over?"

I jump as Sanden drops onto the couch beside me. For a second, I think about hiding the photo and brushing him off, but the instinct is misplaced. I want to protect what Aleks and I have, but what we have is orgasms, and that's not something that needs protecting.

So I tilt the photo Sanden's way.

He laughs and grabs my phone for a closer look. "You guys still hooking up?"

"Sure are."

"Geez, maybe he really will have your babies."

I shake my head, trying not to think about that. "I told you; I want to foster."

"And Aleks?"

"Jesus, I don't know. We're hooking up. It's not like we're even close to having those kinds of conversations."

Sanden passes my phone back and tucks his hands behind his head. "Maybe I'll meet the love of my life on our next job."

I snort. "We're giving a safety talk at a high school tomorrow. I certainly fucking hope not."

"Hey, maybe there's some hot gay teachers who'll want to get me naked."

I pat his arm. "It's healthy to have dreams."

"Fuck you." He picks up the TV remote. "Want to watch *The Office*?"

"Actually … any hockey games on tonight?"

Sanden does a double take. "I thought you hated it."

"Watching sports is boring as hell, don't get me wrong, but …"

I want to learn. To have an interest in the game so when I watch Aleks, I know what the fuck is going on.

Sanden eyes me. "Aleks?"

I groan. "That little hockey player is under my skin. Think you can teach me about the game?"

"I'll teach you everything you need to know. Who knew you were so romantic?"

CHAPTER NINETEEN

ALEKS

"Who's a good Tripp Mitchell? Who's a good Tripp Mitchell?" I coo.

Dog Tripp has settled in with the team so fucking easily, and even though he can't go on the road with us, I love home games where he gets to visit.

He lives with the team's quantitative analyst, but on special occasions like tonight, I get to bring him home with me after the game. Special occasion tonight being that we're playing Vegas in our home arena, and I want Dog Tripp and Human Tripp to meet.

He's so dopey and gorgeous and loving. Uh, Dog Tripp. Not Tripp Tripp.

Everyone loves him, and the media surrounding him and the team adoption has brought in so many donations to the animal shelter. They're not only able to rebuild but to improve on what was originally there.

Gabe may joke about hockey players getting paid a shit ton of money for not doing anything worthwhile, and while it's true we're not out there risking our lives to save others like he is, we do give back. We do use our position to do good in this world, and I'm glad he gets to see it firsthand with Dog Tripp.

"Warm-up," Katz says, and I get to my feet, giving the dog one last pat.

"You be a good boy, Tripp."

"I can't believe they let you keep that name for him," Katz says.

"Technically, they let me keep the Tripp part. Not the Mitchell part. Something about using someone else's likeness in the public being a legal issue or whatever. If anyone asks, his name is Tripp because he trips over his big paws a lot. But really, he's totally the Mitchell brothers. He looks like Tripp but is a huge puppy dog like Dex. It's the both of them in one."

"You're having dinner with them tonight, aren't you?"

"Yep. As soon as we kick their ass on the ice, I'm going to gloat and introduce them to our baby."

We finish gearing up and get out onto the ice to warm up. The stands are fairly empty with how early it is before the game, but my gaze goes to the same two seats it always has this season. It's reflex by this point, and for once, I'm not filled with disappointment.

I know Gabe can't come to every game because of work, but when he does, it gives me magical powers. It's like my inner caveman sees a chance to impress and runs with it.

He's my good-luck charm.

Sanden sits beside him as usual, and they both zero in on me. I give them a wave and then try to focus on psyching myself up for the game. Not that I need much with Gabe in the stands.

We're given our time, we stretch, we skate, we shoot, we get the adrenaline pumping. But as it's time to go back to the locker room, I skate over to the team box, where I know there are some markers for signing.

I take one out, write *come home with me tonight* on my blade, and then hand it to one of the attendants and point to Gabe.

Once I'm off the ice, I turn back, only to watch the attendant hand the stick to Sanden instead.

I face-palm, but when I look up again, they're both smiling at me. I point to my right, indicating I want Sanden to give it to Gabe. Sanden refuses to hand it over. Gabe laughs and nods my way.

Eh, Sanden can keep the stick. I just want Gabe to know he's busy later.

I'm eager for the game to start. Pumped up. And when it comes time for the face-off and I find myself opposite Dex, I give him a smile before taking off past him when Katz passes me the puck.

Quick on my feet, I manage to dodge the two defensemen waiting for me by the net. Then the only thing standing between me and the glory of a quick goal is Human Tripp. He's a solid wall and ready for me, so I don't even try.

I pass off the puck to Katz, skate around the back of the net, and am there waiting when Katz sends the puck sailing back to my blade instead of trying for a goal.

Tripp's too busy trying to block the puck from the net, so he leaves a perfect-sized hole for me to take advantage of.

I shoot, the lamp lights up, and our goal song plays.

Boom. That's how it's done.

"Thanks, Trippy," I taunt.

"That's one," he says. "You only get one."

He's wrong. By the end of the second period, I have another, and in the third period, I scrape in a hat trick right before the buzzer.

A goal in every period? I haven't done that in a long time.

When I lock gazes with Gabe again, he shrugs as if he's not very impressed, but his huge smile gives him away.

Before heading for the locker room, I skate by Tripp and Dex. "Still coming over for dinner, or do you hate me now?"

"Oh, we hate you," Tripp says. "But Collective rules. We'll be there."

"Great. Because I have someone I want you both to meet."

"Would that someone be the hot firefighter strippers in the crowd?" Tripp asks.

"Nope. Someone even more amazing."

They both look confused, but they won't be for long.

-

"Let me get this straight," Gabe says on the way home from the arena. He has his hand on my thigh while I drive, and I fucking love it. It's possessive and affectionate, and it might be my newest favorite thing he does. He glances behind us to the back seat, where Dog Tripp is wobbling all over the place because he can't sit still in the car. "You're excited about tormenting your friend over a dog?"

"What's so confusing about that? Don't you understand brotherhood?"

"Why have enemies when you've got brothers like you?" He thinks about it. "I guess my friends and I are like that, but you hockey guys take it to the extreme."

"Fun, right?"

"Sure. Fun. Not at all egotistical and juvenile."

"Not at all. Glad we agree."

I can practically feel his eye roll from here.

Tripp and Dex have beaten me home, probably because I had a billion interviews to do after my hat trick and then had to find Gabe in the crowd to take him home.

They're waiting on my front doorstep when I pull into my drive. I don't bother putting the car away in the garage, so as soon as I put the car in park, I jump out and open the back door for Tripp.

Being the lovebug that he is, he immediately runs over to greet the new humans who will shower him with love.

"Human Tripp Mitchell, meet Dog Tripp Mitchell."

Dex drops to his knees immediately. "Oh my gosh, he's so cute."

"Of course you'd find Tripp Mitchell cute." I'm grinning. Dex is already roughhousing with the dog, but Tripp's glaring at me. "What?" I ask innocently.

"You named your dog after me."

"You don't see the resemblance?" I ask. "Dex, hold Tripp up to Human Tripp, and let's compare."

Dex picks up the dog and holds him next to Tripp, who screws up his face.

"I told him I didn't get it either," Gabe says.

"First, you kick our ass on the ice, and now you name your pet after me?" Tripp sounds incredulous. "I really only have one thing to say to that."

"I'm waiting with bated breath." Whatever he's going to say, it's going to be sarcastic as hell.

"Why are you so obsessed with me?"

I burst out laughing. "Because you're my favorite of all the queer guys?"

"I can't fault you for having good taste." He brings me in for a handshake and hug.

"I really don't understand hockey players," Gabe says.

"Tripp's balls are so big!" Dex yells from where he's now rolling around on the ground with Dog Tripp.

"Didn't need to know that about your husband," I say.

"No, look!" Dex points to Dog Tripp's testicles.

Human Tripp sighs. "I seriously can't with that dog."

"Don't worry," I say. "He's being neutered soon. Then he will have balls the same size as yours."

Tripp stumbles back, pretending to have been shot. "Shots fired. Man down."

I clap his shoulder. "Let's go inside. Food's already on the way."

"Thank fuck. I'm starving," Dex says, finally prying himself away. "Also, it's official. From this moment forward, my husband will be referred to as Human Tripp."

"I'm so glad you're on my side of this argument," I say, and we walk inside with Human Tripp grumbling the whole way about Dog Tripp versus Human Tripp.

The naming of the dog has already paid off.

Gabe grabs my hand and pulls me back, increasing the distance between Dex, the Tripps, and us.

"What's up?" I ask.

"I might not understand you or your friends or the need you have to set each other on fire or name dogs after each other, but I'm glad you have them. Especially while you still might be working yourself out. They're your support system, aren't they?"

"They are. They've been great. Before, when I was still married, I knew of their brotherhood—everyone knows how tight they are—but ... I didn't really understand it until I joined them. I've always been part of a team, and when you're playing, you have to be loyal to them. Off the ice, it's a different story. So these guys creating the environment they have for out hockey players … it's like I have my own hockey family."

"You're lucky."

I wrap my arm around Gabe's waist and pull him close. "I'm lucky my over-the-top friends decided to set another friend on fire. Because that brought me you."

CHAPTER TWENTY

GABE

Having the dog here has distracted Aleks's friends from giving me the third degree. I'd been nervous on the way over here, expecting to walk into a dinner with more people like Oskar, and it's a relief to know the guy shouting about the roof and the one with his eyebrows growing back weird are almost normal.

As normal as hockey players can be. They're busy dissecting the game, and I'm impressed with myself that I'm managing to follow half of it.

I'm next to Aleks on one side of his giant L-shaped couch, and Tripp and Dex are on the other, with Dog Tripp curled up between them. Dex hasn't stopped scratching the dog's furry head and asking him who's a good boy.

Tripp is watching his husband with a dopey look on his face. "If you start calling me a good boy, we're going to have issues."

"Oskar likes it," Dex says, and that piece of information gets my attention.

I turn to Aleks. "As in, the Oskar I've met?" That is something I never would have guessed.

"We all know *way* too much about that man's sex life," Aleks says.

I rub my jaw. Maybe that would work on Aleks—

As if reading my mind, he points at me. "I'm with Tripp on the good-boy thing."

I laugh and give his knee a squeeze. "Okay, but Human Tripp or Doggo Tripp? Because I think they'd have different opinions about being a good boy."

"Why don't you try it and find out?"

And if I was any more secure in my position with him, I'd take that challenge.

The doorbell rings, and Aleks shifts as though to get up. "Food's here."

I stop him from moving and press a kiss to his head to beat him to it. "I'm a nobody. If I get it, you won't get random-ass stalkers coming around that I have to save you from."

"It helps to be dating a hero."

It gets me every time he calls me that. I know he's playing around, but it's embarrassing as hell because I don't do what I do for that. I got into this job for the least noble of reasons—the thrill, the pace, the adrenaline. Helping people is all bonus, and I love it, but when it comes to *heroes*, Sanden holds that card.

By the time I'm back, Aleks is in the kitchen, and Tripp is pouring drinks by the counter. Dex is with the dog. Lying on the floor. Living his best life.

"I want a dog," he moans. "If I retire, can I stay home and look after all our fur babies?"

"And who will look after me on the road?" Tripp asks.

Dex thinks about it for a moment. "Five years, and then I'll retire, and we'll have all the four-legged kids we can manage."

Tripp hands over his glass, and they tap them together. "Deal."

I join Aleks in the kitchen and help him pull out plates and cutlery. "I like your friends."

"Even Oskar?"

"He has his … charms?" I scrunch my face up, trying to figure out what those charms are. "Actually, he's a big part of why I heard you out. He used the 'it's not you, it's him' line on me, but in a believable way."

"There's a believable way? Damn, I'll have to get him to teach me that."

A sliver of hurt hits me at the thought of all the guys Aleks is going to use that line on after me. I force a smile instead of letting him pick up on it. "Ah, but see? Now I know your trick. You'll have to be smarter than that with me."

"If I'm traded, I won't have to worry about that."

I almost drop the plate I'm holding. "Traded? Is that like being sold to another team?"

"*Traded* to another team. Like a swap."

"You really think that could happen?" Because out of all the ways I saw us ending, it was with him walking away. And I'm embarrassed to say in the back of my mind, I'd always held on to hope I could go after him, convince him to come back to me, even if I had to wait out all the other people, but if he's traded? A whole other city? That would be it for us.

"It's always possible. I've got a good contract with Seattle, and I'm gelling well with my new team, but I don't have a clause in my contract preventing it from happening."

Fuck. I thought our biggest issue was our schedules. I'd never factored into it that dating a professional hockey player could literally upend my entire life. What if we started dating, and once the season was over, he was sent to

… to … *Jersey*? Why am I worried about this when that's a whole lot of *ifs*? It probably doesn't matter, considering we know this is going to end somehow, but now I have another thing to anticipate. Aleks wanting to share his dick with the world, conflicting schedules, and now this: physical distance.

Aleks takes the plate from me, wrapping his arms around my waist. "You look like you want to punch something."

"No, I guess I didn't stop and think about that part." I pinch his chin lightly. "What if they trade you before I'm done teaching you everything?"

"With how I'm playing? The chance that they'll get rid of me is low."

"Then keep playing like that. Hat tricks every night."

"You know how to make that happen?" he asks, tilting his head up so his lips brush mine. "Come to every game."

"You like showing off for me or something?"

"Or something. You could cheer a little harder for your guy though."

Your guy. Fuck. Butterflies. I press into the kiss to avoid having to answer him, caught off guard by what those words are doing to me.

"Can we ask yet?" Dex whines.

Tripp sniggers. "Oh, yeah. *Now* we can ask."

Aleks breaks his gaze away from me. "Ask what?"

The words explode from Dex's mouth. "What's happening here?"

Tripp wraps his arms around his husband and props his chin on Dex's shoulder. "Yeah, you guys are acting more married than we are."

"What do you mean?" Aleks asks.

Tripp looks pointedly at the plates and cutlery we've set out on the counter as Dex says, "I haven't seen you guys stop touching all night."

To prove his point, I pull Aleks back against me. "If you could touch this guy whenever you wanted, wouldn't you?"

"Good point," Tripp says, and Dex turns to him with a gasp.

"I thought I was the only man for you?"

"Honey, I'm gay. I know a hot man when I see one."

Dex pouts and sends what I'm sure is meant to be a terrifying glare Aleks's way, but the effect is ruined by his spikey, barely there eyebrows. "I'm watching you."

"No need when I have a hot firefighter stripper in my bed." He cranes his head to look at me. "You really need to bring that uniform home one day."

"You wanna play emergencies?"

"Mmm, yes, please."

And before Aleks can see me move, I duck down, grab him, and throw him around my shoulders in a fireman carry.

"Fuck!" He scrambles to grab hold, and I give his ass a solid slap.

"Who's hungry?"

Tripp and Dex quickly grab everything from the counter and follow me over to the enormous dining table, where I set Aleks back on his feet. He gives me a flat look.

"You're going to pay for that."

"Ooh, those are fighting words."

"You wait ..."

"All these promises ... think we can kick your friends out now?"

"We're not going anywhere until you've fed us," Tripp says.

"And we don't have a game tomorrow, so maybe not even after that," Dex says angelically.

I turn to Aleks. "I've changed my mind. I don't like your friends."

Aleks pulls out a chair at the table for me. "You'll get used to them."

To get used to them, it means I'll have to stick around, which is maybe the most promising thing I've heard all night.

The four of us dig in, and the seven containers of food we've ordered disappear quickly. Aleks nudges me, smiling through a mouthful of food that he roughly swallows. "I like a man that can keep up with us."

I steal a dumpling off his plate and pop it into my mouth, bringing the three hockey players to a stop.

Tripp's jaw drops. "Did you … take his food?"

"Sure did."

Dex turns big eyes on Aleks. "You must really like this guy."

Aleks rests a hand over the one I have on his thigh. "He's okay, I guess."

I squeeze his thigh, and he squeezes my hand, and then we both smile at each other.

"In all seriousness," Tripp says, "how *are* you doing with it all? I know you were worried about getting back out there. I take it things are going well?"

I'll say.

"Sure are. Thanks to Gabe, that anxiousness is gone."

"That's awesome," Dex says.

"Was it like that for you?" Aleks asks. "When you guys first got together."

Tripp laughs. "I think I was more anxious than Dex was. For a straight guy, he really loved my cock."

"It wasn't about that though," Dex says. "Your dick is part of you. I love you, so therefore, I love your dick. That's all it was for me."

"Same." Aleks's hand tightens on mine again. "It's not about the parts or how they identify, just that I was connecting with someone new. Trying to do that with someone I wasn't comfortable with would have been way too hard. Gabe made it easy."

"Aww, you two are adorable," Dex says. "You should get married."

Aleks smirks at me. "That's Dex's solution to everything. Have a best friend? Get married. Need a tire changed? Husband up."

"Okay, but do you get a new husband for every problem? Or do you need a versatile one to cover it all?" I throw a look at Aleks and pretend to size him up. "Because if I need a lightbulb changed, this little hockey player ain't gonna cut it."

He shoves me, and the three of them start talking smack.

I let out a long breath, glad to have diverted from *that* conversation.

And the reality that it'll never happen.

CHAPTER TWENTY-ONE

ALEKS

I trail my mouth over Gabe's shoulder and whisper in his ear, "How much trouble will I be in if I wake you up?"

"Depends on how you wake me up," he murmurs without opening his eyes.

"By taking you on a date."

"Mm. A reverse date where we start with sex and end with food?"

"I was thinking more of that epic date you were taunting me about. I'm going to show you up."

"If waking me up before dawn is the start of it, you're already behind on the epic scale."

"Just wait. The view alone will kick your romp in the back of a pickup truck's ass."

Gabe's eyes slowly open. "That's big talk. And unless the view is of you naked, I don't know if it could really be better than coming all over each other in the flatbed."

"Hmm, I could maybe work out a way to be naked in front of the amazing view, but it all depends on if Mount Rainier National Park is busy."

"Mount Rainier …"

"Hiking is a cute date."

"I prefer a different kind of way to get sweaty on a date, but it's a nice view up there. If you're new to the city, it's a must do."

"So does that mean we're getting out of bed? Can I bribe you with coffee and breakfast on the way up there?"

Gabe slips out of bed with exaggerated hard effort. "You're lucky you're cute."

I roll out and stand, making my way over to pull some clothes out of my closet. "I wouldn't say I'm cute. Scorching hot. Worth getting up at dark o'clock for. The best date makerer in the whole world. I'll take any of these descriptors over *cute*."

"Not the best date maker yet. Also, makerer isn't a word."

"Sure it is. I said it, so therefore it is now a word."

"That's not how dictionaries work." Gabe pulls on his jeans from the night before.

"You're judgmental when you're tired." I have base layer pants that will be good for hiking, and then I take out a Henley and throw it over my head.

"Do you have a jacket I could borrow that will fit me?" Gabe asks.

"How cold will it be?"

"It's fucking snowing up there, man."

"Oh. Right. In that case …" I rummage in my closet for a sweatshirt and jacket that will fit Gabe. I also have beanies and scarves, so I dump all of them on the bed for him to choose from. "Okay, coffee time."

"I'll take an IV drip." He picks up a San Jose beanie from my old team and puts it on his head.

"You're trying to break my heart, aren't you?"

"What? I like the colors."

"You have no idea what you've done."

He takes the beanie back off and looks at it. "San Jose."

"My old team. You should be rooting for Seattle now." I throw him one of my new team beanies.

159

"Hmm, nah, I like these colors better." He puts the San Jose one back on his head.

"Traitor!"

"Oh no, what will happen? Will the hockey gods smite me again and send you bad luck?"

"Dude. You did not just say that out loud."

"Well, I was talking to Sanden, and he said that if your team doesn't do well during the season, you don't have to go to the playoffs, whatever they are, and it means your summer starts early. What if I want you to lose so you have more free time?"

I blink at him. And then blink again. Even though he's only joking—I hope—it's weird that I'm oddly touched by him wanting to spend more time with me. "If Seattle doesn't make the playoffs now, it will be all your fault."

"I'll gladly take the blame."

"No. Don't do that. The fans will turn on you."

He cocks his head. "They don't even know who I am."

"Yet."

Gabe cocks his head. "What do you mean?"

"Oh, honey." I try to keep the condescension out of my voice, but it's impossible. "Hockey players' social lives are almost as big a news story as hockey itself. People might not know you yet, but if we keep hanging out and seeing each other, they will soon. And if the team goes on a losing streak, you bet your ass fans will be looking for someone to blame. The first thing they'll look at is who has a new partner they're bringing to games. They could be a bad-luck charm."

Gabe screws up his face. "That is the most fucked-up thing I've ever heard. How is someone in the stands accountable for what you do on the ice?"

"Sports are eighty percent mental games. If your head's not in it, if you're distracted, you're going to lose."

He shakes his head. "I don't think I'll ever begin to understand you hockey people. Especially not before coffee."

"Let's get on the road. We have to drop Dog Tripp off on the way." I open my bedroom door, which we had to shut last night when trying to get some sexy time in because otherwise, we ended up having a dog jumping on the bed and wanting to wrestle with us.

Poor naïve thing had no idea why he wasn't allowed to play with us, but once we shut him outside the door, he whined for a couple of minutes and then settled.

Where he must have fallen asleep because when the door opens, his head falls back, and he rolls onto his side.

"You know you're up early when even the dog won't get up," Gabe says.

"How do you handle sleep when you're on shift? Don't you have to be up all night?"

"I mostly get uninterrupted sleep when I'm on shift unless we get a call, and in that case, I have adrenaline getting me through it."

"Okay, so I need to wake you up in a way that gets your adrenaline going, and you won't whine so much?"

"Hey, I know a great way to get a guy's adrenaline pumping first thing in the morning." He stretches his long body out.

"Hiking?"

Gabe laughs. "Sure. Totally what I meant."

As soon as I pick up Tripp's lead, he's all excitable and cute. "I wish we could take him for the hike."

"Will the guy who looks after him full-time even be awake at this hour?"

"Please. Half the team is probably already in the office."

"What?" Gabe seems so offended by that thought.

"It's weights day. A lot of the guys, especially the married ones, get their sessions out of the way early so they can spend the rest of the day with their families."

"Huh." Gabe bites his lip.

"Huh, what?"

"Nothing. I just figured all you hockey players stayed up late partying and slept in. You know, like a frat."

"Oh, we can act fratty. But mostly the younger guys. Us oldies have to be on top of our game before we're phased out."

Gabe's brow scrunches in confusion. "You're not even thirty yet."

"You know how people joke about thirty being fifty in gay years? Thirty in hockey is almost grandpa age. Sure, there are the outliers who are still playing into their forties, but it's rare. When a player hits thirty, it's kind of a 'how much longer do I have in this game' kind of moment. The longer you play, the higher chance of needing hip or knee replacements."

"In your *thirties*?" he exclaims.

I smile over at him. "Are you only now realizing how much strain professional sports puts on the body?"

He averts his gaze and mumbles, "Maybe."

"Have you been paying any attention to the games you've come to?"

"Hmm, probably not as much as I should. I kind of get distracted by one player in particular."

I step closer to him. "Yeah?"

He nods. "Dennan Katz is an amazing player."

I shove him. "You dick."

He heads for the door. "You going to take me on this epic date or what? Maybe then I'll pay more attention to you in your games."

Gabe Crosby might be the death of me.

—

With it going into winter, there are only two entrances to the park open, but I read about this place called Paradise. It has the best views, apparently. It would be better in summer than mid-November because the flowers would be in bloom, but I'm more interested in the view of the mountain.

After we drop off Dog Tripp at Seattle headquarters, where I'm right, and the gym is filled with guys from the team willing to take the dog, we get on the road with coffee and some breakfast.

It's over two hours in the car, where I drive and Gabe has his hand resting on my thigh.

After some caffeine, he perks up and asks me question after question.

"Family? I know you've said you have amazing parents, but do you have any siblings?"

"Nope. Only child."

"Friends other than your pyro hockey dudes?"

I wince. "Gave up custody of my other friends in the divorce."

"Really?"

"My wife and I went to high school together. All of our friends were mutual, and seeing as it was my fault the marriage failed—"

"How was it your fault?"

"I promised her a life together, but even I knew that in the last couple of years, I was there, but I wasn't really present. She wanted things I wasn't ready for. And I know it sounds stupid to be married to someone for ten years and not be ready to settle down, but ..." I shrug.

"Do you think it's because you got married so young that you felt like you settled down too quickly?"

"No. Ugh, maybe. The idea of sowing my wild oats or whatever was appealing, but in the same breath, as soon as I had my chance to do that, I realized it was only the idea of it that made me curious. Given the chance, I didn't actually want to go through with it. So no, that wasn't the main reason. In the end, we just weren't as compatible as I thought."

"Sounds it."

"Okay, enough about me. What about you?"

"Tragic gay story is tragic. Disapproving parents. Got kicked out young. Found my family in the five roommates I used to have."

"Do I get to meet them at some point?"

"If you want to be put through a grueling interrogation, sure."

I laugh. "Tell me about them."

"Madden is a softie. Seven is the scary one, and sorry, boo, but if Christian doesn't approve, it's no go."

"That's how it's going to be, huh?"

"Sure is."

I tilt my head. "If Christian's your best friend, why haven't I met him yet?"

"He's away at the moment. Traveling the country with the play he's in."

The amount of pride in Gabe's voice makes me smile, but I believe him when he says if they don't approve, there's no way forward for us. Not that we've discussed

164

wanting more than our original arrangement yet. But I want to. At some point.

The whole way up to Mount Rainier, there isn't a single awkward silence. Other than when we got onto the topic of music tastes. It honestly took all my strength not to kick him from the car when he said he hated the band Radioactive.

But my interest in Gabe outweighs my love of Jay Jackson's music. Just.

When we get to the Nisqually Entrance of the national park, the trees and entrance gate are covered in snow.

It's so fucking picturesque.

"Damn." I whistle. "Can you get a pic for me?"

Gabe takes out his phone to capture the scenery, and as we enter the park, a fucking deer grazes off the side of the road. A *deer*.

"I think this view alone is already eking out your bonfire."

"Is everything a competition with you?"

"I play hockey. What do you expect?"

"Ooh, you're on, little hockey player. Our next date will be even epic-er."

"Epic-er is not a word."

"Neither is makerer, but if you can make up words, so can I."

Game. On.

CHAPTER TWENTY-TWO

GABE

One epic-er date to the next, we fit them in whenever our schedules will allow. I enjoy my work and the flexible schedule rotations, but combined with Aleks's, it feels like we barely get to see each other. Sometimes we'll luck into two or three days together, but then it'll be followed by his away games, which lead straight into me being on shift.

And I … fuck, I miss him. While he's gone and I'm watching him on TV, sending a bunch of messages for him to find when he gets off the ice, I get this ache of *want*. Of wanting to be there to congratulate or commiserate with him in person. The nights I don't get to catch his games are the worst. It's a good thing I've trained myself to forget all outside distractions while I'm working because thinking about Aleks while I'm on a call isn't helping anyone.

It's not until I'm lying on my bunk, late at night, tired from working all day, that it really hits me. I'm falling for him. All that talk about him not wanting to sleep around, about the public catching on to us … I have no idea what he meant by it all. I have hopes. Hope that it means he's looking at something more permanent between us, but I haven't pushed him to know more. Firstly, I feel guilty for asking him to go from a marriage to settling down with me. Especially since he said he wasn't ready to settle down and that's why his marriage broke up. I'm ready to find my person and start a life together. I'm ready to establish a stable home that I can open up to kids like me who never had that. Aleks and I aren't in the same place.

And second, I don't know if I'm ready for the life that comes with him.

My life is quiet, fulfilling. Dating Aleks will put me in the public eye because he has actual celebrity status. When he's playing like he is right now, he's all anyone in Seattle is talking about.

But I know how quickly that can turn. A string of terrible games and the pressure will pile on. As his partner, I'd have to be the one supporting him through it while trying not to go after anyone talking shit about him.

I didn't know I was signing up for that. I mean, I know *he's* a big deal in the hockey world, but me? Why the fuck would anyone care about us dating?

In the hopes he was exaggerating, I do some general internet searches and see that he's right. The straight players get heat for who they're dating, but the queer ones? I can't believe how many trashy articles there are about Ezra Palaszczuk and Oskar Voyjik, which explains why they were so quick to ask me to keep the story of how I met them to myself.

"Your man was back last night, wasn't he?" Sanden asks from the bunk above me.

And even with all my confusion over what our future looks like, I like that. *Your man.* "Yep, got his message before we went out on that call to move that tree over the road."

"Seeing him today?"

"He's picking me up in the morning."

Sanden sighs. "Must be nice. To have a guy."

"I'll let you know when I have one. Officially."

He sniggers. "You're so dramatic. Aleks is desperate for you. I swear your phone never shuts up."

"We have a lot to talk about." I grin into the darkness.

"Damn, I want that."

"If you play your cards right, I might have some wild hockey players to set you up with."

"Nah, not my type."

I knew he'd say that. He says that about almost everyone. "So what *is* your type?"

Sanden is quiet for so long I think he's fallen asleep. "Just not ... *that*."

"Time to really get the blood pumping."

Aleks shoots me a look across the center console. "Do I need to remind you I've been away playing hockey for five days?"

"Then you can't complain you're not warmed up."

"Do *not* have a good feeling about this," he mutters, turning when I direct him to.

"Trust me ..." I have an arm stretched around the back of his seat, wishing it was his shoulders instead. But, y'know, driving safely and all that. Apparently, it's important. Hard to see the importance of it when I have this incredible man within reach.

Especially when he's not within reach most of the time.

I study his face because while he's gone, my memory only fills in so much. It misses the fine lines by his eyes, the uneven shape of his lips, the dark lashes, and kissable jaw.

He glances over at me and catches me staring. "What?"

"You're pretty to look at."

"Geez, you might as well call me cute again."

"Pretty and puny and cute. Like a doll."

Aleks groans. "You're doing amazing things for my confidence. Really. Continue."

"Nah, gotta keep some of the mystery alive."

He throws me another look. "Last time you stayed over, you waited until I was peeing and pulled up beside me to—and I quote—see who could fill the toilet fastest."

"Bladder battles. It's a thing."

"*So* not a thing."

"Clearly, you didn't get the bonding experience out of it that I did." I hold back my laugh. "Maybe we should hold hands and try it next time."

"You know I have issues when I can't even say no because it means spending more time with you."

"That's the spirit." I clap him on the shoulder as he pulls into a parking lot. "Now, hold that thought."

For our date, I'm going with pure fun. We've done the romance and the dinners and movies and that one time I took him to an NFL game so he could be all sporty while I was all selfless. Yet another thing I didn't know about professional sports players: they like their sport and *only* their sport. Aleks spent the entire game pointing out all the things that make hockey superior.

We climb out of the car, and I take Aleks's hand to lead him inside.

He looks at me, and I'm going to assume his expression is impressed. "Laser tag?"

"I may have gotten wind of a friendly tournament between some of our junior firefighters. And they just so happened to need team leaders, and we're it."

"Explain how this is a date."

"We're out. We're together. And now we're about to get hot and sweaty. Seems like a successful date to me."

"Yeah, except all the kids."

"Okay, maybe not the best context to put it in." But hey, if Aleks and I are going to get serious one day, he needs to know that liking kids is a big thing for me. When the station started the junior program, I was only too happy to get in and help out. These impressionable, confusing years are the ones I like the most.

"If we're doing this, we at least need a wager," he says.

"What? Why?"

Aleks looks at me like I've grown another head. "Because we need to be doing it for a reason."

It's my turn to give him a look. "Yeah. The reason is fun."

"F … un? Does not compute."

I drag him through to the main area, where everyone is waiting for us. "Watch and learn, baby."

There's some initial excitement from a few of the juniors when they spot Aleks, but either most of these guys aren't hockey fans or are too eager to get started because, thankfully, it's over with quickly.

The attendant shows us how to pull on the vests and talks us through safety procedures and what all the lights and sounds mean. For someone who laughed at this idea, he's as focused as the rest of us, and when the attendant finishes up, I catch Aleks's eyes.

"You ready to get your butt kicked?"

"You're adorable." He pulls the gun off his vest and swings it around. "If you ask nicely, I'll go easy on you."

"I didn't think half-assing it was in your DNA code?"

"I can be a total slacker for the right person."

"And I'm the right person? *Aww* …" I nudge his chin with my knuckles. "I'll find you so much hotter if you don't hold back. You know how I like a challenge."

"In that case …" Aleks steps forward and tilts his lips next to my ear. "Winner gets to bottom tonight."

Fuck.

Normally a promise like that, all raspy and sexy, would have me rushing through this game in order to get home, but Aleks bottoming? It's the one thing we haven't done yet. The one feeble excuse I'm holding on to in order to keep him. Once that's over, we'll have to *face things*. Talk. Work out what the hell happens next.

But it's not like I can come right out and tell him I'm scared if he tries my dick, he'll be done with me, can I?

"Deal."

We shake on it, and I spot the determination in Aleks's eye from a mile away. How the fuck am I getting out of this one?

We have a few minutes to make a plan with our teams, which mostly consists of *shoot lots*, and then the assistant opens the door to let us in.

We scatter in the dark, trying to beat the timer to find an area we can hole up in before the game begins. The giant red number counts down along with the voice over the speakers, and I leap a barrier into a section that looks like a fort. To the left of it, the wall comes out enough for me to hide behind.

I duck into the small gap as the alarm sounds, and it's declared *game on*.

I'm in the perfect position to pick off the blue team one by one as they run by. It's dark, with only the occasional laser lighting up the area, and while I'm having fun showing those kids what's what, it's hitting me that maybe

Aleks was right. This isn't exactly date-ish. I haven't even had a chance to shoot at him yet.

Noise is going off all around, the thunder of footsteps, flash of lights, shouts somewhere on the other side of the arena. Instead of hiding, I decide to launch myself out into the fray because even if my team wins, it won't mean anything unless I add Aleks to my body count.

I check the score as I run by, noting that it's wildly close. A group is heading toward me, but I duck into a doorway and down a tunnel to escape them. I'm in stealth mode, that amazing, fun adrenaline hiking through me like some kinda badass army guy, and I don't even notice him sneak up on me.

My vest lets out a loud noise and goes dark, and I spin around to find Aleks behind me.

"Dick."

He winks. "I'll be getting yours later."

I stalk close enough to back him into a wall. He's in no danger with me deactivated for thirty seconds, and he knows it. But through the window to his left, I can see the scores. See the way we go from level, to one behind, to one ahead, to level again.

I press my body against Aleks's. "You have earned it."

"Only because you've made me work for it so hard." His fingers slide into my hair.

We're one behind.

"Bottoming for me is a privilege, little hockey player."

Level.

I bring my mouth down on his, and Aleks sinks into the kiss. His tongue presses into my mouth, exactly the way I've been desperate to do ever since he picked me up from work. It's intoxicating, almost enough to distract me.

Until my vest and gun come back online.

Still level.

"Sorry, baby." I shoot him before he catches on.

And when the alarm goes off and the lights flash on a few seconds later, I get a front-row seat to his clear disappointment.

"A deal's a deal," he says.

And the fact he's trying *not* to sound disappointed makes it so much worse.

The second-last thing I want is to be holding out on him.

But the very last thing I want is to lose him.

I just wish I had the balls to tell him that.

CHAPTER TWENTY-THREE

ALEKS

Fucking hell, this sucks. Longest road trip of the season is here, and I hate it. We're on game four of seven over thirteen days, including a back-to-back against Ottawa last night and Buffalo tonight. Then we have one day off tomorrow where we travel to Boston to play Ezra and Anton the following day, and once we get home, we play back-to-back against Winnipeg and Tampa. Kill. Me. Now.

We're almost midway through the regular season, All-Stars is coming up, and is it wrong of me to want to play the next few games more subdued than usual so I don't get tapped to play in it?

I shouldn't complain. I've been doing amazingly this season. Moving to Seattle has been great for my career, but it's also been eye-opening for my private life. Not just the hot new sex I'm exploring with Gabe but for my priorities as well.

At this point in the season, everyone is starting to flag. We all love our jobs, but it's exhausting. That's expected.

What's not expected is how much these road games make me wish I was back in Seattle. Or, more specifically, with Gabe.

It's surprising because I've never had that before. Hockey was hockey, and home life was home life. They were separate, and it was easy for me to compartmentalize. I've been racking my brain trying to come up with a logical solution to why it's so different with Gabe, but the only sane thing I can think of is that it's because it's new and shiny. I don't think I ever had that with Rebecca because we were so young when we got together.

The insane theories consist of me falling for him, him being the person I was supposed to find all along, and bullshit about soul mates. Definitely can't be any of those things.

I told everyone I was going to play the field once I was single, and I don't want Oskar and Lane to be right. They said I'd fall for the first person I slept with, and I don't want to live in a world where fuckboy Oskar Voyjik is knowledgeable and full of wisdom. Because that's a dangerous combination.

We arrive at the hotel in Buffalo, and one thing I am excited about is catching up with Quinn and Little Dalton.

Asher's having a killer rookie season, but I'm wondering how he and his boyfriend are doing with them being apart. His partner is planning to move to Buffalo but is currently studying medicine in Vermont. Quinn, I'm not so sure about. His season has been … fine, neither great nor terrible, and his private life is more closed off.

Or he doesn't have one. It could be one way or the other. He hasn't been in any media other than to do with his games. I've at least been featured with my fake dates, and a photo even popped up online the other day with Gabe, but they only caught him in profile so haven't identified him yet. Only a matter of time if I keep seeing him.

We're given our rooms and are told to get ready for a practice skate and be back on the bus in twenty minutes. I barely have time to send Gabe a *made it to Buffalo* text before we're shuttled to the arena.

On the way into the visitor locker room, I pass Quinn, Little D, and a few others on the Buffalo team. They must have just come off the ice.

"Ready to have your asses handed to you?" I taunt.

"Like you did last night?" Little D quips.

"Hey, that loss was close, Little D." There was only one goal in it, and it happened in the last minutes of the game.

"Eat shit and die," he says and storms off.

Quinn shakes his head. "He loves that turn of phrase. It mostly comes out when puck bunnies hit on him. Or if people call him Little D."

"Note to self. Always call Asher Little D."

"Oh, and make life *so* fun for me? Thanks."

Our teammates pass on either side of us while we're paused in the middle of the corridor.

"How are you holding up?" I ask.

"Doing okay. Not having the best season." He runs a hand over the terrible mustache he's still sporting.

I lower my voice. "Is it the pressure of being out? It hasn't been as bad for me as I thought it would be, but I'm sure once word gets out about Gabe and me, that might change."

"Nah. Well, maybe. I'm probably overthinking the game. I need to show that my gayness doesn't affect my playing, but the more I try to prove that, the worse I play."

This is exactly why I said to Gabe that hockey is mostly a mental game.

"Will you judge me if I use that knowledge to my advantage? We need a win after the loss last night."

Quinn laughs. "Aww, you're such a great friend."

"Hey, out here, I am your friend. That only changes once we're on the ice."

"Noted."

"I'll see you out there. And before I have to go into enemy mode, here's my advice as your friend. Forget everything but hockey. Do what you love and you won't overthink it."

But now that I've been *nice*, if we lose this game tonight because of Quinn, I only have myself to blame.

–

The game is a tough one, but thankfully, it's going in our favor. For now. By two goals. Buffalo has had an amazing season—for them—but tonight, they can't find the net. At least Quinn's game has picked up in the sense he's had the most shots on goal. It's just that none of them are landing.

Considering how exhausted we are, we've done well to put two away. They weren't particularly great plays either. It's a difficult question to answer, really—are we doing well, or are both teams collectively doing badly? Hard to say.

Little D manages to put one past Chenkin, but it's late in the third period, and they need two more miracles to pull this off.

All we have to do is stop them from scoring. So instead of a strong offense, Coach tells us all to go on the defensive for the last couple of minutes. It's risky because if any of us fuck up and get a penalty, we'll be giving Buffalo the chance to score on a power play.

Playing defense also means playing in their zone, which means we're close enough for them to pull off a fluke.

In the scuffle of madness, watching that tiny disc soar across the ice, pass after pass, my hockey brain kicks in and sees an opening. It's lightning fast, but my reflexes are faster. In a move that's so blurry even to my own eyes, I manage to get the puck and fly.

I'm vaguely aware of Quinn hitting the ice behind me, but I'm on a breakaway that I can't stop. I see Katz out of the corner of my eye, catching up to me. I pass to him, and Buffalo's goalie turns his body toward Katz to protect the net, which Katz immediately sees and passes back to me where I'm waiting to take my shot.

The puck sails through the air, passes the goalie's shoulder, and hits the back of the net.

Katz crushes me in a hug, pats my helmet, but that's when I look back and see Quinn limping off the ice with Little D helping him.

"Fuck, what happened to him?" I ask my teammates, who are still celebrating around me.

Injuries happen. It's hockey. But ever since last season when Oskar took a skate to the face and almost lost his eye, every tiny injury makes my breath catch. We still don't know if it was my skate or Rostel from Chicago that did it—I've replayed the tape so many fucking times, but we were all limbs and scrambling for the puck, and both Rostel and I were right there, our feet by Oskar's head. The reality that I might have almost ended my friend's career weighed me down for the rest of the season.

Quinn's taken off the ice and led down the chute. I really fucking hope this wasn't my fault too.

For the rest of the game, which is only a couple of minutes, I'm on the bench, and I'm thankful because I can't get my mind off Quinn. It might be overreacting, but maybe I'm having some PTSD.

At least with Quinn, there was no blood. He didn't pass out—that I know of. And he got back up. Oskar didn't. He had to be carried out of there.

Once back in the locker room, I beg Frank not to choose me to do the press conference, skip the cooldown, rush through showering and getting dressed, and then head for the home locker room.

The boos hit me as soon as I walk in. I try to laugh when wet towels are thrown at me but can only manage a smile instead.

"Where's Quinn?" I ask.

"Physio room," Müller says and points.

I make my way in there, where Little D is by Quinn's side, and their team's trainer has Quinn's leg in the air, stretching it out.

Quinn's face is bright red, and his face is scrunched up in pain, but Little D has a smirk on his face.

"Can I assume he's going to be okay, or does someone else's pain just make you happy?" I ask. With Asher, it's hard to tell.

He goes to open his mouth, but Quinn cuts him off.

"I'm fine. It's a lower-body injury."

"What is it? Hip, leg, glute, groin?"

Quinn gives me a look on that last one, and I try not to smile.

"Stop it!" Quinn cries out. "I'm going to be out for at least eight games, if not more."

I hold my hands up. "I'm not saying anything. I feel for you, man."

"Cold compress, massage, and rest," the trainer says.

Little D puts a finger on his nose. "Dibs not being the one to massage Quinn's *groin*."

"Ha, ha." Quinn rolls his eyes.

"Don't worry about that," the trainer says. "I've got you covered."

I swear Quinn's face turns even redder, and after the trainer leaves us in the room, I find out why.

Little D bursts out laughing.

"What am I missing?"

"Quinn wants to climb Vance like a tree, and now his hands are gonna be all over his body."

Quinn closes his eyes. "This is mortifying."

I do feel for the guy, but more than that, I'm happy his injury isn't serious.

How much longer is left of this damn road trip?

CHAPTER TWENTY-FOUR

GABE

The knock on the door is unexpected, and I'm only fifty-fifty committed to getting off the couch. I've been out all day, trying to keep myself busy and not think about Aleks flying in today and that I won't get to see him.

With back-to-back home games, Sanden and I split the tickets. He gets to go tonight, taking someone for their birthday or whatever, and I'm going tomorrow night when I'll actually be able to go home with Aleks afterward.

And now that I'm comfortably relaxing in my sweats, I *really* don't want to get up and answer the door to a salesman. Or someone from the church.

The knock comes again, louder this time, and I resign myself to the fact it's probably one of my old roommates wanting to drag me out of the house. It would be a good distraction, but I'd rather sit around wallowing over the fact I don't get to see Aleks. Dramatic, much? I'm basically the tail end of a rom-com at this point.

So when I open my door and he's standing on the front porch, I have to check I'm not hallucinating. I reach out and poke his cheek.

"You feel real."

"I should hope so."

"Fuck, baby." I grab his hand, tug him inside, then slam the door and back him up against it.

"Maybe you should check again," he suggests, voice deep. "I hear my mouth is a good way to test if I'm real."

I bring our lips together, cupping his face and pressing my body against his. Chest, abs, groin, legs. It takes all of a second for him to harden, and then it's a race to see who can get it up first. His kiss is addictive, and I sink into the way it makes me feel, scared of the feelings building in my chest but tired of running from them.

"Still real," I say, pulling back enough to break our kiss but still keeping us locked together. "What are you doing here?"

"Coach sent us home for downtime before the game. I was going out of my skin not seeing you."

And it shouldn't, but hearing him admit that brings the biggest smile to my face.

"Hmm, to shamelessly obsess over your dimples or be offended that my misery makes you so happy? Hard choice," he says.

I huff a laugh. "Sorry. As you can tell by this greeting, I missed you too."

"I didn't say I missed *you*. It was your dick. *All* your dick."

He goes to grab me, and I take a step back. I'm not smiling anymore. For one foolish second, I'd gotten caught up in the moment, and Aleks swiftly brought me back down again. At least there's no doubting where his head is at.

"Right, well, we better get you two reacquainted, then. I'm guessing you don't have much time."

He hums and slides his hands around my waist, reeling me back in. "I have a few hours to kill. And I was thinking

..." He leans in so his words are right by my ear. "I want you to fuck me."

My whole body stiffens, and I know, without a doubt, that there's no getting out of it this time. But I try anyway. "You really want to be sore before a game?"

"I've just played one of the hardest weeks of the season—I'm already sore. This won't make a difference."

"Yeah, but you wouldn't know—"

He steps back and tilts his head. "Is something going on? Do you not want to, or ... I'm sure you've mentioned fucking me before, so I guess I kinda assumed you didn't bottom all the time, but if you're not into that ..."

Ah, fuck. Aleks's face is scrunched with confusion and doubt, and even though I don't *want* to have this conversation, looks like it's happening.

I scrub a hand through my hair. That uncontained need to *move* burns under my skin, but instead of pacing like I'm desperate to, I fall against the wall and pull him closer.

"This will sound incredibly dumb," I warn him.

"Okay ..."

"I've been avoiding topping you because, well ..." My hand finds my hair again. "If we do that, that's it. There's no reason to keep doing this."

Aleks takes a moment for that to sink in, and as it does, his eyes narrow. "No reason ... Other than we both want to."

"What?"

"*What?*" He scowls at me. "I'm not exactly running away here."

"But this was all a sex thing."

"Really? Because I know I take a lot of hits to the head, but from memory, pizza at the fire station, chasing down

183

those animals, hiking, that stupid football game you took me to, laser tag, I don't recall sex at any of those things."

"No, but …" Is he saying what I hope he is?

Aleks's face softens, and this time, it's his hand in my hair. "Have you really been holding off on fucking me because you were scared I'd ditch you the next day?"

"When you put it like *that* …"

"Kinda pathetic." He grins.

I pinch his side and make him squirm. "I'm sorry I caught feelings for you."

"I'm not. Well, I *am*, but only because this means Oskar was right. I don't think I'm ever going to be over that."

"What do you mean?"

"He and his boyfriend said that I'd fall for the first guy I slept with." Aleks makes a buzzing noise. "You're it."

"You're falling for me?"

His gorgeous bluish-green eyes meet mine. "I'm trying really hard not to think about it, if I'm honest."

My voice drops to a whisper. "Think about it."

"I have, and I'm scared."

That's all I need to know. "So am I, but the fear outweighs how good it could be."

I move first, but Aleks is half a breath behind me. Our mouths collide, all hot, urgent need. An outpouring of all the things we haven't said and want to say, but it can all wait because if he's willing to try for something even though he's scared, then I sure as hell can work through my issues.

All we need to concentrate on right now is us.

And getting him as naked as humanly possible.

I yank his team jacket off his shoulders and break the kiss to pull his shirt over his head before my mouth comes down on his neck. His skin is cold from outside but rapidly warming from our shared body heat. He tastes salty and smells like something I've smelled on him before and never been able to place. I press my nose to the spot where his shoulder and neck meet and inhale. "What is that?"

"Hmm, what?"

"It's, I don't know. Buttery? Vanilla-y? I'm shit with scents."

"Ah … I think it's the locker room soap."

I moan and sniff him again. "It's all you."

"And about twenty or so other guys."

"Yeah, but I'm not planning to stick my dick in any of them."

"You sure about that? Bilson teases me about my *hot fireman* often enough I'm starting to think he wouldn't mind."

I take a fast step back. "Well, in that case—"

Aleks thumps me, then tugs my sweats down in one fast movement. My dick slaps back against my abs, and Aleks's stare zeroes in on it. "That's all mine."

"Oh, I think I like possessive on you, little hockey player."

He pouts up at me and *fuck*. How can a man this sexy pull that look off? "What about needy? Because I need you so much."

I reach out and undo his jeans, then slip my hands down the back, under his briefs, and grab an ass that's pure muscle. "I can honestly say I've never been with a man who has an ass like this." I squeeze his cheeks. "I can't wait to see the exact moment your virgin hole takes my cock. To see it stretch around the head, to see the way your ass moves as I pound you."

"Those are a lot of words for someone who hasn't topped in a while."

"You have nothing to worry about."

I kiss him again, walking him backward across my small living area to the bedroom. As we walk, I push down his jeans, and Aleks steps out of them, pressed against me, my hands steady on his back. His briefs go next, and then it's all naked skin, hard muscle, and our cocks sliding together.

He laughs into my mouth. "How does this feel so right?"

"I know what I'm doing."

"No, just … you. I've never missed anyone before, but now …"

I kiss him again to save him from trying to find the words. This is new for us both. He has to come to terms with being in another relationship so soon, and I need to come to terms with some hard truths. Dating my dream man means losing the privacy I've always taken for granted.

It'll be an adjustment, but for him, it's a change I'll learn to make.

Against everything in my body screaming at me to hold him tight, when we reach my bed, I finally let him go.

"Lie down," I say as I grab the lube.

Aleks does exactly that, his long, lean body looking like fucking art against my rumpled bedding. His tattoos, his light body hair, his swollen cock. Those *eyes*.

He's going to be the death of me.

"I'm going to be as patient as I can, but I'm telling you, you're really making it difficult right about now."

Aleks slowly strokes his cock. "Is this better?"

He lets his legs fall open.

"You don't play fair."

"I play to win."

I can guarantee the man is winning tonight.

I take my time, kissing down his body, lips skimming skin and muscle, taking extra time to trace the bruises left by his games. His breathing deepens in a way I'm coming to get addicted to. Every time we're together, whether it's hard and fast and rushed, or slower, quieter, like this, I take a moment to commit everything about him to memory.

I was not prepared for Aleksander Emerson, but thankfully, I'm good at going with the flow.

My kisses reach his pubes, and I bury my face into the base of his cock.

I blindly click open the lube and coat my fingers, then lean up and suck the head of his cock into my mouth while my fingers find his hole.

Aleks's breath stutters for a brief second, but I turn all my attention to his swollen tip, running my tongue over it, playing with the underside, alternating between soft and hard sucks before letting my teeth lightly scrape over the sensitive skin. While I work, I let my fingers rest against him, let him get used to the feeling, and when I've got him sufficiently distracted, I start to work open his hole.

"That's it, little hockey player," I coo, running my tongue over his length. "You wanna take my cock? You gotta let me in."

He exhales heavily and flexes his hips toward me. A clear invitation for me, and I take it. I'd give Aleks whatever he wants at this point, and that's the problem. I really am falling for him. I want to convince myself that this is fresh and new and that we have plenty of time to learn who the other is, but my heart is racing ahead of that. I'm not in control. There's nothing calm and careful about the way my feelings are full speed ahead for him.

It scares me. I should be smarter than that.

I'm not.

And considering I'm used to staying levelheaded in stressful situations, that's saying something. I sink into the taste of him, into his scent, listening and reacting to every sign he gives me when to keep going and when to give him a minute. When my index finger breaches him for the first time, his hiss slows me down. When the tension melts from his thighs and the grip around my finger loosens, I stroke inside him slowly. In and out. Gently at first, then firmer, opening him up for another finger, then a third.

I suck on his balls, loving the tight grip he has around my fingers as I work them in and out. I want to replace them with my cock so bad, but I'm determined to make this good for him. He needs to be well and truly ready to be fucked before I stick my cock in him because I'm barely going to be able to hold back.

I'm already leaking all over my sheets, desperately pressing into the mattress every few minutes to lessen the need. But this is *Aleks*, and the combination of how attractive I find him and how much I feel for him is making this so much harder than I ever thought it would be.

My brain wants to tap out and let the rest of me take over, but I need to hold out for him to be completely ready.

When he's good and stretched, I pull off him and replace my mouth with a lubed hand. I keep my fingers lodged inside him while I crawl up the bed on my knees, stroking slowly until he looks at me.

"We good to go?"

"Yeah, just remember, I'm still in the rookie league. And I play later. Don't hurt me."

I press in until I find his prostate, and Aleks's groan rumbles in his chest. "I know what I'm doing."

His hole is still perfectly stretched and ready for me when I pull my fingers out and lube myself up. And as much as I want to be greedy and shove back in, I position myself at his entrance and turn my attention back to him.

I seal my mouth over Aleks's, taken back to that very first kiss. The one that started and almost ended everything between us. The promise, the lust, the possibility. The thrumming band of sexual tension that was right on the edge of snapping. This is a thousand times better than that.

Now I know how he tastes and how he kisses. Now, when I wrap my hand around his cock and use every trick in the book to keep him hard as I push in, I know what moves will work. I know which ones will make him desperate and distract him. With every grunt, with every time his hands tighten in my hair, with every flex of his hips stirring me on, I *know* him.

I give one final thrust, sealing us together. I've been inside him for less than a minute, and it's already hands down the best sex I've ever had. Every time I'm with him, it's the same. I never realized how much having this deep connection with someone could make every experience heightened. Like life on steroids.

Sex in fucking candy land.

I keep kissing and stroking him as I start to thrust. Slowly at first, testing him out, letting him adjust, until I sense the moment he's comfortable.

"Your sexy hole is strangling my cock," I rasp into his ear. "Feel that?" I bring us together hard enough to send a jolt through him. "I'm so hard for you. So ready. Gonna blow inside your ass."

"Shit yes."

"Time to mark you the way you marked me."

And so fucking help me, Aleks actually whimpers.

I kiss him again, this time zero plans to stop until we're done. Our tongues fight for dominance as my thrusts pick up, hard and fast. Aleks takes over stroking his cock, so I plant my hands on either side of him, knees digging into the mattress, and fuck him like my life depends on it. And with how hard my orgasm is building, I'm not convinced it doesn't.

He's long past rookie league, with his heels digging into my ass, urging me faster, hand that's not gripping his cock dragging scratches down my back. His tongue filling my mouth, the smell of sweat and sex around us, his hard body wrapped around mine.

I want to hold out, but the pleasure is too much. He feels way too good. I love bottoming for him, but topping is fun in a different way. The high I feel about getting to be with him like this, that he trusts me to make this incredible, it's too much.

My orgasm hits me, spurt after spurt shooting deep inside him as I try to milk out every last drop. Aleks's thighs grip my waist a second before he follows me over the edge.

I pull out of him, sweaty and tired and so fucking satisfied, before I flop onto the bed beside him. We both take a moment to catch our breath, the smell of sweat and sex all around us. I've never loved anything more.

Still wrapped up in my high, I turn my head toward him and find him already watching me. My knuckles run over his hip, needing to touch him. "You okay?"

"Yeah. You?"

Is he serious? I just blew my load and had amazing sex with someone I'm really growing to care about.

Aleks's hand finds mine, fingers sliding down my palm. "No freak-outs, I mean? No wanting to get rid of me?"

"None. I was the one freaking out about that, remember?" And feeling like I'm pushing my luck, I ask, "So we're really doing this? Dating or whatever?"

"I figure we basically have been this whole time. Why mess with a good thing?"

"That might be the smartest thing you've ever said to me."

"Not bad for a little hockey player."

I squeeze his hand. "Don't worry, I won't get used to it."

CHAPTER TWENTY-FIVE

ALEKS

Okay, so maybe losing my ass virginity right before a game wasn't my greatest idea. Even though Gabe took his time and did everything right, the aching twinge every time I move makes me wince.

Luckily, hockey isn't a sport that involves much movement. Oh, wait …

I'm moving slower than a fucking pylon, and my teammates know it. When Katz tries to send the puck my way and I'm not where I'm supposed to be, he throws me a frustrated look. When it gets intercepted and Winnipeg scores because of it, everyone on the team scowls at me.

Or in general. I can only assume that it's at me because I'm fucking up more than a rookie in his first-ever game. At this point, if we had a five-on-three power play with no goalie in the net, I'd still miss.

Note to self: no more bottoming before a game. Ever. Maybe Gabe and I can come up with some kind of schedule. A fucking schedule. Sounds so romantic. He can have my ass in the off-season, and I can have his all the other times. Sounds fair … if, you know, the off-season wasn't so short.

My gaze finds him in the stands as I skate by the home team's family seats. When he'd said Sanden was taking the season tickets tonight, I offered him one of the couple of tickets we get comped. I should be focused on the puck, but hey, that hasn't actually helped me all game.

Out of nowhere, Fensby—an asshole who used to play for Vegas before he was traded—bodychecks me against the boards.

I don't even have the puck.

The penalty is called, but I'm fucking pissed. I probably wouldn't be if it were an accident or I didn't know how much of a homophobic dickweed Fensby is.

I shove him. "What the fuck, man?"

The next second, his gloves are gone, and it's on.

I'm not a fighter on the ice, but I'm not a turtle either, and if he's expecting me to drop to the ice and cover myself from the blows, he's as delusional as he is an assface.

Whether he has a problem with me because of my new connection to the Collective or if he saw me as weak and just wanted to feel like a big man, I'm not sure, but I also don't care.

Fensby grips my jersey with one hand and throws a punch with the other. It connects to the side of my helmet.

Nice shot, dumbass.

When I throw a punch, I at least hit my target. A satisfying crack sounds when my fist connects with his jaw.

His next move is to knock my helmet off my head.

The whole arena has paused, everyone watching as two grown-ass men fight like little boys, but the crowds die for this. I don't usually live for fighting, but with Fensby, any free shot I get, I will take.

I punch him in the gut, but his pads soften the blow. He finally manages to clock me in the face, sending a sting through my cheek. His rough-as-fuck knuckles break skin.

What is probably only a few seconds feels like minutes until teammates decide to step in and pull us off each other.

Fensby and I are both sent to the sin bin for five minutes, and yeah, maybe I should have been the bigger person and not retaliated—considering I've contributed nothing to this game, the least I could've done was give us a power play, but with all the frustration of playing badly and knowing Fensby is a dick, I took my shot. At least we're both off and the play is still even numbers.

Once in the box, I do nothing but stare at the ice and think about what I've done. Yes, kids, even grown-ups get time-outs too.

Fensby chirps at me, some crap about having a terrible game, but hey, it's true, so I don't let it get to me.

It's the longest five minutes of my life, and when we're finally released back onto the ice, the need to prove myself and make up for the shitty play I have been doing tonight outweighs the tiny ache in my ass.

I hit the ice like lightning and charge down to our offensive zone, where my teammates are frantically trying to put one in the net, but no matter how hard we fight, no matter how hard we scrimmage, none of us can find the fucking net.

There's a moment where Katz and I lock eyes, and for the first time in maybe my entire career, I hope the puck doesn't land in my position. The others have scored tonight. I haven't. I've done nothing but slow us down.

With reluctance, he passes me the puck, I shoot, and of course, it's fucking blocked.

I'm disappointed and downright pissed at myself when the buzzer goes, and we walk away with the loss. Throughout the cooldown and showering, getting dressed, I'm convinced I can't get any lower than this moment.

That is, until Frank asks to see me in the empty press room before I leave for the night.

That can't be good.

I text Gabe to tell him I'll meet him back at his place because the big, scary PR manager wants to see me.

> Is it about the fight?

Aww, that's cute. I reply:

> Nope. That's hockey. I have no idea what this is about.

If it were a simple publicity opportunity, that could have waited until tomorrow or next practice.

The only reason I move so fast is because I don't want to keep Gabe waiting long. It's a rare night where we'll get to sleep in tomorrow because he's off work, and I have another home game tomorrow night, so the only obligation I have in the morning is a light workout to keep warm.

I enter the room and stop in my tracks at the sight of a woman next to Frank. She's got caramel-colored hair with blonde highlights and extensions. She's the kind of natural beauty that has the makings of a supermodel, and she looks about twenty.

"Aleks, meet Natasha Grigorieva."

She smiles at me. "It's so nice to finally meet you."

"Uh … okay?"

She cocks her head at me, and I shake out of my stupor and shake her hand.

"Sorry. Hi."

"Natasha's an up-and-coming model and needs some publicity."

Model. Called it.

I'm momentarily confused until I realize what he means. "Oh. As in, me and her …" I wave my finger between us. "I thought I was done with that?"

"You haven't been seen with anyone for a while."

Natasha steps closer. "My agency told me about you. How you're playing the bi rep, and I understand completely about needing to keep your image a certain way. It's the same in my industry. We could help each other."

"Pansexual." I frown. "I'm kind of seeing someone though."

"You are?" Frank asks.

"Actually, not kind of—we just made it official."

"Before that game?" Frank points to the closed door leading back into the bowels of the arena.

"Yeah, why?"

"Whoever they are, after the worst three periods in your career, you might not want to go public with that knowledge yet."

"But you want me to go on a date with Natasha."

"That's a date, and I guarantee there will be speculation about her effect on your game."

That's the last thing I want for Gabe.

"The fans won't hate me forever, will they?" Natasha asks.

"There isn't a lot of crossover between hockey fans and fashion," Frank says. "Shocking, I know. If anything, if they think you're bad luck, your name will appear more times on social media than if you merely go on a date with him."

"But I have a boyfriend now," I say. "Like, this isn't even a discussion."

"Boyfriend?" Frank asks. "So, it's a man."

"Yes. And we're together, and—"

"You know we told you the team and organization would be supportive when or if that was to happen, and don't get me wrong, because we are ready to handle that situation."

That it's a "situation" at all pisses me off, but I know it's not Frank's fault. It's sports in general. Welcoming and mostly supportive, with a few remaining standouts who live back in the nineties when it was normal to call people the F-word and fear the gayness. Or, in my case, pan-ness, which back then "didn't exist" to some fucknuggets.

Times are changing, that's for sure, but we're still not there yet.

"But?" I ask.

"But all I'm saying is go out with Natasha tonight, take a few weeks to get your game back on track, and then we'll release the pink, yellow, and blue banners around the arena and make the entire team use that color tape on their sticks."

My eyes widen, because what the fuck?

That's when Frank smirks. "I'm messing with you about the tape and the banners, but one hundred percent support."

"Once I'm not sucking on the ice? What do you need? A hat trick? Pull off an Anton Hayes and get six goals in one game?"

"I'll let you think about it." Frank steps closer and grips my shoulder. "But in answer to your question, maybe save stepping out with your boyfriend to a night where you don't trip over your own skates, get into a fight, and give up a power play because of your ego."

Touché.

"You two talk. I'll be outside waiting."

Frank leaves Natasha and me to stare at each other awkwardly.

"Sorry, I didn't know about your boyfriend," she says softly.

"No one does. Yet."

"I'll understand if you don't want to go out tonight. My agency's just trying to get me out there, you know?"

"I get it. More than most people probably would." Do I really want to go on a fake date with her? No. But Frank has a point that fans are batshit crazy. And okay, he didn't use those exact words, but in some cases, it's true.

The fandom of hockey—or any fandom, really—has the ability to go overboard, and with hockey, if your team isn't winning, the fans will turn on you. They'll blame every little thing. They'll stalk social media to find out what's happening in your private life and talk smack to try to pinpoint where it's all going wrong.

Someone's wife isn't holding their hand in public? Marriage is on the rocks? Bam, it's their fault the team isn't winning. Seen out drinking the night before a game? You're an alcoholic, and your disease is bringing down the team. Everything is overinflated, and if they can't find anything true, they'll make up lies.

I don't want to pander to them by going through with this charade, but at the same time, I want to protect Gabe from that.

"I don't know what to do," I say.

"Why don't you call your boyfriend and ask him what he thinks?"

"Sure, because that phone call will go down so well. 'Hi, honey, I know we just made it official and stuff, but can I go on a date with a supermodel? Thanks. Love ya, bye.'"

She giggles. "It's cute you think I'm a supermodel, but I see your point. Explain the situation, then. Tell him there's nothing between us, and I'm just using you to get my damn photo on some gossip sites."

"I don't think that's any better, but that might prevent my balls from being ripped off."

"Talk to him, and let us know. I'll be outside the door with Frank."

Really, what's the worst that could happen? He could say no. Natasha's right. I should run this by him. Maybe he'll understand.

But if that's the case, why am I so fucking nervous about calling him? I stare at my screen, telling myself he'll still be on his way home … even though I was his ride.

Oh, fuck, I was his ride, and I told him to leave.

That alone has me hitting Dial.

CHAPTER TWENTY-SIX

GABE

Aleks telling me he'll meet me back home rather than at the arena doesn't seem like a good sign, and when my phone lights up with a call from him, I work out why.

"Hey." He lets out a heavy breath. "I just had a meeting with PR, and now I'm confused."

My eyebrows rise. "What do you mean?"

"I played like shit tonight."

"Did you?"

He laughs. "Did you miss the part where I was sent off? The fight? I had two left skates and couldn't have found the net even without a goalie there?"

"I think you're being hard on yourself."

"Not what the fans will say."

"Fuck the fans." And I mean it. If they're that angry over one game, they're no fans. "Everyone has off days. And it's not like hockey is life and death."

Okay, I really know something is up when he doesn't react to *that*. I was expecting a gasp, maybe a threat of smite from the hockey gods again, but he doesn't.

"Unfortunately, fans are a big part of why I have a job, and they're vicious. Remember what I told you about them lashing out at any change being the cause of a bad game?"

It clicks where he's going with this. "You don't think it's because of us? Because that's taking superstition a step too far."

"*I* don't, but they will. And Frank had an idea … my PR guy. See, Natasha is an up-and-coming model who wanted to use dating me for publicity, like what I was doing at the start of the season. And I told Frank I was seeing *you* now and that I wasn't interested in that, but he has a point. People will be looking to blame someone for how badly I played, and I don't want that person being you. She knows the deal. She's fine with it. It would literally all be for show."

Aleks talks fast, but the more words he says, the more the ringing in my ears tries to drown him out. *She* knows the deal? *She's* fine with it?

"What are you saying?"

"They want me to take her out on a date tonight. A fake one. Totally fake. People will assume I'm dating her, and then when we fake break up, they'll be happy, and I'll come out saying I'm dating you, and you'll be safe from all the hate."

A pit is growing in my stomach at the thought of Aleks with anyone but me. He's going to, what? Go out with her tonight on the one night we have to spend together after not seeing each other for way too many days? Will there be photos? Will I have to see them together? What happens if his game keeps getting worse?

Insecurity is clawing at me, and there's nothing I can say.

My jaw tightens. "What do *you* think?" Somehow my tone comes out almost normal.

"I think it's probably smart."

"Well, if it's *smart*, I guess that's it, then."

"Gabe—"

"No, it's fine. Enjoy your date."

"I'll come over straight after."

"You know what, Aleks, it's late." I'm really struggling to keep my tone level. "I'll just see you at your game tomorrow."

"You get why I have to do this, right?"

"Of course."

He's quiet for a moment. "If you're sure."

"Yeah. See you." I hang up before I can say anything else. My blood is *boiling*. Hands actually fucking trembling as the pit in my gut grows. I'm so goddamn jealous I can barely see right, and it's not that I think he'll cheat or anything because Aleks is better than that. It's the fact he had a choice between spending time with her or me … and he didn't choose me.

Even though we've been apart for almost two weeks and just made things official. He plays tomorrow night, then his day off conflicts with my day on, then he's gone for another four days.

This was our only shot for almost a week.

I'm not his priority.

It's his career.

It's saving face and making the fans happy.

I let out a bitter laugh, remembering how worried I was about being dragged into the spotlight, and here Aleks is trying to protect me from that, and I'd prefer literally anything else.

If he'd bothered to ask me how I felt about being blamed for his game, I would have told him I don't care.

I would have chosen *him*, no questions asked.

It's a blow to know we're not on the same page.

He's always said he's not a settling-down type, but I thought he was as desperate to see me as I was to see him. This taste of reality *sucks*. Especially when I remind myself that I knew what I was getting into; I'd just chosen to ignore it.

The driver pulls up in front of my house, and somehow I manage to thank him and get out. I pace inside my tiny, crappy house that I was so proud of being able to afford all on my own, but now I compare it to what Aleks has and worry we're fooling ourselves.

Do we actually have a real shot?

Aleks is worried about the fans coming after me, and let's face it, they have a lot to come after. I'm poor and disowned, and those things will never change about me.

Maybe the media scrutiny won't be too much for me but for *him*.

I strip off and rage shower, hoping it will calm me down.

It doesn't.

By the time I climb into bed, Aleks hasn't messaged or called, and my brain is working overtime. Thinking of him out. Eating dinner. Talking and joking. Enjoying himself and not even taking a second to spare me a single thought.

I fucking hate how whiny and irrational I'm being, but I can't make it stop.

I barely sleep a wink all night.

—

You coming tonight?

> Of course I am. And don't worry, to keep
> up appearances I'm bringing a date. I'm
> hoping the kiss cam will be thrown our way
> x

Petty? Whiny? Hurt? Yup, I'm feeling all three as Madden and I pull into the arena parking lot. I waited all day to see if Aleks would text me, but I get the feeling he was playing the same game because my phone was radio silent. I'm sick with this *thing* between us, and all I wanted was to call him and tell him I'm being an idiot and I miss him. I just couldn't work out how to do that without coming across as a stage five clinger.

All I know is that the past twenty-four hours have made it very clear to me how deep my feelings go, and if Aleks isn't right there with me, I need to walk away. I *have* to. For my own sanity.

Madden pulls into a parking space and switches off the engine, then turns to pin me with a look. "You sure about this?"

"Nope." Not even a little bit. I scrub my hands back through my hair over and over. "I don't know which is worse. Him being hurt at the thought of us on a date ... or him not giving a shit."

Madden pulls me into a hug. "It's not a real date though."

"Neither was his. Still hurt."

Especially since I spent my morning torturing myself by looking him up. The woman he was out with was fucking gorgeous, and I wondered, more than once, whether it would be fairer on Aleks to not get started on this thing between us at all. Literally the only thing that helped me keep it together was that in all the photos I saw, they weren't touching in any of them. Not even holding hands.

It's the one thing that helped me breathe.

"Okay," Madden says. "Let's go show him how dumb his plan was last night."

Probably as dumb as mine. Holy fuck, I'm nervous.

We purposefully arrive later than usual, missing the warm-up skate, and by the time we walk from the back of the parking lot, the arena is filling up, and no one's on the ice.

I already know that no matter how hurt I am, I'll be finding him as soon as this game is over. Staying away all day has been painful, and my resolve is at the very goddamn end. I work early tomorrow, and then he leaves again the next day. If he tells me he has another date set up tonight though, that will be it. I can't do it again.

I'll sit in angry silence with him all night if that's what it takes to spend time with him.

I drop down in the seat beside Madden, feeling drained.

"So," he says. "If the kiss cam *does* land on us, we're not actually doing it, are we? You know I love you, and I will if I *have* to, but the thought of your hockey player boyfriend punching me in the face isn't enjoyable."

I eye Madden. "You guys are probably the same size. You could take him."

"A professional bruiser? Doubt it. Maybe in my college ball days."

I think for a moment before shaking my head. "Nah, no kiss. Not even for the kiss cam. No way would I risk losing him over something stupid." But if he doesn't actually care, that'll be a whole other conversation.

"In that case, if it lands on us, lean in like you're gonna, then I'll kiss you on the forehead."

"You're the best."

He doesn't miss a beat. "I know."

Almost as soon as the game starts, Madden is so invested he forgets all about me sitting next to him. He's constantly on his feet, cheering Seattle on, but I'm so overly aware of Aleks and what he's doing I have no idea about the rest of it.

God, he looks good out there.

My whole dumb body aches for him, and I wish I could go back to this time last night. I would have waited at the arena and told him I didn't give a shit about the fans. Only him. Maybe I would have gotten my answer then around how serious he is, and maybe I wouldn't have, but sitting here in complete limbo is maybe the worst feeling ever.

Aleks plays an incredible game, like always. Last night was one of those nights where things went wrong, and yeah, I saw the types of comments he was talking about all over his social media, but those people will be eating their words tonight.

They might even beg those two to get married after a game like this.

I tell that stupid voice to shut the fuck up.

I've beaten myself up enough for one day.

Both teams suddenly head for their team boxes while they resurface the ice, and Madden drops back into his seat. His elbow jabs my side as he points up.

"Kiss cam time, baby." He wraps his arm around me, probably to try to get whoever picks the couples to focus on us.

Suddenly, I'm dreading this even more than I was.

206

Music fills the arena, and Madden bounces in his seat.

I tell myself the chances of being on this thing are small and to calm the fuck down, and with the first two couples, I begin to believe it. But then my gut fills with dread as my face appears on the screen.

Holy fuck.

"C'mere, baby," Madden says. His grin is enormous as he grabs the front of my Emerson jersey and tugs me closer. His lips are pursed, mouth inching slowly closer, and I know he said he'd divert and kiss my head, but before he manages to lift his chin, a thunderous *bang* makes us jump apart.

Then I'm looking up into the murderous face of my boyfriend.

He pounds the glass again, then points at Madden. "Don't you dare!" The side of his fist hits the glass, and after a moment, he turns his stare on me. "Touch my boyfriend and see what happens!"

Madden's jaw hangs open, and my eyes are goddamn huge. I'd been *hoping* for a split second of jealousy from him before he caught on to us messing with him, but this? I'm low-key in shock that Aleks is causing a scene, even as this twisted balloon of *something* grows in my chest.

Something morbidly happy.

Something that I really shouldn't be feeling but can't help feeling anyway.

The crowd is screaming.

And it's lucky that glass is between us because if it wasn't? I'd kiss him in front of this whole goddamn arena.

Because I'm ready for everyone to know that man is all mine.

And after all that? Apparently, he feels the same.

CHAPTER TWENTY-SEVEN

ALEKS

"Caveman much?" Katz asks when I sit back down in my seat.

The crowd is still going nuts, even though the kiss cam has moved on, and yeah, maybe that was over-the-top, but it was effective. In more ways than one.

"Gabe was letting me know how much I fucked up last night by going out with some model Frank set me up with."

"Wow. You did that and he still turned up? That man has got it bad for you."

Yeah, feeling's mutual.

"He brought another guy," I point out.

"Probably to show you how it feels."

"It worked."

Katz slaps my shoulder. "Use that rage out on the ice, and let's finish this."

I do as he says, and it's an easy win. It's a good game all round by all of us, one of those times where everything works.

Without fail, though, every time I leave the ice, my eyes connect with *him*. I swear he hasn't stopped smiling since my display, and hey, at least that might mean he's not too pissed at me anymore. I still have some groveling to do though. And I'm going to do it. As soon as I'm done here.

But when we head down the chute, Frank motions for me to follow him back into that tiny conference room we were in last night. I'm almost expecting to see Natasha in there waiting for us, but it's empty.

"Decided to scrap the whole plan, I see."

"No offense, but it was a stupid plan, and I shouldn't have agreed to it. Instead of protecting my boyfriend from the fans, all it did was piss him off. And I get it."

"Ah, so that's what the show was all about."

"We can still spin this. We can say Natasha and I are friends—which, after last night, I'd like to think we are—and that I've been dating Gabe for a few months now, and we're happy. Except for when kiss cams try to come between us."

"Of course. Are you willing to go to the press conference tonight and clarify all that with the public?"

"Uh, can I talk to Gabe about it first? He might not be okay with me going out with someone else, but he still might not want to be in the spotlight like that."

"Go change for the press conference and text Gabe to meet me at the players' entrance so I can bring him to you."

Okay, time to face the music, I suppose. Time to put my groveling hat on.

The first thing I do is text Gabe and then change into Seattle sweats and a cap to keep my sweaty hair somewhat tame.

There are reporters taking interviews with players in the non-naked part of the locker room, but I bypass them all, even when they see me and throw questions about my public outburst.

I take my phone with me back to the spare press room and wait. Gabe hasn't replied, and he doesn't have the read feature on, so I can't even tell if he's seen it. I'll give him a couple more minutes before I try to call him.

That proves to be a mistake, though, because as soon as I decide not to call, I notice the notification tally going up on my Twitter app. I have the alerts for it switched off, but I can see that number in red going up and up and up.

I don't want to look.

I look anyway.

And okay, it's not horribly bad. It's not great, but at least there's no one story being run. No one knows who Gabe or his friend are or why I'd be mad about them kissing. Some even accuse me of being homophobic. They're either late on the news that I'm pansexual or think I was lying. Either way, they suck.

"What are you doing?" Frank asks.

I lift my head, and "Twitter" absentmindedly falls from my mouth when my gaze lands on Gabe.

But unlike the smiles he's been sending my way during the last half of the game, his face is unreadable.

"I'll leave you two to discuss." Frank turns on his heel and leaves, pulling the door closed behind him.

It's my turn to talk. To say everything I should have said to him last night but didn't.

I open my mouth, but no noise comes out, so I try again. "I made the wrong choice."

He runs for me, almost knocking me over as he takes me in his arms.

"That was a lot less groveling than I thought I'd have to do."

He pokes me in the ribs. "If you think for a second you've made it up to me, you're in for a rude awakening.

This just means I'm not mad at you anymore." Gabe looks down at me, his bright blue eyes shining. Then he leans in and kisses me, hard and rough.

I want to take him right here against the press conference table, but I force myself to pull back. If I need to go out in front of a room full of people, it's going to be without a hard-on.

"I'm sorry," I whisper. "I was trying to protect you, but seeing you with that guy tonight, I get it. I get why you were pissy."

He snorts. "Couldn't hide that, huh?"

"To be fair, I don't think you even tried."

"Yet, you still went out with her knowing I was mad."

"I thought you were mad at the situation, not at me. Not seeing you today or hearing from you, I figured I'd majorly fucked up. And then your text about your date—"

He almost looks sheepish as he says, "That was Madden."

"The Madden? Your ex-roommate Madden?"

Gabe nods.

"You manipulative shithead," I say, but I'm laughing while I say it. "I tip my hat to you because it worked. I wanted to kill that guy."

"Well, you can't. Sorry."

"I bet I've made the best first impression on him."

"Could've been better. Could've been worse though. He could've kissed me and you wouldn't care. That's what I was afraid of."

I shake my head. "That wasn't even a possibility. Without sounding all possessive and toxic, no one gets to touch what's mine."

I've never been so possessive over someone before, and if I'm honest, I'm scared of it because I told myself I wouldn't fall so easily or fast. With anyone. But Gabe's been different from any expectation I had from the very start.

Gabe leans in to kiss me again, but once I start, there's no way I'll be able to stop.

"I have to do the press conference," I say. "And you need to tell me what you're okay with me saying. That's why Frank brought you back here."

"Oh no. Is that like being sent to the principal's office at school?" He starts talking baby talk. "Someone got angwy, and now he's in twouble."

"Exactly. And it's all your fault. But the truth is, the questions have already started about who you and Madden are and why I would have a problem with you two kissing. The story Frank and I came up with—"

"I don't want stories," Gabe says, frustration leaking into his voice. "I want the truth. I don't care if the fans hate me. I don't care if they think I'm a bad-luck charm. I only care about what you think. What you want."

"I want you."

He smiles. "Then go tell them you have me."

I have him.

And I intend to keep him.

—

I wake up to an empty bed after Gabe had to leave before dawn to go home to his place to get his work stuff and start his shift at six. I preferred it when he'd work from 6:00 p.m., not a.m., but apparently, they shuffle rosters around occasionally.

I'm sleepy, kind of out of it, and I'm flat-out exhausted from road trips and back-to-backs.

I'm praying I don't get tapped for All-Stars, which is being announced in the next couple of days. I need the break.

I also need self-making coffee machines to be a thing. If I can get a voice-activated light switch, blinds, and TV, surely there's a coffee machine you can ask to make a coffee for you.

There's a vibrating in my brain and it takes me one second too long to realize it's my phone on my nightstand.

It stops, and when I pick it up and see Oskar has already called three times, I know that when it starts up again, I have to answer it.

And yep, on cue, the phone vibrates again.

"New phone, who this?" I say.

He doesn't buy it. "Someone's in looooooove," he taunts.

"And someone's a dick."

"Your point?"

"You should be happy for me."

"Oh, I am. I totally am. I want you to be happy, and I swear it's only ninety percent because I love being right and ten percent because I'm a good friend."

"That checks out."

"Where is he? Can I gloat to him too?"

"Oh no, so sad, he's at work."

"Fine. I'll call back tomorrow."

"Really, it's okay. You don't have to do that."

Oskar scoffs. "Yes, I do. It's the law."

"Mmhmm, the law. Got it."

"Hold on, Lane wants to talk to you."

Lane gets on the line. "Hey, Aleks—"

"Let me guess, you're going to say you were right too."

"Actually, no. I want to know if you've given your new PR manager a coronary yet, and if he needs any help to tell him to call me because between you and Oskar, it's a miracle I survived last year."

"By sucking my dick!" Oskar yells somewhere in the background.

"I'll let Frank know," I say.

"It's serious, then? Between you and the firefighter?"

"I think so, but I've already fucked up, so there's that."

"Ah, basically threatening to kill the guy he was with at the game last night is a bit of a fuckup."

Lane's not going to like this next part. "No, that's what made him happy. I went on a date with a woman the night before—"

"You what?"

"For show. And now, looking back on it, it was stupid of me to even do it. Frank got into my head about image and bad luck, and I thought I was protecting him, and I hurt him. I seem to be good at hurting people I'm supposed to love."

"Do you?" Lane asks. "Love him?"

"I don't fucking know. I thought I found the love of my life with Rebecca, but I still didn't love her as much as I love myself. My career. My everything. She had to bend to my way. What if … what if I'm not cut out for love? What if I fuck up again somehow because I'm selfish?"

"Everyone fucks up. It's what makes us human. It's how you handle the fallout that matters."

"What if I don't want a fallout at all?"

Lane hums. "I'd say you'll either be walking on eggshells for your whole life waiting for something bad to happen, or you'll not face any problems and one day explode. Can't say either is healthy."

"Who cares about healthy?"

"I would say every medical professional in the world, but you do you."

I slump back on my pillows. "Is there such a thing as a perfect relationship?"

Lane bursts out laughing. "You do know who you're asking, right? Have you met my boyfriend?"

"Lane!" Oskar sounds even further away now. "Where'd you put that butt plug I like?"

"The scary thing is, he's not even in the room yet still timed that perfectly," Lane says.

"Point taken. I guess I'm terrified of fucking up again and again and again until Gabe realizes I'm not worth the fight."

"You should be with someone who does see you as worth the fight, and if that's not him …"

I want it to be him. So badly. But going from one relationship to another with nothing in between, I worry I'm not experienced or equipped to deal with adult relationships.

"Found it!" Oskar's faint voice says. "It was in the freezer."

I really don't want to know what that's about, but at least I'm not alone. Maybe no hockey players are equipped to deal with adult relationships.

CHAPTER TWENTY-EIGHT

GABE

I stretch out on one side while wrapping my other arm around Aleks. He got in yesterday, and as soon as I finished work last night, he picked me up for us to begin our days off together.

Three. Whole. Days.

It almost doesn't feel real.

He burrows his face into my neck, stubble scraping me deliciously. "I have a great idea." His voice is low and sleepy. "Let's stay in bed all day."

"You know what? I bet that standing up my friends would be the perfect first impression."

He groans, which only makes me laugh.

"If it helps, *none* of them will mistake you for a stripper."

Another long groan and he buries his face in deeper. "I'm going to be spending a long time making that up to you, aren't I?"

"Sure are." My palm connects with his bare ass. "Now, get up and get moving."

He rolls onto his back, whipping the sheets off. His cock is standing at attention, practically begging me to help him out, and all it takes is needy eyes from Aleks before I'm on him.

"To be clear, I know what you're doing. It's going to make us late, and I don't even care."

Then I swallow him to the back of my throat and give the best *good morning* to his morning glory that I can manage.

Aleks comes hard and fast, fingers gripped in my hair and ass rising up off the bed. Once I've drank him all down, I pull off and send him a gloating smile.

"Best boyfriend ever, am I right?"

Aleks shrugs. "I have nothing to compare you to, so …"

"Fucker."

He throws a pillow at me that I narrowly dodge. "Where are you going?" he calls as I leave the room. "It was my turn!"

"If you're fast, I'll let you give me a handie in the shower."

I've barely stepped into the bathroom when Aleks slams into the back of me, crowding me into the shower and turning the water on over the both of us. I gasp at how cold it is for a moment before warming up.

"Someone's impatient."

He hugs me close, hand slipping down between us and wrapping firmly around me. "I have a best boyfriend title to win back."

"By all means, give it your best shot."

And when my cum fills his fist, I'm ready to hand the title over to him on bended knee.

Best. Boyfriend. Ever.

On the drive to meet my friends, my hand finds Aleks's thigh, like usual. It fits perfectly and gives me this wave of satisfaction, of contentment. I never thought I'd be this happy with another person, but goddamn, it feels right.

I lean back and turn a dopey smile his way. "You're cute, little hockey player."

"And you're adorable, ginormous firefighter."

I squeeze his leg. "They're going to love you."

"Yikes, thanks for the reminder." He huffs a breath. "It's like this is a whole meet-the-parents situation."

"It basically is. These hot messes are my only family, but as long as I'm happy, they're happy. It's all we care about." We've been through a lot. All of us lived together for years before I moved out, bonded by the fact our families wanted nothing to do with us. Even Christian, my best friend, is flying in to be here today.

"And you're happy?" Aleks checks.

"As long as there are no more supermodel dates, we're good."

"Another thing I'll never live down."

I might tease him, but I'm already over it. He made a mistake, and I didn't know how to talk to him about it, but we had our moment and moved on. Sometimes things need to be broken down a little to be fixed, and since then, it's like another layer between us has been removed. We're closer, the trust tighter. "I told you I'm over it, and I meant it. But so you know, everything is fair game when it comes to teasing."

"I've given you too much ammunition already."

"Tell me, did you keep that flappy dress? Maybe we can pull it out to celebrate our anniversaries."

"Wow, already talking a year ahead? Careful, Gabe, you're smothering me."

And even though it's a joke, I do know there's a tiny grain of truth to his words. I'm not going to push him to be ready for more than he is. "Don't worry. I know where your head is at. I'm perfectly happy to do the dating thing. For now."

"That sounds ominous."

"Just saying, if we decide to move on to something more serious, I'm here for it. No rush. Getting to be your boyfriend has more than enough perks to keep me going."

He thinks for a moment. "What does serious look like to you?"

That's an easy question. "Living together is a big one. Shared goals for the future. One hundred percent commitment to be in this thing and, if issues come up, to work our way through it together. To *want* to make it work."

"That, uh …" He clears his throat. "That's maybe the most simple way I've heard it described."

I give his knee another reassuring squeeze. "What about you?"

"I think that's the problem. I don't really know. It was always get married, buy a house, have kids. All these restrictive rules like a five-point flow chart and then, what? You hit all those targets, and what the hell is next?"

"You did the first two of those things. Did it make you feel fulfilled?"

He scrunches up his gorgeous face. "I feel like I'm being an asshole to Rebecca by saying this, but … no. It made me resent it."

"Well, just putting it out there—it's *your* life, Aleks. It's allowed to be whatever you want it to be."

"You make it sound easy."

"That's because it's supposed to be."

Aleks pulls into the street where I used to live, and I direct him to the front of Big-Boned Bertha. I miss this house. The feel of family whenever I'd come home. But

I don't regret my decision to move out, as much as I miss them all.

I'm about to get out when Aleks's hand tightens over mine. "Is that because *you're* easy? It takes one to know one type of situation?"

That little fuck. Laughing, I lean over to kiss him. "I think someone has forgotten that we're with my friends now. We might not be hockey players, but they sure as shit will tease you mercilessly if I ask them to."

Aleks's eyes widen. "Ah, you're so clever. And pretty. And good in bed."

"That's more like it."

We climb out and approach the house. Even though I told Aleks he had nothing to worry about, I'm nervous about introducing him to the rest of the guys. I know they only want what's best for me, and there's every chance they're going to love him, but if they *don't* like him? Fuck. That would be a nightmare.

I'm not giving him up, but trying to balance my friends and relationship separately would be a lot of work. I don't only want Aleks involved in all aspects of my life; I want him to *want* to be. And if *he* doesn't like *them*?

I'm sweating just thinking about it.

We walk up the stairs, and he points at the Big-Boned Bertha plaque by the front door. "Story here?"

"Not really. The owners had it up, and it never occurred to us to take it down."

Then before I can second-guess this whole idea, I throw the door open and yell out, "He's here!"

Aleks mutters something I miss before following me through the door.

Xander appears first, his blue hair freshly dyed, and he launches himself at me in the hall. He jumps into my arms, legs around my waist, and squeezes hard. "It's been forever!"

"I saw you last week."

"But I dreamed you *died* last night. You were hit with a hockey puck, and they took you to the hospital, where you stopped breathing and they couldn't revive you."

I set him back on his feet. "Here I am in the flesh. Revived and alive." I know better than to ask Xander if he's okay because that'll only make him think about it, and within ten seconds, he'll be struggling to breathe. Or having a heart attack. Or asking at what age Alzheimer's can kick in.

"Give them space," Seven says, wrapping an arm around Xander's shoulders and pulling him away from us. "So this is the hockey player, huh?" He eyes him, and as far as Seven goes, it's a friendly look, but Seven isn't the friendliest-looking guy. "I thought hockey players were big?"

"Did you tell him to say that?" Aleks asks.

I hold up my hands. "I didn't, I swear." But Seven is about the same size as me, and to us, everyone is small. He's also tattooed to all hell and rocking a bunch of piercings, so it's no wonder Aleks is keeping his eye on him.

"I'll only come out if he promises not to punch me in the face," Madden calls from the front room.

I grab Aleks's hand to pull him around the others and into the house. Madden and Christian are sitting on a couch—Madden thankfully having remembered to pull on clothes—and as soon as he sees us, he grabs my best friend and pulls Christian across his lap.

"I'm not here."

Christian shrugs him off. "Yes, he is. Here, I'll even hold him down so you can get a good shot in."

They start jostling back and forth, acting like total animals, and I turn big eyes on Aleks. "And these were the guys you were scared of."

"Right? What was I thinking?"

"Don't get too comfortable, little hockey player," Seven says, joining us.

Aleks throws me a look. "You *definitely* told him to say that."

"I *didn't*." As soon as Aleks turns away, I throw Seven a wink.

It's possible I gave them the heads-up to *not* be on their best behavior. Hey, if Sanden and I had to deal with Ezra's bad attempt at porn music, he can get through this.

There's only one person missing from the mayhem, and that's Rush, but he's late to literally everything, so I wouldn't be surprised if he shows up an hour late, with no idea what's going on.

I flop onto the ground and pull Aleks down between my legs.

"Guys, this is Aleksander Emerson. I'm told he's kinda a big deal, but I don't see what all the fuss is about."

"That's not what you said in the shower," he throws back.

The guys laugh, and it warms me to the core. "That was private," I whine.

"Then be nice."

"That's not what you tell me in bed."

Christian snorts. "Listen, we know way too much about your sex life from when you lived here, so let's skip this part of the hazing."

"Says you. The only reason I moved out was because I couldn't get through another night of you screaming Émile's name."

Christian rapidly turns red. "Okay, that's just mean."

"When were we nice?" Xander asks, face screwed up.

"I think it happened on the tenth of … February?" Seven says.

"Almost a year." Madden nods. "Might be due for that again."

Christian sighs. "I miss being literally anywhere but here."

And just for that, Madden tackles him again, and they fall off the couch with a *thud*. I yank Aleks out of their path.

He relaxes back into me, watching them wrestle as they almost drown out the sound of Xander and Seven bickering about whether Xander has suddenly developed diabetes.

My arms tighten around my boyfriend. "This okay?"

"Somehow, I feel right at home."

Rush walks in, carrying a board game, the same vague look on his face that he gets when he's been working all day and doesn't remember what is going on. "Who's up for Monopoly Monday?"

"It's Thursday," I point out.

"Shoot."

Christian and I share a grin. "But we're all here, so why not?"

Aleks fits right in with my family, and relief settles in my chest. I breathe in the stench of sweaty dudes in a share house, which weirdly has a calming effect. It's familiar. It's home. And Aleks is sharing it with me for the first time.

Things couldn't be any more perfect. But then halfway through the game, Aleks's phone goes off with an alert, and when he checks it, he lets out a loud *whoop*.

"I'm not playing All-Stars."

"Are you saying what I think you're saying?" I ask.

"I get an entire week off."

Okay, now everything is perfect.

CHAPTER TWENTY-NINE

ALEKS

Despite being nervous about meeting Gabe's found family, they prove to be a bunch of immature guys who would rival the Collective in the stupid shit they do. Of course, no one wore a dress, got drunk, and set a fire, so we have that edge over them.

Gabe and I have fallen into a pattern of spending every possible moment together, which, admittedly, isn't a lot because of our schedules, but we're making it work.

With All-Stars coming up, the Collective are scrambling to make plans to meet up like they do every year, and all I know is that I want Gabe to come. Hang out with me and my friends. Together.

I know I don't have much to compare us to relationship-wise, but I think the reason we gel so much and it's easy together is because Gabe has a life outside of me. My wife never had that. She had friends, sure, but she didn't work, and she didn't have any hobbies. Gabe has his life at the fire station, his friendships with both work colleagues and the guys he used to live with, and if the night of playing board games with them tells me anything, it's that he has other interests than being on a hockey player's arm.

Hockey is *my* life, but I'm realizing it doesn't have to be my partner's. Separate interests outside of each other is healthy.

Look at me acing this relationship thing.

Maybe that's why I wasn't cut out to be the next manwhore of the NHL. I'm too good at loving someone.

And while I'm not totally convinced that I'm there yet with Gabe, I can't deny I'm falling hard and fast.

Gabe recently switched back from a.m. starts to p.m. starts, and honestly, the whole fire department's scheduling system has to be on drugs. There doesn't appear to be any rhyme or reason to it, though Gabe has tried to explain it on many occasions. It makes sense to him, at least. That's the important thing. The good thing about him starting at 6:00 p.m. and ending at 6:00 p.m. is that as soon as I finish practice and go home and shower, I can pick him up from work and take my man to dinner.

I get to the station just in time for him to clock off, so I scramble out of the car with the single red rose I picked up along the way and stand outside waiting for him.

Sanden sees me first. "Aww, that's so cute. First, you give me your hockey stick, and now a rose? You're an amazing man, but I've already told you hockey players aren't my type. Stop smothering me."

Gabe shoves him, hard, and Sanden almost tumbles over.

"No need to resort to jealousy and violence," I say to Gabe.

He smiles, and I'm guessing he's anticipating me to say something claimy. I want to, but I'm trying to play it cool. Sanden's only joking about smothering him, but what if Gabe actually thinks I am?

"What Sanden and I have is so pure," I add at the end with a grin.

"Are you both trying to piss me off?" Gabe asks.

"It's not our fault you look adorable when you're mad," Sanden says. As he passes me, he holds out his fist for a bump.

Gabe narrows his eyes. "I don't like you two getting along."

"Does this make it up to you?" I hand Gabe the rose.

"A little." He steps closer and kisses my cheek. "Thank you."

"That's not all I'm here for. I'm going to take you out to dinner. Somewhere nice." I roam my gaze over his navy fire department T-shirt and navy pants. "So maybe we'll have to swing by your place first."

"Ooh, Mr. Famous Hockey Player is taking lil ol' me somewhere fancy?" Gabe takes my hand as we walk toward my car.

"Yup."

"Is this another date challenge I'm going to have to top later?"

"Ergh. Don't say top later and not follow it through with a promise." I wink.

"What happened to only wanting to bottom when you're not playing hockey?"

"No, no, I want to bottom again, but it's not good for my game."

Gabe steps closer. "You sure about that? It was your first time. Maybe next time, you'll be more … looser."

"My ass?"

He laughs. "I meant afterward, but sure, that works too."

I unlock my car, and I drive to his house with his hand firmly on my thigh. I'll never get used to the owned feeling it gives me to have it there, and I don't want to.

"Question. If, theoretically, you were to top a fancy date at a fancy restaurant, what would you do?"

"I'm not giving you any ideas. You could steal it for yourself."

"Hey, I'm an honorable man. I don't cheat. I play to win. The only way to be the best is to beat the best fair and square."

Gabe shakes his head. "Tell me, how can your huge ego fit in your tiny little body?"

I grunt. "I'm not fucking small, damn it. I am bigger than all of your friends … except that Seven guy, but he's intimidating all round."

"I'm so going to tell him you think he's intimidating. He'll love it."

We pull up to Gabe's place soon after, and I tell him to go change into a suit while I wait for him in the car.

"You're not coming in?" he asks.

"No. Because if I do, we'll be late, and I made reservations."

"Reservations? Wow, this really is a proper, thought-out date."

"Only the best."

His gaze narrows. "You just want me to admit you take the crown for the best date makerer ever."

"I might be above cheating, but I'm not above playing dirty." I give him a nudge. "Now, hurry up."

While he's gone, I check my phone. Ever since the press conference where I said the man in the stands was my boyfriend, there's been photos of Gabe and speculation about who he is.

They haven't gotten his name yet—I said in the press conference to respect his privacy because I signed up for the life of a hockey player; he didn't—but I know it's only a matter of time before it is leaked. I've been randomly checking every day, and there has been nothing, but it looks as though that's all about to change.

There was an article posted seven hours ago.

They not only got his name, but they've also found a photo of him from his fire station's website and done a write-up about how he's a hero.

Good news, it paints Gabe in a good light.

Bad news, there's no going back now.

The passenger door opens, and I jump. Do I tell Gabe everything now before our date or ruin his spirit tomorrow morning? He says he doesn't care about what's said about him for being with me, but I thought the exact same thing when I began to make a name for myself in hockey. I wasn't going to let any of the online critiques get to me. Then I started reading them.

It's easy to say it won't bother you, but until it happens, you really have no idea how you'll react.

"What's up?" Gabe asks.

I meet his eyes and force a smile, but it stays on my face when I take him in. How have I never seen Gabe in a suit before? He should wear one all the time. I'm making it a law.

"You look amazing."

Gabe leans across the console and presses his lips to mine. "Thanks, but I'm starving, so let's go."

Waiting until the morning it is, then.

I drive to our destination and find a nearby parking lot. Because of the location in the center of Seattle, there's no way Gabe can guess where we're going, but it becomes obvious as we walk toward the tall, skyward structure.

"Space Needle? Really?" he asks.

"Is that disappointment I hear?"

He puts up his hands. "No, no, not at all. It's an amazing view."

"But?"

"It's a little obvious, isn't it?"

"Why don't we head up and find out?"

We walk into a relatively empty lobby, minus the staff, and Gabe looks confused.

"Where is everyone? It's usually busier than this."

The person who greets us says, "Welcome, Mr. Emerson and Mr. Crosby. Right this way."

Gabe leans in and whispers, "Mr. Crosby. I sound important."

It wouldn't be a big deal had it not been for the minor detail that I didn't give them his name.

Tomorrow. I just have to get through this date, and then tomorrow, I can tell him.

We're led to the elevator, and I put my hand on the small of Gabe's back. He smiles over at me, melting away some of my anxiety.

Our greeter hits the button to the level for the revolving restaurant at the top and gives us a wave as the doors close.

"I don't think I've ever been here with the elevator empty before," Gabe muses.

Yeah, there's a reason for that.

The doors open to the very expensive-to-rent-out empty restaurant, and the look on Gabe's defeated face was worth it.

"Okay, smarty-pants. You win this round of date wars, but only because you cheated by flashing your giant bank account around."

"Nuh-uh. Didn't cheat. Played dirty."

Gabe steps closer to me, grips my shirt, and pulls me against him. "You can play dirty with me anytime."

"That's a promise I'm going to make you keep."

He moves in, his breath ghosting my lips, but when I think he's going to kiss me, he pats my cheek instead. "I'm good for it."

Then he turns on his heel and follows the restaurant host to the candlelit table they've set up for us over the glass-bottom floor.

If this is the only private date we get in a while, I'm going to make it worth it.

CHAPTER THIRTY

GABE

Dinner is fucking fantastic, and despite what I said about the Space Needle being a cliché, I can see why this would be the date to top all dates. The view is incredible, even at night.

My feet are tangled around Aleks's under the table because my hands are occupied with eating, and I can't stop myself from touching him.

Probably because I don't want to stop. The closeness is everything, and it's like my body is telling me to touch him while I can. The small pockets of time we have together are too random to play it cool. To act standoffish or whatever it is guys are supposed to do. He's getting me, completely, and I'm pretty sure he's giving me the same.

No matter what Aleks claims about being bad at relationships, he's putting in the effort. More even than he needs to, but I'm not exactly going to tell him that when we're here together, uninterrupted, on top of Seattle.

"I think I have to give you the win," I tell him.

"What do you mean?"

I gesture at the room around us. "There's no way I can top this. I could probably get us *higher* with, like, skydiving or something—"

"Nope. No skydiving. I'm, uh, you know … contractually obligated not to do anything that can get me hurt. Yep."

I lift an eyebrow at his sudden outburst, and he holds up a hand.

"True story."

"And burning down your house wouldn't get you hurt at all, would it?"

"Not when sexy firefighters show up to save the day."

I pin him with a look. "You better not be talking about Sanden again."

He can't keep a straight face as he says, "Who's to say?"

"Sanden might find himself accidentally in a new team," I mutter.

"You'll have to get me his schedule."

I can't hold back my laugh anymore. "Wow, and here you are, supposed to love me, and you're keeping your affair with my colleague to yourself. At least let us share you around."

Aleks's face falls. "You'd do that?"

"If we both get to sleep with him? Hell yeah."

My clever boyfriend suddenly doesn't look so playful. "Are you doing that thing again where you show me what a dick I'm being by doing the exact same thing back to me?"

I wink. "No idea what you mean."

He snatches my hand up before I can reach for my drink, and it makes me grin.

"You gonna get all claimy now?" I ask.

"I'm starting to think you like it."

"It's good for my ego." I lift his hand and press a kiss to his knuckles. "Who doesn't like some light jealousy now and then?"

"Feel free to give it back."

I glance around to make sure our servers are all still a distance away and drop my voice. The last thing Aleks needs is for people to know his new boyfriend has a dirty mouth. "Every time I see you hug your teammates, I want to throw you over my shoulder and carry you off the ice. All I can picture is getting you home and fucking your face or your ass until I've filled you up with so much of my cum there isn't room for anyone else."

His eyes have widened, and his tongue swipes over his lips. "Maybe we can try that in the off-season."

"Ooh, we're going to have so many sexcapades. You'll be bow-legged by the time we're done."

"Something tells me my team won't be happy about that."

"It's okay, they can make you the team mascot, and Dog Tripp can take your place."

"The way you overestimate my abilities really makes my heart warm."

"If there's one thing you can always count on, it's that I will never appreciate hockey the way you do."

Aleks pouts. "Every time you say that, a Zamboni somewhere dies."

"Good. Fewer machines to rise up against us."

"Those poor, widdle zam bams."

I pat his hand that's holding my other one. "They're in a better place. The big ice rink in the sky."

"Just saying ..." Aleks's lips twitch. "You better not talk like this at the All-Stars party in Buffalo."

"Buffalo?"

He squeezes my hand. "Yeah, I was hoping you could come? The Collective members who aren't selected for it get together for All-Stars week each year, and we're having it in Buffalo since Quinn is still having some issues with his … lower-body injury."

Even though I've spent time with Aleks's friends and met them when they were at their worst, this feels big. I'd be meeting them on purpose. As the boyfriend. It both excites and terrifies me—and not only because I know what that group is capable of. "When is it?"

"Week after next, so I understand if you can't rearrange your work schedule."

"I'd have to see if it lines up with my days off. If not, I could ask someone to cover for me."

"It's not a big deal if you can't." He shakes his head. "No. What I mean is, it *is* a big deal, because I really want you there, but I also understand why you might not be able to get time off."

The clarification makes me smile. "How do they feel about you inviting me?"

"Little D said, and I quote, 'good, then I'll bring my boyfriend so I'm not stuck with you losers all day.'"

"Wow. He really loves you guys."

"Losers is a step up from him calling us the Babysitters Club-ective, so I'll take it."

I snigger into my cup. "I think I'll like him."

"Do me a favor and *please* pretend like you think Ezra's his boyfriend."

I cast my mind back to the other tall, dark-haired man, who looked formidable, even in a bikini. "Ah, yeah, hard pass on that. I'm not going to fuck with Ezra's boyfriend."

Aleks's jaw drops. "*He's* the one you find scary? Not me, not Oskar, *him*?"

"Oskar's bigger than the rest of you, but he's also … how do I say this nicely?"

"A hot mess?"

"Bingo. He's a disaster. His boyfriend also has him on a leash, so I'm not worried about him. You, my big, bad hockey player, wouldn't hurt a fly. Sorry, but it's true. You can check people into the boards and have those little tussles on the ice all you like, but you're a sweetheart to your core."

"Baby …" Aleks clasps his hands to his chest, and at first, I think it's because he's all *naw, Gabe's so sweet* … but then he opens his mouth. "You spoke hockey to me."

"Wait. What?"

"Checked into the boards?" Dear God, Aleks is making eyes at me. "Have you been …" He swipes a fake tear. "*Learning?*"

I deflate in my seat. "I knew that was a mistake."

"Do you know what a puck is?"

"Can we move on now?"

"And a *hat trick*?" Aleks gasps. "You're finally living up to your last name."

"And *you're* having too much fun with this."

"Hey, I'm just relieved I don't have to be embarrassed by your terrible taste in sports anymore."

"Don't get me wrong, hockey still sucks."

"You take that back," he warns.

"Make me."

"You're going to regret that when we get home later."

I lean across the table. "What are you going to do?"

It's not so much the question that takes him by surprise but the tone I ask it in. Because if Aleks is going to punish me, yeah, I'm interested in knowing what that would look like.

"I … umm … it's a surprise."

I crack up laughing. "Pity. If you'd told me, I probably would have let you do it."

236

"Really?"

"Uh-huh. You can have my body any way you like."

He exhales loudly. "I fucking hate all the time away."

"Me too. Which is why I'll use everything at my disposal to try and come to Buffalo with you."

"You will?" The way his face lights up makes me realize I'll call off sick if I have to. I'm going. I don't give a shit.

"After the last time you were all together, I think it'd be smart to have emergency response on-site at all gatherings."

Aleks stands, slides his chair around next to mine, and falls down into it. Then his mouth is on mine. I lean into him greedily, not caring that it's semi-public, that our servers could easily be taking photos, that this is how gossip begins.

I just kiss him.

Like we're two men.

Falling.

Happy.

Together.

He pulls back and smiles, my face still cupped in his hands. "Apparently, the thought of spending time with you makes me happy."

"Well, that's a weird emotion from a boyfriend."

His hands slide to my neck, my shoulders. He's not quite smiling, but he looks happy. "No, I mean ... With Rebecca, it was always a guarantee we'd be together. I'd get home, she'd be there. Even before that, while we were at school. Class would finish, we'd hang out. I never felt like I was going out of my skin to get to her. Don't get me wrong, I *liked* her. Like, I'm not an idiot. I wouldn't have married her if I didn't, but ... This isn't coming out right."

I lean into his ear, wanting these words to be for him and only him. "I'm sitting here, right now, with you … and I already miss you."

Aleks turns, those gorgeous green eyes finding mine. "Yeah. Exactly like that."

My thumb strokes his stubble. "I know."

His head tilts forward, and he rests his forehead against mine. He's warm, solid, dependable. And I'm fucking screwed. Because I mean it. I already miss him, just knowing I have to work and he has to travel. If Aleks ever decides I'm not who he wants … that's going to wreck me.

I pull back and try to lighten the mood. "Well, if people didn't know who I was before," I say, glancing at the servers who are lingering, "they will now."

His gorgeous face falls. "Yeah, about that …"

"Uh-oh."

Aleks throws me an apologetic look before reaching for his phone. He opens an app and searches for something before holding it out to me.

My name stares back at me from the screen.

I'm torn between the strangest urges to either throw his phone or read whatever the hell this is about.

Then I glance up at him, at his worried expression, and … it doesn't matter.

"I know you weren't sure about being in the public eye," Aleks says. "And I stupidly want to apologize for dragging you into it, even though you knew what you were signing up for."

I did.

I knew this whole time that we'd face this moment, and I didn't care. Not if I have Aleks.

238

So instead of leaning into either of the emotions surging through me, I take a deep breath. Hold it. Let it out.

Then I lock his phone and set it on the table.

"I don't want to know."

He frowns. "What do you mean?"

"Nothing they have to say will change my mind about you. If it's good stuff about me, that's great. But if it's shitty—and there *will* be shitty things because people can't goddamn help themselves—then I don't want to know. It'll only make me feel like crap, and no offense to all those strangers on the internet, but … they have no right to have that effect on me."

"Wow. Who knew strippers could be so wise?"

"Literally everyone not shoving dollar bills in their panties."

He laughs, and it's only now that I realize he's been subdued most of the night. I'm only picking up on it now that weight is gone.

"I will also try not to look," Aleks says.

"It's up to you. Just try not to read into everything you see. Don't give them that power."

"I'll do my best."

"Good." I move closer, snaking my hand behind his neck. "Now, let's give them the kind of kiss they won't be able to ignore."

CHAPTER THIRTY-ONE

ALEKS

Considering Gabe could only get one night away to come with me for All-Stars, I'm pissed that our flight to Buffalo is delayed. I almost told the guys I couldn't come, but Oskar called me after Ezra ranted to him about it becoming a Collective tradition, and the only excuse to miss it is if we're dying. And even then, it's conditional.

In Oskar's imitation of Ezra, his exact words were "Bullet holes heal, Emerson."

By the time we land, check in to our hotel, and then get to Quinn's house, the skills portion of All-Stars would be almost over, so there was really no point schlepping all this way when I could've been inside Gabe. In bed. Racking up as many orgasms as we could manage.

I lift my hand and knock while holding Gabe close to me with my arm wrapped around his shoulders.

"So, seeing as we're late, on a scale of one to ten, how messy are they going to be in there?" he asks.

"I can't say."

Little D opens the door, his permanent scowl on his face.

"What, you live here now?" I ask.

"Quinn put me on doorman duty because he broke his dick."

"Not my dick!" Quinn calls out from inside.

"Groin, dick, same thing," Little D yells back and then says to us, "Come on in."

We follow him inside Quinn's two-story older-style home, where the living room is off to the right of the entryway.

"Your partner is a med student," Kole, Little D's boyfriend, points out. "You should know better than that."

Little D just laughs, approaches Kole, and kisses the top of his head.

"For anyone who hasn't met my boyfriend yet, and for those who can't remember him because they were passed out in a bikini on my lawn"—I glance in Anton's direction—"this is Gabe. Gabe, this is everyone."

Gabe rubs his chin. "You know, I'm disappointed. You all look *sober*."

Foster Grant stands from his armchair that he's sharing with his adorable, introverted partner, who's sitting half on Foster's lap. I've only met Zach once while I was on the road and playing against Montreal, but they make a cute couple.

Foster shakes Gabe's hand. "I can't tell if I should be happy I couldn't make that party or disappointed I missed it all."

Gabe looks at me. "I can't say I was disappointed for witnessing it."

I smile. "Then you never would've met me or got season tickets and learned to love hockey. What would your life be like?"

He lifts his hands and weighs them up. "Happiness without hockey or happiness with hockey. Hard choice."

"You wouldn't be happy without me," I say. "I'm the best thing that's ever happened to you."

"Hmm, let's see. I have my job, my friends who are like my family, my—"

I cover his mouth with my hand and face the group. "He's obsessed with me."

He bites my hand.

"Motherfucker." I shake it off, but he's left damn teeth marks. "You're vicious."

"We like him," Ezra says.

"Unfortunately, so do I." I take Gabe's hand and lead him to free beanbag seats in front of the TV. "So, how did drills go?"

"Tripp won the shootout, blocking every attempt, and Dex choked with the speed drill. He came in last." Anton snickers.

Last season, there were two members of the Collective at All-Stars, and this year, there's a married couple. It's fucking amazing for representation, even if it means Tripp and Dex couldn't be here. Soren, Ollie, and West—the retired guys—aren't here either. Apparently, the loophole to get out of meeting up for All-Stars week is to either get shot or retire, and I'm not doing either of those things anytime soon.

Then again, if everyone was able to make it, it would be a full house. We're taking over the league. Next step: World. It's not only the Collective that's growing but the partners and boyfriends too.

I brought Gabe, Little D brought Kole, Foster brought Zach, but Oskar didn't bring Lane.

I turn to my old teammate. "Where's Lane? He let you off your leash?"

"He's the one on a leash this time back at home. It's okay, I cracked a window and left some water out for him." Oskar winks.

I nod. "He's working, isn't he?"

"Yes," everyone else says.

Thought so.

"What drills are left?" I ask. The TV is currently showing recaps of the night so far.

Ezra hands Gabe and me some beers. "Accuracy and passing."

"Dex will kill that," I say.

"Only because I'm not there," Anton boasts.

We all groan, but Ezra takes it one step further and takes the half-eaten bowl of popcorn off the coffee table and throws pieces at him. "Can't even swat popcorn away, babe."

Anton growls. "You're going to pay for that later."

Gabe leans in. "Is everything a competition with you guys?"

I think he's trying to be quiet, but he fails because everyone laughs.

I nudge him. "Hey, I played Monopoly with your friends. I know how competitive you can be."

"Ooh." Ezra dramatically covers his mouth. "Your boyfriend's friends must be tight. Even we know not to play Monopoly. That's how friendships and relationships fall apart."

"They're basically my family," Gabe says. "We're stuck with each other through the best and worst of times."

"And Monopoly with his friends is the worst of times."

"We're half as bad as you guys," Gabe argues.

We really can't refute that we are highly competitive. It's in our blood; it's in our nature.

Gabe understanding that side of me, him getting along with my friends and vice versa ... the more time Gabe and I spend together, the more he fits into that perfect-for-me box. He's everything I want and everything I didn't expect.

The next drill starts on-screen.

"What's with the tiny goals?" Gabe asks.

"It's accuracy drill," I explain. "Players have to hit each of the five goals in the fastest time."

Even though Gabe claims to hate hockey, he's glued to the screen. "This is so much more fun than watching a game."

Little D's partner, Kole, slashes at his throat. "Dude. Never let them know how much you hate the sport."

Little D lifts his head. "What?"

"I love hockey, almost as much as I love you." Kole wraps Little D in a hug and glances over at us with an almost imperceptible shake of his head.

We drink and cheer on our teammates but not as loud as we cheer for Dex when he's on screen. He nails it and takes out top spot, holding on to it until the very last player, who beats him out by half a second.

When Gabe's beer is finished, I jump up to get him another one.

Oskar follows me. It's on the opposite side of the entry, but everyone is being so loud we can still hear everything they're saying, and I'm thankful when Kole engages Gabe in conversation.

It might be the best thing about this group. They're all welcoming. With the WAGs and the straight couples, anytime someone would bring a new girlfriend into the fold, there was a process before the women would welcome them.

Here, it's no questions asked. I love it.

"You didn't follow me in here to gloat some more, did you?" I throw our empty bottles in the trash and move to the fridge to get two more.

"Nope. Just to be a very supportive friend and see how everything is with you."

I narrow my gaze. "You want details of our sex life."

"I'm so sad we're not on the same team anymore. You really know my soul."

I shove past him. "You're getting nothing from me other than it's amazing."

"Do I hear second-marriage wedding bells?" he taunts, smile stretching the scar running down his cheek from his accident last season.

I let out a "Pfft" in response.

At the same time, I hear Ezra joke to Gabe. "What are your intentions toward our new valued member of this association?"

I pause where I am, just around the corner from the living room where the guys shouldn't be able to see us.

Oskar whispers, "We're an association now? Did Ezra actually go and legally register the Collective as an entity?"

"Wouldn't surprise me." But I'm more interested in what Gabe will answer.

"That's really up to Aleks."

Why is it up to me and not *us*?

"He's already done the serious relationship thing, so he might not want to follow my life path."

"What does your life path entail?" someone else asks, but it's a bit muffled, so I can't tell who it is.

"Big house—"

"Aleks already has that," Ezra says. His voice is so distinct with his Boston accent.

"I want a house with lots of bedrooms, not so much the large living space he has. I need rooms to fill with kids."

And that's when my heart stutters, screeches to a halt, and then drops into my stomach.

Kids.

"Uh … did he just say what I think he said?" Oskar asks.

"Yup."

"He wants kids?"

"Yup." I seem to only be able to say that one word.

"Did you know that?"

"Nope." It's still relatively early. We haven't needed to have that discussion. When we've discussed the future and having the same goals, I can't recall babies ever being mentioned. Other than when I drunkenly said I want to have his.

Oh shit.

"Aren't kids the reason you left Rebecca?"

I swallow hard. "One of." But if I'm honest, it was probably the main one.

I wasn't ready. I might never be ready.

Kids is a huge step, and I keep waiting for that parental gene to kick in. Yearning or something. What happens if that never comes?

During one of Rebecca's and my many, many fights, she screamed at me that I'd wasted so many years of her life and that if I didn't want kids, I should have told her sooner.

The thing is, I didn't know sooner. I still don't know now.

I don't want to waste Gabe's time. I don't want to waste anyone's time.

"What are you going to do?" Oskar asks under his breath.

"I don't fucking know."

CHAPTER THIRTY-TWO

GABE

It's amazing to me how *easy* Aleks's friends make everything. And I'm not only talking about their apparent sexual exploits. Given how I first met most of them, there could be awkwardness, or hostility, or more threats about me not selling the story, but other than a few earlier jokes, it's all but forgotten.

We've fallen into conversation, and as much as these guys try to pretend like they don't give a fuck about anything, it's obvious they care about each other. A lot.

They can give one another shit all they like—the way they're questioning me about my relationship gives them away.

I'm sipping beer, actually enjoying the skills stuff playing, and while I'm struggling to keep up with who is who, these guys are pretty cool.

"So, you have to tell me," Kole says, leaning forward, "how drunk was Asher the night you met him, and was he depresso drunk or fun drunk?"

"Ah …" I glance at the guy sitting in front of me, trying to picture a *fun* version of him. "I … don't really remember," I hedge. His glare softens. "But he was wearing a ridiculous hat."

Kole starts laughing as Asher—Little D—whatever, narrows his eyes in my direction.

"And *you* were there as the entertainment."

"I dunno." I rub my chin. "You guys had that part covered."

"Aleks, your boyfriend sucks," Asher says as Aleks and Oskar rejoin us.

Aleks drops down next to me, and I have to really reach across for my hand to find his thigh, but when it does, the muscle under my palm goes tense.

I glance up at Aleks, whose focus is on my hand before he glances away. "Here." He holds out a beer in my direction, and something feels off. He's not looking at me, and clearly, something about me touching him isn't welcome.

When it was totally fine before.

Reluctantly, I draw my hand away.

"Stripper or not, this is exciting," Kole says. "Zach and I have been hoping we can expand our group."

"Group?"

"Please leave me out of it," the small guy with ridiculously big glasses says. "This is *not* my group."

"But you named it," Kole insists, and something about his smugness reminds me of his boyfriend. I'm suddenly understanding what the happy, friendly guy is doing with someone like Asher.

"I did not," Zach splutters, turning to his boyfriend—Foster? "I did *not*."

Foster smiles indulgently. "What's the name?"

"I don't want to say."

"Zach …"

Zach drops his face into Foster's shoulder and mumbles something I miss but Foster apparently finds hilarious. "Okay, no, he didn't name that."

Kole shrugs. "Your boyfriend's a freak. Deal with it."

"Oh, he definitely is. But only with me. There's no way he came up with that name."

Zach reappears, face flaming. "*Thank* you. It was *meant* to be husbands and boyfriends, but the HABs was taken, so we reversed it to—"

"The BAHs," Kole says.

I was expecting way worse. "Okay, what's so wrong with that?"

Zach lowers his voice. "It's not boyfriends and husbands anymore."

"That was too exclusionary. Like WAGs. So *we* changed it—"

"—*not* we—"

"To blowjobs, anal, and handies."

I bark out a laugh as Ezra turns to Anton and says, "Babe, can I *please* join their group? Technically, one of us should. In support."

Anton narrows his eyes. "I don't think the name of the group is their initiation ritual."

Ezra turns to Kole, looking for confirmation.

Kole glares. "It's like you *want* my boyfriend to murder you."

"If I get a blowjob out of it first …"

Anton kisses Ezra's head. "Or I could give you one without the threat of murder."

"Like, now?"

"Later."

Ezra huffs. "This day keeps on disappointing me."

"You know," I say before this can get any weirder than it already is, "technically, that's not totally inclusive."

"What do you mean?" Zach asks.

"A lot of ace people don't like those things."

His face falls. "Oh my God, you're right. My best friend is demi—he'd kill me for not thinking of everything."

"Lucky you've got a smart guy like me around."

"So, we're, what?" Kole scrunches his face. "Blowjobs, anal, and ... hugs?"

Ezra throws his hands up. "Eww, hugs. That's me out. You'll need to recruit Gabe."

Kole scowls, once again reminding me of Asher. "He's literally the only one I'm trying to recruit."

"Hey, wait," Aleks says quickly. "Can you give the guy a minute? He's *just* meeting everyone, and you're already trying to recruit him into your husbands club? Like, chill."

There's a second of silence that Ayri jumps in to cover up with "The next challenge is starting," but it's too late to hide the awkwardness.

Or the weird look Aleks and Oskar share.

I'd thought there was something off going on earlier, and this all but confirms it.

Whatever the hell Oskar and Aleks were talking about in that kitchen has made him change his mind about something.

And that something feels a lot like me.

—

Unlike when Aleks chose the fake date over spending time with me, I'm not at all mad he's staying behind with his friends while I have to fly back home. Because *this* decision makes sense.

These guys are his family, like my friends are to me.

He doesn't get to see them often either, and while Aleks originally planned to fly back today, when Oskar

251

begged him to stay, I pointed out that I have to work tomorrow morning and I'd be leaving him alone anyway.

I'm happy he gets this time with them.

The thing that has me on edge is the way we leave things.

Aleks was extra attentive this morning before he could drop me off at the airport, but there's this *vibe* I'm picking up on that I really hope I'm overthinking.

The attentiveness has felt … sad. Almost clingy. Where he didn't want me to touch him yesterday, today it's like he's swung in the total opposite direction. His confusion is coming through loud and clear, and I'm worried.

It almost feels like he's getting ready to let me go.

Whether he wants to or not.

And if that's his choice, I'm going to have to let him. I can't force him to stay.

But with every mile that stretches between us, the discomfort in me grows. Gnaws at me.

Fuck, I wish we'd had the morning to ourselves so I could ask him what the hell is going on. What Oskar must have said.

Like, he wingman-ed for us. Surely he hasn't changed his mind? Hasn't convinced Aleks I'm not good enough?

And I all but pushed Aleks to stay with them.

Fuck, Gabe, you're a supportive idiot.

Nope, I refuse to regret that.

As much as I'd love to be some man's top choice one day and I'd love for that man to be Aleks, it's not going to be because I'm his *only* choice.

I'll be here if Aleks wants me and, like I said to the others, if his life plans line up with mine.

I'm hopeful. There have been hints during our time together. I know he's conflicted about marriage, and I'm cool with it. I can take it or leave it. Moving in together? Negotiable. Prenup? I'd totally get it. Whatever concerns he came to me with, I'd be happy to talk it through.

There's only one path for my life that I've always seen as something I'd fight tooth and nail for: kids.

Not my own though.

As it is, being a father isn't something I've thought about a whole lot, but ever since I was younger and came out to family right before being shown the door, I vowed it had to end. The preteens, teens, and young adults who have nowhere to go. Who sleep on the streets because the shelters are full. Who choose to end it all rather than look for direction. Who go through hell because of people who are *supposed* to love them.

Looking after *them* is more important to me than any man.

Even Aleks.

As much as it hurts me to say.

And fuck, it hurts. Because in the few months we've had together, I'm pretty sure I've gone and fallen for the guy.

I cling to the idea that I'm making the weirdness into more than it actually is. That once he's back, everything will be the same as it always is. Jokes, cute dates, hot sex, and quiet, peaceful moments.

Like, fuck. If Aleks cares about me the way I think he does, I can't see anything Oskar has to say as being enough to come between us. He can go off all he likes about cheap sex and playing the field or whatever, but that's not Aleks. That's not something he wants or cares about.

So, if it wasn't that, what the hell else could have happened in that kitchen?

All I know is this is a discussion we have to have in person, so these next few days will be unbearable.

Unless a miracle happens, and when Aleks calls tonight, everything is all back to normal. Easy. Happy.

I cling to that hope, even though it feels foolish.

CHAPTER THIRTY-THREE

ALEKS

I think Oskar begged me to stay the extra night with the Collective purely for my benefit, but I regret staying the minute I drop Gabe at the airport. I was tempted to leave Quinn's car there, forget my bags back at the hotel, and leave with him, but maybe we need the break so I can get my head on straight.

When I'm with him, the rest of the world doesn't matter. He sucks me into this bubble where nothing could ever get to me.

Or I thought nothing would ever get to me. Nothing that would make me question our possible future.

It has to be the kid thing messing with my head. I'm in a weird state of limbo where I want to be with Gabe no matter what, but the bigger part of me is yelling at me to run now before I'm in too deep.

On the outside, Gabe and I shouldn't fit together. Our schedules mean we rarely see each other. He hates hockey. He wants kids. He's the first person I've been with since getting out of a long, long, *long* relationship. That alone should tell me to end things now.

But the problem with all of that is I don't care that I don't get to see him often. Sure, I'd love to see him more, but that means that when we are together, we don't sweat the small stuff. We're engrossed in each other and get lost in the heat of us, a burning fire neither of us wants to extinguish. I don't care that he hates hockey. Despite hating it, he's there at my home games whenever he can be. He doesn't have to love my job to support it. Just like I don't like the idea of him risking his life and running into burning buildings, but I admire him for it. He's brave as fuck. I don't even care that I've never been with another man or anyone else other than Rebecca. I've already realized I'm not the hookup type, and maybe I only thought I should be that way because society—especially the sporting world's toxic masculinity—says I should do that. I don't need to experience other people to know that I fit with Gabe.

Which means the issue of having children is the only thing holding me back.

How do I get over something like that? What if I give in and down the line, we have a kid and I resent it? How is that fair to a child?

What if Gabe compromises and hates *me*?

Kids aren't really something you can compromise *on*.

All these questions run through my head on the drive back to Quinn's place, and when I enter his house, everyone's already piled around the TV again for the actual All-Star games to begin. Though Kole and Zach are missing.

"He get away okay?" Oskar asks.

Everyone stares at me for a reaction, and I get the impression they all know something's up.

"Yeah, good. Fine."

A few faces pinch, and even Little D frowns.

I turn to Oskar. "You told them, didn't you?"

"That we heard their conversation with Gabe last night and that you don't want kids, and now you're being an asshole to your boyfriend because you don't know what to do? That? Yeah, I told them."

I slump on a beanbag chair. "I don't want to talk about it."

"Kids is kind of a big issue," Ezra says. "I'm the worst at relationships, and even I know that. I'm lucky Anton is as anti-kids as I am."

Anton pinches Ezra's thigh. "Remember when you begged me for a baby, and then we looked after Tripp and Dex's niece for, like, less than a day, and by the end, you were begging me to never want any of our own?"

Ezra shudders. "I have PTSD from the mere mention of that spawn of Satan."

"Really selling me on the kid thing," I say.

"She was cute." Anton shrugs. "But that's the thing. We're not trying to sell you on anything. You need to decide what you want."

"I want Gabe."

"And if Gabe came with a side of child?" Ezra asks.

Oskar shakes his head. "Why are you making it sound like he's ordering off a food menu?"

"Because Ezra doesn't only suck at relationships. He also sucks at being a normal human being most days." Anton says that, yet still looks lovingly at his partner.

I glance at Quinn, Foster, and Little D, who are suspiciously silent. "What do you guys think?"

"I'm twenty-four," Quinn says. "Stop with the pressure cooker."

"I'm only twenty-eight," I point out.

"I mean, I'd need to find a boyfriend first. One who—" His mouth slams shut.

"One who what?"

He waves me off. "Let's just start with boyfriend. Serious boyfriend."

Little D sneers. "Good luck. You wouldn't know potential boyfriend if he slapped you in the face with his dick."

There's an image.

"Shut. Up," Quinn says.

"Last week, we went out after a game, and this dude was totally hitting on Quinn. He had no idea. Completely clueless."

"He said he was a sub. I thought he meant substitute teacher!"

Little D cracks up laughing. "So fucking funny. Especially when you asked how he enjoyed subbing for kids. I thought he was about to call the police."

"So glad my small-town naivety is hilarious to you. But also, how are you supposed to react to that?"

Oskar touches his heart. "Oh, Ayri, honey, sweetie. You say kiss my feet and force him to his knees."

Poor Quinn looks horrified.

"Definitely clueless," Little D murmurs.

I'm thankful for the distraction of the millions of baby thoughts running through my head, and I'm excited to think they've dropped it, but they haven't.

Little D eventually composes himself and turns to me. "Back to the baby thing. I practically raised my siblings. I've done the child thing, and I'm not going to lie, it's fucking hard. If your heart's not in it, it'll only be harder."

Foster sits up. "Wait ... *you* have a heart?"

For the first and only time since I met Little D, his features are soft. And when he says, "For my family, yeah. I'd do anything for them," nearly all of us fall off our seats.

Then he adds, "They're fucking disasters. They need the help."

There he is.

Foster turns his gaze on me. "You need to work out what you're willing to do to keep Gabe, and it doesn't stop at kids. What would happen if you were traded and Gabe wasn't willing to move away from Seattle? Could you do long distance, or would you give up hockey?"

Gasps from every direction fill my ears, but Foster has a point.

How far am I willing to go for a man I can't stop falling for?

–

You know what a six-hour flight with a layover in Chicago is good for? Not being able to run away from your thoughts.

And that's all I fucking do all the way back to Seattle.

I've never been a pros-and-cons kind of person, but Foster made me think. Pros of staying with Gabe: I get to have him in all the ways I want him. Cons: I might be stuck with a child, and all those doubts that I have, that constant unreadiness ... what if I regret it? It might sound selfish to only think of what I want, but fuck, Gabe knows what it's like to have terrible parents. What if I don't have that gene?

Pros of leaving Gabe now instead of later: I save us both major heartbreak than if we were to be together for twelve years and then suddenly realize we're not what the other needs or wants. I've been there, done that, have the T-shirt. Cons: ... I fucking lose him. Considering that's the only thing I can think about—that I don't want to lose him—I know I'm being selfish again.

I was selfish in my last relationship, unwilling to bend anything in my life. Not hockey, not kids, nothing.

So instead of focusing on what I wasn't willing to do for Rebecca, I look at what I am willing to do for Gabe.

Millions of scenarios run through my head, from being traded, to Gabe being injured in a fire and needing constant care, and everything in between. And when I reach my answer, I fill with dread because I realize I'm going to have to tell him.

As soon as I land.

I don't even allow myself to go home first to drop off my duffle bag because I know I'll chicken out of this.

My heart hammers wildly the whole Uber drive to the firehouse, where I know he'll be, but when we pull up outside, the trucks are gone, which means he's out on a call.

The waiting only builds the anxiety, and by the time I see that bright red monster of a fire truck coming down the street, I almost want to hurl.

I stand by the open garage door after the truck pulls in and firefighters start pouring out. When Gabe's feet hit the concrete, he sees me.

He's so fucking sexy in his full getup. Black pants with a yellow reflective stripe on each ankle, black suspenders over his navy Station 40 T-shirt.

Sanden nods to him to come over to me, but my body moves on its own, and I meet him halfway.

He doesn't smile, though I think he attempts to.

"That look on your face tells me you're not here with good news …"

God fucking damn it, my heart is about to give up, roll over, and just stop working. "Depends on what you'd consider good or bad news."

"Just tell me, Aleks. I'm a big boy."

"I overheard you. At Quinn's. Telling the guys you hope I want the same life path as you—"

"And it was too soon? I get it. And that makes so much more sense than what I thought you were freaking out over."

"No, it's not that. Well, it is too soon to be thinking too far into the future, but I'm not scared of you being some clinger or whatever."

He goes to open his mouth again, but I stop him.

"Let me get this out?"

His work colleagues are mulling about, packing away whatever they have to and getting out of their full getup. Gabe doesn't pay them any mind. He stands in front of me expectantly. Waiting for me to spill my guts.

"I think I told you … or maybe I didn't. But one of the reasons—the main reason—my marriage ended was because Rebecca was ready for kids, and I wasn't. I worry that the parental gene is not something I was born with. She said she felt like I had wasted her time, and I don't want to waste yours."

Fuck, he looks so sad.

"The way you were talking to the guys, it seemed like it was nonnegotiable for you, and that scared me because I can't know if I'll ever be ready for that life."

"Okay, so you're ending it, then. Got it." Gabe turns to walk away, but he pauses when I yell out to him.

"I'm in love with you!" Okay, that got everyone's attention.

He slowly turns back but doesn't make a move to come back closer to me.

"I went through every scenario in my head. Every possible future. And I realized that if I got traded and

261

had to move, and for whatever reason you didn't want to move away from your found family or you couldn't get transferred to another city—I don't know how the firefighting department works—but say you couldn't leave Seattle ... I would give up hockey for you."

"I'm not asking you to give up hockey."

I step closer. "I know you're not." Another step. "But I realized, with crystal-clear clarity, that if I am willing to put hockey on the line—the thing that makes up ninety-five percent of who I am—for you, then why would I hold back from something I thought would happen eventually, but I've been waiting for that moment where I realize *I'm* ready. I might never be fully ready, but is anyone?"

Gabe steps closer now. "Do you mean that?" He's beginning to look hopeful.

"I do. It's scary as fuck, but ... I want to have your babies."

The smile that was trying to break free dies on his lips. "Wait, what?"

"Babies. Kids. Big family. Whatever you want."

Oh, look, apparently, it's Gabe's turn to look like he's almost going to puke. "Uh, I don't want to have babies with you."

It's like one of those nightmare times where you're in a loud space, but everything quiets at just the right—or wrong, depending on how you look at it—moment, and everyone hears it all.

The blanket of silence is suffocating.

"This is fucking awkward," Sanden says.

I don't know what to say other than, "I'm confused."

"I'm taking five," he calls out and then grabs my hand and pulls me outside.

"Something tells me you're not going to push me up against the wall and kiss the fuck out of me like you did last time I came to visit."

Am I an idiot here? How did I fuck up what he said so clearly?

"What did you actually hear?" he asks.

"That you want kids. Everything went blurry and panicky after that."

"And you assumed kids meant babies?"

"Well, yes."

Gabe laughs. "If you had kept listening, you would've heard me say how I want to be a foster to teenagers who get kicked out of home for whatever reason—LGBTQ teens, specifically, but I'm not only open to that. Anyone who needs a home like I did growing up deserves one, whether it's short-term emergency placement or longer stays. They deserve to know they're loved for who they are and that they can be whoever they were born to be."

"Oh." My chest warms at that idea. He's not talking about settling down and *raising* kids—he wants to be the safe space misplaced ones can land. Older kids. Admittedly, that might be even harder than having little ones together, but the panic has completely left me. "That ... actually sounds like a great idea. And less scary, somehow. Sure, you're probably going to get difficult teens who lash out because they've lived through too much trauma in a short amount of time, but taking them off the streets is better than letting them live in the hell of having no one to turn to. Nowhere to go."

Gabe lets out a loud, relieved breath. "You know, this whole freak-out could have been avoided if you used your big ears more."

I gasp. "I do not have big ears."

263

"I'm surprised your helmet fits on your head."

I fold my arms. "I take it back."

"Take what back?"

"That I love you."

His lips purse, and he steps toward me, running his hands up my arms, from my wrists to my shoulders. "I'm pretty sure the I love you confession is a no-backsies kind of situation."

"I disagree. I can take it back whenever I want." I pluck at the air. "This is me grabbing it and tucking it in my pocket."

Gabe quickly grasps my wrist before I can put my hand in my pocket. "Keep it out."

"Why?" I croak, my throat suddenly dry.

He smiles. "Because I love you too."

CHAPTER THIRTY-FOUR

GABE

After Aleks's fucking incredible arrival, I still have six hours of my shift to go.

Six.

Hours.

All I want is to call an Uber and head off early, but I'd never let my team down like that. It'd be just my luck that a huge emergency would happen the second I stepped out the door. As it is, we get a callout with half an hour to go, and I'm back later, grumpy that it's eating into my time with Aleks.

Objectively, I get that my work is more important than my personal life, but watch me pout about it anyway.

"Please say you'll drive me to Aleks's," I beg Sanden as we jump out of the truck and start to strip down.

"You don't want to shower first?"

I know I *should* because it's been a busy day and I stink, but I'm desperate to get moving. After all that sweetness, I need him within arm's reach. I need to hear him say it again. It was basically drive-by I-love-yous, and all I want for the rest of the night is to hear those sweet words in my ear while his cock splits me open.

"Put it this way," Sanden says. "You're not getting in my car smelling like smoke and sweat. Your choice."

265

I all but race him to the showers. I make it fast, then sit there pelting him with chunks of soap until he finally shuts his water off.

"Anyone ever told you how annoying you are?"

"You're holding me up from my boyfriend's diiick," I whine.

Sanden doesn't look swayed. "You really expect me to feel bad for holding you up from your regular sex? Some of us aren't getting it at all."

"You could easily hook up if you wanted to."

"Shut up and get in the car."

But once we get to the parking lot, it turns out I didn't need Sanden after all. Aleks is sitting in his shiny, fancy car, and I barely spare Sanden a goodbye before jogging over to it. I'm in the passenger side before Aleks has even spotted me, and my mouth cuts off his surprised hello.

"Someone's happy to see me," he says when I finally let him up for air.

"Someone told me he'd give up hockey for me, and have my babies, and love me. Then *left* me for hours. *Someone* needs to get driving." I snake my hand between his legs to grip his cock. It's not hard, but it's trying. "Because in the next half an hour, this thing is going to be inside me, I don't care where we are."

Aleks's eyes fly wide, giving me a perfect view of his blown-out pupils. "Put your goddamn seat belt on."

I laugh and do as I'm told. "Just so you know, even if I went through your windshield, that time limit still stands."

My gorgeous boyfriend curses and peels out of the parking lot. It's not far to his place, but every minute that passes is torture. My cock has been half-mast since I climbed into the car, the smell of his bodywash igniting my senses. Everything about Aleks gets me going though:

his voice, his smell, his tattoos, the vulnerability in his eyes. Talking to him, joking with him, touching him, fucking him—I've never met someone I'm so wholly obsessed with. Now he's given me the go-ahead, now he's all in, I'm not going to hold back. I offered him an out, he didn't take it, so now I'll fight tooth and nail to keep him.

My hand finds his thigh, and Aleks throws the most breathtaking smile my way.

Oh, yeah, he's mine now.

We make it back in record time, even though the red lights and traffic made it impossible to speed, and once Aleks gets the door unlocked, I take his hand and lead him inside. I might want to go at it like rabbits, but that's not what tonight is. Tonight is for healing the pain of almost losing him and for taking my time to enjoy the body I hope will be mine for years to come.

The body I want to know every detail of.

The body I want to keep. Forever.

He follows me up the stairs and into the hall, where I finally pull him against me. Our lips meet softly, lazily, his arms wrapping around me and holding me like … like I'm special.

Like he knows me and accepts me and still loves me.

Outside of my chaotic friends, I've never had that. Total love and acceptance. And I've never had it from someone where that feeling was all for me. I don't have to share it or to live up to it or to earn it. I will, because that's what he deserves, but he's giving himself to me freely.

I unzip his athletic jacket, then push it off his shoulders and let it fall to the floor. Aleks's cold fingers sneak under my shirt, making me hiss. He chuckles into my mouth before pulling back for a second so he can push my shirt up over my head.

Somehow we make it down the hall, kissing and touching and losing items of clothing on the way until we're both completely naked. Aleks steers me backward into his bedroom, hard cock skimming against mine with every step. Normally I like to ride him, to watch his face and figure out how I'm driving him wild, but from the gentle way he's guiding me, I get the impression he wants to be in control tonight.

When he presses me back into the bed, I go easily, chasing his mouth and holding him as close as I can manage. His body blankets mine, slotted perfectly in the space between my legs, our dicks finally trapped together, delicious pleasure building inside me.

Our kiss deepens, Aleks rutting on top of me as his hands map their way across my abs, and this time, there's nothing sweet about it. It's hot and deep, all tongue and teeth. He feels around beside us before grasping the lube. It lights me up to think of him tossing it there ready before he left to pick me up.

The click of the lid is loud and promising.

"Spread your legs," he demands before his mouth finds my neck.

I groan, head falling back and legs falling open. Whatever he asks, I'll do it. And I know he wasn't sure about asking me to exclusively bottom while the season is on, but he underestimates how much I love having him inside me.

Aleks's lubed fingers slide along my crease, teasing me with light brushes over my hole.

"Don't be a dick," I complain.

He sucks a spot into my neck as he presses one finger inside. The dual assault heightens everything, and my poor cock is making a valiant effort to stop from going off.

My knees pull closer toward me, giving him better access, and Aleks takes the hint. A second finger joins the first, and he immediately starts to fuck me with both. He stretches me open with every stroke, nudging my prostate and drawing my pleasure out until my nails are digging into his shoulders and my balls are pulling tight.

"Urgh, stop," I gasp. "Fuck, I'm gonna shoot if you keep that up."

His fingers immediately disappear. "No coming until you're full of me."

"Look at that—we're already on the same life path."

Aleks smirks, pouring lube into his hand before slicking himself up. "You ready for me?"

"Always."

Aleks settles back between my legs, his weight on one arm while he holds his cock against my entrance. Right before he pushes inside, his eyes flick up to mine, and our gazes lock, a beat of something heavy and inevitable passing between us.

Then his cock breaches me, and *holy fuck*, the stretch.

I bear down, letting him in, loving the way he splits me open. His cock is goddamn perfectly sized to give me that initial burn that I crave before quickly melting away to mind-numbing pleasure.

When Aleks's hips press against my ass, his forehead rests against mine.

"G-Gabe ..." His voice shakes. "This is terrifying."

"Having sex with me? Not doing great things for my ego."

He laughs and pinches my side, dick moving deliciously in my ass. "You idiot. I just ... I really meant it. You're everything to me. What ... what if I lose you?"

"Then I also lose you. And that's not something I'm going to let happen."

"But you might get sick of me not being any good at relationships."

"I know who you are." I cup his face. "I know what I'm in for. I'm a very patient guy, you know?"

"I know, but—"

"Are you a hockey player, or are you a hockey player?"

He frowns at me, clearly confused.

"I thought you guys played to win?" My lips brush his. "So play to win, Aleks."

He all but tackles me as his mouth seals over mine, tongue pushing into my mouth as he starts to thrust. Every move is consuming; every touch sets me alight. I don't fight him, just let him set the pace, let him follow his need and turn me inside out as he does.

I'll never get over this. Never get sick of him. He can have doubts all he likes; I'll make it my mission to break every one of them down. I wasn't talking shit when I said I know what I'm getting into. He's vulnerable. Wary. Scarred from the divorce of a relationship that was supposed to be forever.

And after all that, I imagine forever would be hard to promise someone again.

So I'll promise it for us both.

His thrusts pick up, get harder and faster until he's pounding me into the mattress and panting in my ear. Tremors are racing down my legs to my toes, making them curl over into the sheets, and each thrust is sending me higher.

"I'm not gonna last."

"So close," he gasps. "Gonna fill you with my cum. Mark you. Make you mine."

His.

The word fries my brain, and the thought of being marked, claimed, wanted so badly has me scrambling for my cock. I jerk off hard and fast, my cock leaking, begging for more.

"Show me how much you love my cock," Aleks says, and that's all it takes. Hearing him take over with the dirty talk does some very filthy things to my brain—and my dick. My balls tighten, and the pressure finally releases.

Pleasure sweeps over me as I shoot spurt after spurt of cum onto my abs, the lust sending waves out to my limbs. As my muscles start to relax, I can tell Aleks is getting close. His grunts are erratic, his grip on me tight, each pump of his hips fast and shallow.

"*Hrgh*, Gabe …"

"Do it. Come in me."

He cries out, whole body locking up, and I sink into the feel of him pulsing inside me. The feeling is one of my favorite things on earth.

Aleks lets out a long breath and collapses on top of me. "That was some good I–love–you sex."

I slap his bare ass cheek. "Now, how about I make us some good I–love–you dinner?"

"Fuck, you're perfect." He pushes up so he can see me properly.

The compliment bubbles in my postorgasm love haze. "Speak for yourself, little hockey player." I lean in and whisper, "*Zing.*"

His soft laugh brushes my lips. "How didn't you run that night?"

"I did." Our eyes clash. "Right to you."

EPILOGUE

ALEKS

"This is the one," I say, opening my arms wide in the expansive living space. I love this house. I *want* this house.

"You say that about every one." Gabe is the pickiest when it comes to where we'll be settling down. He's had this vision of his future for so long he wants everything to be just right. Even though I've told him numerous times that anything is changeable. We don't have to buy the house as is, and I'm willing to pay for remodeling before we move in, but no. He says when he sees the one, he'll know, but we've seen about a billion houses since the start of the off-season, and here we are, months later, and he has liked maybe one house in that whole time. He ummed and ah'd about it for so long it was sold from underneath us. I'm due back for training camp in mere weeks.

They say if a relationship can endure a trip to IKEA, there's nothing that can tear that couple apart. I'll match IKEA and raise you house hunting. If I ever had any doubt that Gabe and I could be in this long haul, the fact I still love him after enduring this kind of hell means there's no stopping us.

"This is the one," I say again. "I'm so confident I even invited Sanden here to talk you into it."

"Why Sanden?" he asks.

"Because I already know what any of your Big-Boned Bertha ex-roommates would say: it's not Bertha. Why don't we kick them all out and buy that house?"

"I do love that house, but no. I want this to be ours." His blue eyes meet mine. "But good call on not asking one of them to come."

"Come on." I take his hand and lead him to the back deck on the White House-inspired mini-mansion. It's not what he had first envisioned—we went to a lot of run-down older-style homes with cute wraparound porches and a homey feel. But none of them met his standard, so I took things into my own hands. And maybe that was a mistake because it gave Gabe more options to be fickle with. "It has eight bedrooms, six baths, seven thousand square feet, it's in the heart of Capitol Hill—Seattle's gayest neighborhood—" I gesture outward. "Partial view of the Space Needle and Puget Sound, and the best part is, everything is already done. I asked, and even though the house was built in 1906, it's been modernized to within an inch of its life."

Gabe chews on his lip and glances around. "Okay, show me the rest of the house."

"Yes! Okay, follow me." It's hard not to get excited because the last house I took him to, he didn't even go inside.

To save arguments, I stopped bringing him to houses at all until I thought I found one that could work.

According to him, "It had a bad vibe." At least he's going to see all of this one.

"Reading or study nook for the kids." I open two sliding doors just off the downstairs living room, which is right next to the open-plan kitchen and dining room. I take his hand and drag him through the amazing kitchen.

"Self-explanatory." On the other side. "Laundry that doubles as a butler's pantry to hide all the messy dishes teenagers will most likely have."

I'm too scared to look into Gabe's eyes because I'm almost convinced I'll see doubt, disgust, or indifference.

"There's one small bedroom and bathroom on this level, tucked away past the stairs, where I thought new fosters could stay short-term. They'd have their own bathroom, privacy until they got to know everyone else. And then ..." I practically run up the stairs, dragging him the whole way.

Him not saying anything is a good sign. Or maybe it's a really bad sign. Maybe it's defeat.

"Up here, we have seven, count them, seven bedrooms—with dual bathrooms to four of the rooms—one living room, and my favoritest part ever." I open a door to a tiny study nook that has a balcony with a view similar to the one downstairs.

"This tiny room?"

"Can't you imagine the Stanley Cup sitting right here?" I exclaim.

"Oh, how you know me so well," Gabe deadpans.

"That wasn't the best thing. Just something to observe because I guarantee I'll be bringing it home next year." This season was a bust, but the team still went far. If it weren't for some pesky Buffalo having the season of its life, we might have made it all the way. I blame Little D and Quinn. "Go over to the bookcase."

"O ... kay." He does, and I close in behind him to reach above his head and pull.

The secret door opens, and there's the grandest of all hideaways. It's as big as the master bedroom. "We can hide from the kids when they get too much! And it can double as a panic room. Ooh, or a sex room."

Gabe sighs. "Because who doesn't want a panic room as the place you sleep every night?"

"Okay, fine. We can take the master. This can be the time-out room, then."

"I'm starting to regret asking you to foster with me."

"I'm sure I'll be fine. Teenagers are way less scary than babies."

Gabe gives me that look that he gets sometimes. I notice it's whenever I say something so obscenely wrong that he doesn't have the heart to tell me.

I shrug. I have been through PR training and charity events, junior days where I meet younger athletes. Teenagers to me are a breeze.

And sure, we're not actually planning on fostering anytime soon, but I wanted to buy the perfect house now my lease is up. One where Gabe and I can plan for our future. The future that involves each other, the jobs we love, and helping those in need.

When I think about each of those things, I don't get scared. I don't have any doubt. I've never been more confident in anything before.

I finish the tour in the boring master suite with no secret doors. "I could see us being happy here." Then I hold my fucking breath.

His eyes fill with tears, and oh fuck.

"You hate it that much?" I throw my hands up. "I give up."

Gabe takes hold of one of my flailing hands. "No, no. I … love it." A tear drops onto his cheek. "I love it. It's perfect. I've been waiting for something to jump out at me as a deal breaker, and there's nothing."

I sag in relief. "Thank fuck." I seal my mouth over his, kissing him hard and deep. "I'm going to put an offer in right now."

Gabe steps back. "Uh, about that. What's the asking price? I know it has to be over the budget I set."

Yeah, the budget he set for us was utterly unrealistic. We're buying this house together, and he says he wants to contribute, but he earns shit all doing hero's work, and I earn more than enough for the both of us. I think he's worried about long-term. We only met each other a year ago, so this is fast compared to some relationships, and I get why he's hesitant to go all in on this massive purchase when anything could happen to tear us apart.

But if that were to happen, not that I think it will, but on the off chance it does, there's no way I'd punish the foster kids by making Gabe buy out my half. He wants to do something amazing, and I want to give him the means to do it. I'm lucky enough to be in a position to give it to him.

"Aleks?" Oh no. I know that doubtful look.

I grip onto his shoulders. "Okay, it's a little, teeny, tiny bit over budget." If by little, teeny, tiny, bit, we mean three times over. "But let me do this for you. For us."

Before he can answer, there's a voice calling from downstairs.

"Hello? We're here."

It's Sanden.

"Oh, have to get that, glad we agree about the budget thing, okay bye." I make a run for it and fly down the stairs. Gabe might be big, but I'm fast. I barely notice Remy next to Sanden and grab Sanden's bicep. "He likes this one," I whisper. "He actually likes this one, so even if you hate it, say you fucking love it."

Sanden laughs. "Dude, you don't need to sell me on it. I was sold before I even walked in the door. This is amazing." He steps back and winks. "When do I move in?" he yells.

I turn to see my gorgeous man, who still has shiny eyes, strolling down the steps.

"Never," Gabe says. "This is our house." He comes up and wraps his arms around me.

Our house.

Remy's phone lets out a loud shrill, and he takes it out of his pocket so fast I swear he might be the Flash. "Where are you?" he asks and walks outside onto the back deck.

"What's up with him?" I ask.

"This is weird," Gabe adds. "You. With him. Alone, without Eman."

"Eman didn't come home last night. Remy's freaking out because they're getting married next weekend."

"We know. We're going," I say.

"You were invited?"

"I was invited to the engagement party."

Sanden shakes his head and stares after Remy. Gabe says Sanden hates Remy, but I don't see hate in his eyes. Concern, maybe. Care, definitely.

"I'm sure it's all pre-wedding jitters. From what I recall, I was a mess. Should've known it was a warning sign." My eyes widen. "Uh, but your friends are going to be fine. Super fine. But I mean, for me. Personally. You know, fuck marriage and all that stuff." I glance at Gabe. "Uh, right? Like, we're on the same page about that, aren't we?"

"You saying that even after we foster kids together, maybe even adopt—"

I gasp.

277

"—if the opportunity is right and we both want it. Stop freaking out."

I breathe again.

"But you mean to tell me, after all that, you won't want to make an honest man out of me?"

Oh, look at that. There is a way to make me all panicky again.

Gabe bursts out laughing. "Holy shit, you should see your face. I'm totally fucking with you. Marriage has never been high on my list of priorities, and to me, it's only a legal advantage, but even now you can register your domestic partnership and have it be recognized by foster agencies. I don't need the piece of paper to tell everyone who I belong to." He leans in and kisses my lips softly. "Because it will always be you."

And I will always belong to him.